Dieppe's

by Newm

This is a work of fiction. Similarities to real people, places, or events are entirely coincidental.

DIEPPE'S REVENGE

First edition. November 12, 2023.

ISBN: 979-8223909835

Written by Newman Skyles.

Also by Newman Skyles

Peter Carter & The Seekers
Peter Carter & The Seekers - The Lost City of Atlantis
Peter Carter y los buscadores - La ciudad perdida de la Atlántida
Peter Carter & The Seekers Alexander The Great's Treasures

Standalone
Time Eclipse
◇ ◇ ◇ ◇
Peter Carter y los buscadores Los tesoros de Alejandro Magno
Eclipse de tiempo
Dieppe's Revenge

Watch for more at https://www.spartankingenterprises.com.

Table of Contents

This is dedicated to the love of my life, my wife, Susan.

The Battle of Dieppe, also known as Operation Jubilee, was a significant World War II military operation that took place on August 19, 1942, primarily involving Canadian and British forces against German-occupied Dieppe on the northern coast of France. The operation was a major Allied raid aimed at testing and gaining experience for larger amphibious assaults in the future, particularly the eventual D-Day landings in Normandy. Some of the background for the Dieppe invasion. The primary goals of the Dieppe raid were to gather intelligence about German coastal defenses, disrupt their coastal radar installations, and gain experience in large-scale amphibious operations. Most of the attacking force comprised Canadian troops, with British and some American and Free French units also taking part. The Royal Navy provided naval support, and the Royal Air Force (RAF) and the Royal Canadian Air Force (RCAF) provided air cover.

During the planning and preparation, the Allies decided Dieppe was chosen as the target because of its proximity to Britain, which made it a workable location for a raid, and its significant German presence, which would provide valuable intelligence. They decided the raid would be scheduled for August 19, 1942, during the hours of dawn, to minimize the chance of detection by the Germans.

The plan involved a seaborne assault with three major objectives: the main landing at Dieppe, a smaller attack at the nearby port of Puys, and an attack on the coastal radar station at Pourville.

The operation began with a naval bombardment of German coastal defenses, followed by air support from the RAF and RCAF. However, the element of surprise was lost when the naval force encountered a German convoy en route to Dieppe, resulting in a battle that alerted the Germans.

Despite being detected, the Canadian, and British forces landed at their designated locations. The major assault on Dieppe faced heavy resistance, with well-prepared German defenses, machine-gun nests, and artillery positions. The raid at Puys was also met with fierce resistance. The attack on the radar station at Pourville achieved some success, but ultimately could not destroy the station.

The Battle of Dieppe was a costly operation for the Allies. Of the approximately 6,000 men who took part in the raid, over 3,600 were killed, wounded, or captured. The Canadians, in particular, suffered heavy casualties, with many taken prisoner.

Despite the high cost of lives and equipment, the Dieppe raid provided valuable lessons for the Allies. They realized the importance of better planning, coordination, and intelligence gathering for future amphibious operations. These lessons were applied in the planning of the successful D-Day landings in Normandy in 1944.

The diversion of German resources to defend the coast following the Dieppe raid had the unintended consequence of easing pressure on the Eastern Front, where the Soviet Union was engaged in a brutal struggle against the German Army.

The Battle of Dieppe was a significant but ultimately unsuccessful raid in World War II. While it resulted in heavy casualties for the Allies, it provided valuable insights and experience that were crucial to the success of larger amphibious operations later in the war, such as the Normandy landings in 1944.

Perhaps the most significant application of the lessons from Dieppe was in the planning and execution of Operation Overlord, the Allied invasion of Normandy, on June 6, 1944, commonly known as D-Day. The meticulous planning, careful reconnaissance, extensive training, and coordinated assault used during D-Day were direct results of the experiences and failures at Dieppe.

The Battle of Dieppe had a profound and enduring impact on military strategy and planning, influencing operations in subsequent conflicts and contributing to the development of modern military doctrine. It also serves as a poignant reminder of the sacrifices made by Allied troops during World War II and the importance of learning from history to ensure the success and efficiency of future military operations.

The Battle of Dieppe underscored the importance of international cooperation in military operations. Allied forces, including Canadians, British, Americans, and Free French troops, took part in the raid. While the operation faced significant challenges, it highlighted the need for unified planning and coordination among different nations when conducting joint military actions. This lesson was crucial as the Allies continued to work together on a global scale throughout World War II and beyond.

The Dieppe raid played a pivotal role in shaping the development of amphibious warfare doctrine. It became a textbook example of what not to do in terms of amphibious assault planning and execution. This painful experience prompted military leaders to refine their tactics, improve training programs, and establish clear principles for future amphibious operations. These developments led to more successful large-scale landings in the later stages of World War II, such as the liberation of Western Europe.

The lack of accurate intelligence about German defenses at Dieppe was a critical factor contributing to the failure of the operation. The Allies recognized the necessity of intelligence-sharing and improved reconnaissance in subsequent operations. This led to the establishment of more effective intelligence networks and the exchange of information between Allied nations, enhancing their ability to plan and execute successful military actions.

The Battle of Dieppe serves as a poignant reminder of the human cost of war. The sacrifices made by the soldiers who took part in the raid, especially those who lost their lives or were taken as prisoners of war, are a testament to the bravery and dedication of Allied forces. The raid reminds us of the importance of striving for peaceful solutions to conflicts and the need to prevent such devastating battles in the future.

The Battle of Dieppe had far-reaching consequences that extended beyond the immediate military sphere. It influenced international cooperation, shaped military doctrine, improved intelligence-sharing, and contributed to the formation of NATO. It remains a powerful symbol of the sacrifices made by Allied soldiers and serves as a sobering reminder of the human toll of war.

There are so many sad stories during World War 2, and this, my friend, is only one of them.

Chapter One

Montreal, Wednesday, August 18, 1942, Brian O'Bryan was heading to McKibbin's Irish Pub on Bishop St. He promised his best friend Brendan Murphy that he would meet him for a beer around 9 p.m. He was already late as he walked along Saint Catherine Street. He eventually arrived at the pub by 9:30.

The pub was unusually quiet for a Wednesday. It was usually full of military servicemen out on leave, and brawls were the normal entertainment of the night.

"Well, look who was kind enough to show up. It's Mr. O'Bryan our Irish most elite," expressed Brendan Murphy as he bowed.

"Hilarious Brendan, hilarious."

"I'm glad you finally showed up, Sean. I want you to meet a few fellow Irishmen."

Brian looked toward a large circular table in the back of the pub.

They approached the table. Brian sat down to the right of Brendan as he glanced around the table.

"Brian, I want to introduce you to some members of our group."

"Our group. What group is that, Brendan?"

"The Montreal chapter of the Irish Republic army, that's what."

Brian sat quietly as he looked around at the group of men around the table. He knew they were not IRA. Just a bunch of drinking delinquents.

"Let me introduce you to our comrades. Starting on my left, Brian Kelly, Cian Walsh, Fionnuala Smith, Gobnait Ryan, Blaine

O'Connor, Alistair McCarthy, and finally Doyle O'Reilly," said Brendan Murphy.

"Well, that's very interesting Brendan, so why did you invite me to this so-called IRA gathering?"

"Because, my friend, I want you to join us to fight these British pigs."

"What the hell are you talking about? Britain, Like Canada, is fighting the Nazis' swine."

"That is not our problem. They are not attacking Ireland, are they? So why should we be worried about the British?" said Brendan.

"Do you guys seriously believe that once they take over Britain, they will not have their sights on Ireland?" questioned Brian.

"They're not interested in Ireland, just England," yelled Brian Kelly.

Brian glanced around the table and expressed, "This is Montreal, Canada, not Dublin, Ireland. My brother is fighting over in Europe, in the Canadian 4th Infantry Brigade. He's risking his life to save you Irish trash so that you can sit in a pub ranting your propaganda."

"You British lover that you would betray your country, Ireland," hollered Brian.

"First, my country is Canada, born and bred in Montreal. So my loyalty is Canada, not Ireland."

"Why you son of a bitch," screamed Brian Kelly, as he, got on the table to attack Brian, but was quickly grabbed by Brandan.

Brian stood up quickly, with his chair falling over.

"I'm sorry to hear you say that, Brian. I guess I made a mistake. I think you should leave."

As the tension in McKibbin's Irish Pub escalated, Brian's decision to confront Brendan and the members of the so-called Montreal chapter of the Irish Republican Army (IRA) hit a nerve. The other patrons in the pub took notice of the commotion, and a sense of unease settled over the once-quiet establishment.

Brendan struggled to restrain an enraged Brian Kelly, whose face was flushed with anger. Brian, his chair knocked over, maintained his composure but also recognized the potentially dangerous situation he was in. He knew that the consequences of his words could be severe, especially considering the deeply held convictions of these acting IRA members.

"Doyle, Alistair, Gobnait, let's go," Brendan finally said, attempting to defuse the situation. "We'll talk outside."

Reluctantly, the group of IRA members disengaged from the confrontation and followed Brendan out of the pub, leaving Brian standing amidst the scattered chairs. The other patrons exchanged nervous glances and whispers as they watched the scene unfold.

Brian righted his chair and took a deep breath, trying to regain his composure. He knew he had taken a considerable risk by openly opposing the IRA's agenda, but his loyalty to Canada and his belief in the fight against Nazi tyranny were unshaken.

As the pub slowly returned to its usual ambiance, Brian couldn't help but wonder about the choices he had just made. He had put his friendship with Brendan on the line, and he wasn't sure if their bond would ever be the same. He couldn't ignore the fact that he might have made some enemies within this new IRA branch, a group known for its unwavering commitment to its cause.

As the evening wore on and Brian sat alone at the bar nursing his beer, he reflected on staying true to his beliefs, even when faced with vehement opposition. He hoped his actions would make Brendan and the others reconsider their extremist views and that they would ultimately choose a path that aligned with the greater fight for freedom and democracy.

Little did Brian know that his decision that fateful night at McKibbin's Irish Pub would have consequences that reached far beyond the pub's dimly lit interior, affecting not only his friendship

with Brendan but also the course of events in Montreal during those
tumultuous times.

AUGUST 19, 1942, THE 2nd Canadian Infantry Division, led by
Major-General J.H. Roberts, formed the bulk of the infantry assault
force. Had finished embarking on the transport that would bring
them to their destination. Launched across the English Channel
from southern England, Operation Jubilee was underway.

During the Dieppe Raid, several types of ships were used by the
Allied forces[1]. The naval forces included 237 ships and landing craft,
including eight destroyers[2]. The main assault troops were convoyed
in large mother ships, with their LCPs or Landing Craft Personnel
hanging from davits ready to be lowered into the water a few miles
offshore[3]. The two main types of ships used during the raid were the
Landing Craft Assault LCA and the Landing Craft Tank, or LCT[4].
The LCA was used to transport the assaulting infantry, while the
LCT was used to transport tanks[5].

Two of the soldiers were constantly criticizing each other
without mercy.

"You stupid frog, Ribbit, Ribbit," screamed Pvt Bill O'Brady.

"You stupide chien anglaise. That is stupid English dog for you
English that are too stupid to talk more than one language," hollered
Pvt Marcel St-Louis.

"Will you two shut the hell up, now?" ordered Sgt. Mike
Armstrong.

1.   https://en.wikipedia.org/wiki/Dieppe_Raid

2.   https://en.wikipedia.org/wiki/Dieppe_Raid

3.   https://en.wikipedia.org/wiki/Dieppe_Raid

4.   https://jemesouviens.org/en/landing-crafts/

5.   https://combinedops.com/Dieppe.htm

Both Pvt saluted as they clicked their heels screaming, "Yes sir, Sgt. Mike Armstrong."

"You idiots, you don't salute a Sgt. How many times have I told you?"

"Do you mean today or forever, Sgt., sir?"

"I hope the Germans take you both prisoners. I guarantee they'll surrender in a week," commented the Sgt.

"Mon bien-aimé Sgt., vous me blessez," complained Pvt St-Louis.

"God damn you St-Louis, stop talking French. This isn't the French Foreign Legion, it's the 2nd Canadian Infantry Division," yelled the Sgt..

"Are you sure, Sgt.?" Pvt St-Louis responded sarcastically.

The Sgt. was going to choke Pvt St-Louis, but he knew that the division frowned on the practice of choking your men, so he walked away while cussing a flurry of obscenity.

"You realized, my friendly frog, that if we keep bugging the Sgt., he might end it all by falling on his bayonet," said Bill.

"He loves it when we bug him. It keeps his heart alive if he has one." Said Marcel.

"Yeah, right, he loves us like his children," stated Bill. "Listen, if his wife had given birth to us, he would have strangled her to death." As they both busted laughing.

Bill took out his pack of export plain cigarettes and gave one to Marcel.

Bill O'Brady and Marcel St-Louis were inseparable. They grew up together at the east end of Montreal on Dorion Street. They went to school together, played hockey, chased girls together, and they were always in fights against the English boys or the French boys or anybody else who was stupid enough to attack either of them. Once they were in a fight with a neighborhood gang when Bill's younger brother Brian came flying in to help his older brother. Bill grabbed the scruff of his younger brother Brian's neck and told him to go home right now. Bill didn't want his younger brother to be hurt and then had to explain it.

As the Allied forces, including the inseparable duo of Bill O'Brady and Marcel St-Louis, steered their landing craft closer to the haunting silhouette of Dieppe's coastline, the atmosphere inside the vessels grew increasingly charged with tension. The dim, pre-dawn light cast eerie shadows on the faces of the soldiers huddled together, and the weight of the impending mission bore down on them like an invisible shroud.

In those quiet, anxious moments, the men aboard the 237 boats could feel the gravity of their undertaking. They knew that the operation ahead was a perilous gamble, a bold attempt to breach the formidable defenses that guarded the French coastal town. The intelligence had suggested heavily fortified German positions, but this was war, and uncertainty clung to the very air they breathed.

Bill O'Brady, his fingers clenched around his rifle, stole a glance at Marcel St-Louis, his closest friend and confidant since their days growing up on the streets of Montreal. The unspoken understanding between them was palpable. They had been through countless skirmishes together, their unbreakable bond forged in the crucible of battle.

The rhythmic hum of the boat's engine seemed to echo the steady heartbeat of the men aboard. Each of them knew the risks—the imminent danger as they approached the unknown shore, the deafening roar of enemy gunfire, and the chaos of combat. But they were soldiers, and they were prepared to confront whatever challenges lay in their path.

For now, the churning waters of the English Channel separated them from their destination, and the weight of anticipation hung heavy on their shoulders. They braced themselves, steeling their nerves, for they were about to embark on a mission that would etch their names into the annals of history.

The unexpected encounter with the German naval group had sent shockwaves through their ranks. High-pitched whistles pierced the air as shells from both sides screamed through the sky. The surrounding sea erupted in chaos as the exchange of fire intensified.

Brian and Marcel crouched low in the confines of their landing craft, the cold steel beneath them contrasting with the fiery chaos that raged around them. The air itself seemed to tremble with the thunderous symphony of battle, as if the very world had been engulfed in a tempest of violence.

Overhead, the sky was painted with fiery streaks of artillery fire, each explosion casting an eerie and fleeting light that briefly illuminated the grim faces of the soldiers. The reverberations of the blasts coursed through their bodies, a visceral reminder that they were but tiny figures in a cataclysmic clash of nations.

The engines of their vessel added their voice to the cacophony, a relentless growl that permeated every fiber of their beings. It was a mechanical beast, forging ahead into the heart of a maelstrom, driven by the unwavering determination of the men it carried.

Around them, their comrades shouted orders and words of encouragement, their voices a desperate counterpoint to the unrelenting chaos. They were a brotherhood, bound by a shared purpose and a shared fate, and in their eyes, Brian and Marcel could see mirrored reflections of their resolve and fear.

Their exchanged glances spoke volumes, a silent acknowledgment of the path they had chosen, the sacrifices they had made, and the uncertainty that lay ahead. Amid this tumultuous symphony of war, they clung to their determination, knowing that their mettle would be tested like never.

Amid the chaos of the approaching shore, a nearby landing craft became the unfortunate target of an enemy shell. In an instant, the sea exploded into chaos as a monstrous plume of dark smoke and fiery debris billowed upward, clawing at the sky. The deafening blast reverberated through the very marrow of their bones, and for a moment, time seemed to freeze.

Their vessel quivered under the impact as if recoiling from the brutality of war. The shockwave of the explosion jolted the soldiers within, sending them stumbling and grappling for balance. The stench of acrid smoke and burning metal clawed at their throats, and their ears rang with the clamor of devastation.

It was a grim and sobering spectacle, a stark reminder of the perilous theater in which they were now actors. The sea, once serene and calm, had become a frenzied battleground, and the price of victory loomed ominously in every plume of smoke and shard of debris. In that fleeting moment, as the remnants of the stricken craft rained down around them, the soldiers knew that their journey into the heart of danger had only just begun.

Surrounded by the relentless chaos of war, the soldiers huddled aboard their boat, their faces etched with the weight of their training and their profound belief in the mission they were about to undertake. Each man clung to the camaraderie of his comrades, a lifeline in the turbulence of uncertainty.

They understood with an unwavering clarity that the fate of the amphibious assault on Dieppe hung in the precarious balance of this moment. The German defenses loomed before them like an unyielding fortress, bristling with the machinery of war and willpower of the enemy. The success of their mission relied on their ability to pierce through these formidable barriers.

Amid the deafening harshness and the heart-pounding tumult, they drew strength from the bonds they had forged, from the knowledge instilled in them through relentless training, and from the fervent belief that their sacrifices would pave the way for a better future. Each man held fast to his duty, knowing that the crucible of Dieppe would test not only their mettle but also the very essence of their purpose.

Amidst the relentless fury of battle, Brian and Marcel found their thoughts drifting back to the loved ones they had left behind. The images of distant faces, letters never sent, and promises unfulfilled flickered like candles in the darkest corners of their minds. These memories were their refuge, a source of strength amidst the chaos that engulfed them.

As the deafening tumult of war raged on, their shared purpose to honor the fallen comrades from past battles burned like an unquenchable flame within them. It was a promise etched in their hearts, a vow to ensure that justice would be served, no matter the cost.

Their resolve remained unshaken, even when confronted by overwhelming odds. In the crucible of Dieppe, their purpose was obvious, their duty unwavering. With every shell that exploded around them and every shout that echoed through the air, their commitment to seeing the mission through blazed brighter than ever. They were soldiers bound by a sacred oath; soldiers who would not falter until their mission was accomplished.

The waters surrounding Dieppe became the stage for a harrowing and desperate struggle, where the bravery of these soldiers would be put to the ultimate test. They were not merely fighting for their survival, but also for the very fate of Europe itself.

As they approached the shores of Dieppe, their hearts pounded with a mixture of anxiety and fortitude. The sea, once a symbol of tranquility, now mirrored the turbulent uncertainty that gripped their souls. The weight of history rested upon their shoulders, and they bore it with unwavering tenacity.

Faced with overwhelming odds and the relentless onslaught of enemy fire, they pressed forward. Each wave that crashed against their boats seemed like a chorus of nature itself, bearing witness to the valiant struggle to unfold upon its surface.

For these soldiers, the battle transcended the immediate dangers they faced. It was a clash of ideals, a fight to preserve the freedom and future of an entire continent. The sacrifices they made on that fateful day would echo through history, a testament to their courage and unwavering commitment to a cause greater than themselves.

The allied boats pressed on, their progress toward the shores of Dieppe marked by a palpable sense of dread and anticipation. Bill, Marcel, and their comrades clung to their weapons, their knuckles white from the tension, as they mentally prepared for the fierce battle that awaited them.

The once-calm sea had transformed into a turbulent flurry of chaos. Shells screeched through the air, their deafening whistles echoing in the hearts of the soldiers. Explosions erupted, sending geysers of water and acrid smoke billowing into the sky. The ocean, once a symbol of serenity, now churned with turmoil, mirroring the turmoil within the men on board.

Every passing moment felt like an eternity, and the soldiers exchanged determined yet anxious glances. Their faces, smeared with dirt and soaked by the relentless sea spray, bore the weight of their shared mission. They knew the odds were stacked against them, but they were resolute in their commitment to the cause.

As they neared the perilous shores of Dieppe, their collective firmness only grew stronger. They were soldiers of different backgrounds, united by a common purpose. The impending battle was not just a test of their courage, but also a testament to the bonds forged in the crucible of war.

Bill's mind raced with memories of his fallen comrades; their faces were vivid in his thoughts. He couldn't shake the solemn promise of revenge that he had made to himself and their memories. Each wave that crashed against the boat seemed to echo with the voices of his lost friends, urging him to press onward.

Marcel, his steadfast companion on this perilous journey, shared the burden of their mission. The weight of the lives lost, and the sacrifices made hung heavily in the air. They both understood that they were part of something larger than themselves, a grand tapestry of courage and sacrifice woven by countless individuals.

As the danger intensified, their fortitude burned brighter, an unyielding fire in their hearts. They knew their actions would help shape the course of history, and the memory of their comrades spurred them forward. Amid chaos and uncertainty, their doggedness remained unbroken, a testament to the enduring spirit of those who fought for a just cause.

The German naval group proved to be a formidable adversary, unleashing a torrent of fierce resistance against the Allied forces. The air crackled with tension as the enemy's relentless barrage of fire rained down upon them. Explosions rocked the boats, sending plumes of smoke and debris into the air, adding to the chaos and confusion.

Amidst this maelstrom of violence, shouts of urgent orders pierced the discord, struggling to be heard above the tumultuous din. The cries of pain from wounded soldiers mingled with the deafening sounds of battle, creating a nightmarish symphony of suffering and strife.

It was a harrowing ordeal, a terrifying dance of life and death in the open waters. The soldiers clung to their training and their unwavering steadfastness, knowing that the success of their mission hinged on their ability to withstand this brutal onslaught.

Recognizing that they were vastly outnumbered, the German naval group swiftly disappeared into the shroud of darkness that enveloped the night. With a sense of urgency, they radioed ahead to warn their fellow defenders on the shores of Dieppe about the incoming Allied forces, their voices crackling over the airwaves to prepare for the impending assault.

As the enemy vessels melted away into the obscurity of the night, the Allied soldiers aboard their boats were left with a tense anticipation of what lay ahead. The uncertainty of what awaited them on the shores of Dieppe added an extra layer of apprehension to the already perilous mission they were about to undertake.

As the Allied boats steadily closed in on the shore, the soldiers could feel the weight of the impending peril pressing upon them. The tension in the air was intense, each man acutely aware that the most treacherous phase of the operation loomed just ahead—the landing itself. While intelligence reports had suggested that the beach might not be bristling with formidable German defenses, the specter of confronting entrenched enemy positions sent shivers down their spines.

With the shoreline now within sight, a sense of both dread and resolve settled over the troops. They had meticulously trained for this very moment, rehearsing every step and scenario, and their collective determination remained unyielding. The sea, once tumultuous, now seemed to hold its breath in anticipation of the impending clash on the sandy shores of Dieppe.

Amid the deafening chaos that enveloped their boat, Brian and Marcel found a moment of respite. Their eyes met, and in that shared gaze, unspoken words conveyed the profound understanding of the gravity of their situation. Their bond, forged through countless battles and shared hardships, had never been stronger.

Aware that their survival hinged on their ability to function seamlessly as a team, their unspoken communication spoke volumes. They knew distractions could prove fatal, and their unwavering focus on the mission was paramount. With their minds in sync, they braced themselves for the imminent landing, ready to face whatever awaited them on the beaches of Dieppe.

The resounding clang of the landing craft's ramp hitting the pebbled beach served as a grim overture of the impending chaos.

It was the concerto of war, and with hearts racing and adrenaline surging through their veins, the soldiers surged forward onto the unrelenting shore.

Each step they took carried them further into the heart of the battle-scarred town of Dieppe. The air was thick with the acrid stench of smoke and explosives, and the once-quaint streets were now a twisted labyrinth of destruction and danger. With determination etched across their faces, they pressed forward, resolute in their mission, and prepared to confront whatever horrors awaited them amidst the ruins of Dieppe.

The beach unfolded into a nightmarish tableau of pandemonium. Bullets zipped through the air like angry wasps, their menacing whirr merging with the harshness of battle. Explosions ruptured the shoreline, hurling geysers of sand and debris high into the heavens. Amidst this tumultuous symphony of war, the soldiers of the 2nd Canadian Infantry Division and their resolute allies exhibited unwavering valor.

They pressed on, their advance a testament to their unyielding grit, even in the face of the daunting and unexpected odds that beset them. The beach, now a battleground of chaos and destruction, bore witness to their indomitable spirit as they fought fiercely to secure a foothold in the heart of enemy territory.

Bill and Marcel, their hearts pounding in rhythm with the relentless staccato of gunfire, joined their comrades in a desperate scramble for cover. The beach, strewn with debris and punctuated by makeshift barricades, became their refuge amid the frenzy of battle. The unyielding barrage of German fire pinned them down, making any advance a perilous endeavor.

Aware of the urgent need to breach the enemy's staunch defenses, they exchanged glances filled with grim resolve. Each shared an unspoken commitment to finding a way through this hellish crucible. The fate of their mission and their comrades depended on their ingenuity and unyielding courage in the face of overwhelming adversity.

Amid the chaotic symphony of warfare, Sgt. Mike Armstrong's authoritative commands cut through the dissonance, guiding his men with precision through the perilous landscape. He urged them to advance with cautious determination, taking every available scrap of cover to shield themselves from the relentless onslaught. The beach reverberated with the staccato rhythm of machine gun fire, punctuated by the haunting cries of wounded soldiers, creating an atmosphere of unrelenting tension.

Bill, his fingers wrapped tightly around the stock of his rifle, felt the weight of both his weapon and the gravity of their mission. His heart raced, fueled by a potent mixture of fear and will power. Despite the chaos that threatened to consume him, he clung to the burning resolve within him—a mission to avenge his fallen brothers-in-arms. It was a promise he intended to keep, no matter the cost.

With every cautious step forward, Brian and Marcel exchanged glances that conveyed more than words ever could. Their eyes held the fierce purpose of soldiers who had weathered the storms of war together, forming a bond that transcended mere camaraderie. It was a connection born of shared experiences, countless hours of training, and an unspoken understanding of each other's strengths and weaknesses.

Amid the tumultuous battlefield, this unbreakable bond became their lifeline. They expected each other's movements with an almost telepathic precision, seamlessly navigating the treacherous terrain. Bill covered Marcel as he advanced, and Marcel returned the favor, creating a harmonious rhythm amidst the chaos of battle. Their actions were a testament to the unwavering trust they placed in each other, a trust that had been forged in the crucible of war and adversity.

Amidst the unrelenting resistance from the German defenders, the Allied forces displayed unwavering resolve as they painstakingly advanced. The beach, once a scene of chaos and confusion, now bore witness to their tenacity and courage. Each step forward was hard-fought, every yard of ground gained a testament to their determination.

They fought valiantly, surmounting the formidable obstacles that littered the beach, from hastily constructed barricades to the ever-present threat of enemy fire. The soldiers pressed on, their hearts aflame knowing that the success of the mission hinged on their ability to secure a foothold in Dieppe and advance beyond.

The outcome of the operation hung in the balance, and the lives of countless soldiers depended on their collective will and unyielding spirit. It was a battle against the odds, a test of their bravery, and they were determined to emerge victorious, no matter the cost.

The battle for Dieppe was far from over, and Bill, Marcel, and their fellow soldiers knew acutely that the most challenging and perilous phase of their mission loomed on the horizon—their assault on the heart of the town itself. Here, amidst the narrow streets and looming buildings, the genuine horrors of war awaited them.

As they fought their way off the beach, the soldiers couldn't help but feel the weight of the task before them. The town was a labyrinth of uncertainty, where danger lurked around every corner. The echoes of gunfire and the acrid smell of smoke filled the air, creating an atmosphere of tension and dread.

The fate of the mission and the lives of those who had landed on the shores of Dieppe rested on their shoulders. They knew that the battle had only just begun, and the challenges they would face in the urban warfare that lay ahead were daunting. But they were determined to push forward, to confront the enemy on their turf, and to achieve the objectives that had brought them to this war-torn town.

The battle-hardened soldiers steeled themselves for what lay ahead, their resolve unshaken by the perils that awaited them in the streets of Dieppe. They were warriors, and they were ready to face the crucible of urban combat, where courage and comradeship would be their most potent weapons.

As the Allied forces fought their way off the blood-soaked beach and advanced into the labyrinthine streets of Dieppe, the intensity of the battle surged. The German soldiers defending their positions did so with unwavering resolution, transforming the town into a deadly maze of urban combat.

The echoing disjointed gunfire reverberated off the weathered stone buildings, drowning out all other sounds. Smoke and dust filled the narrow streets, reducing visibility to mere meters. The soldiers moved cautiously, every step fraught with the peril of enemy ambushes from hidden corners, windows, and doorways.

Buildings scarred by war loomed overhead, their shattered windows and crumbling facades bearing witness to the brutal struggle for control of Dieppe's streets. Shell craters pockmarked the cobblestone roads, serving as treacherous obstacles to both sides.

Amidst this chaotic urban battlefield, the soldiers of the Allied forces pressed on, their determination unwavering. They knew that victory hinged on their ability to dislodge the tenacious German defenders and achieve their objectives within the war-ravaged town.

Each corner turned, each alleyway traversed, brought them one step closer to their goals, but it also exposed them to the unrelenting danger of close-quarters combat. The fate of the mission hung in the balance, and the soldiers of Dieppe fought with everything they had, their lives intertwined with the destiny of this war-torn town.

The relentless artillery fire had left a trail of destruction, reducing once-proud buildings to heaps of rubble that obstructed the narrow streets. In this grim tableau of urban warfare, Bill and Marcel found themselves entrenched in the heart of the brutal struggle.

They darted from one shattered building to the next, their boots crunching on broken glass and debris as they sought precious cover from the ever-present threat of enemy fire. These ruined structures, once symbols of civilian life, now offered a precarious shield against the onslaught.

Amid the chaos, the two soldiers engaged in harrowing close-quarters combat with their German adversaries. The tight confines of the battered city streets amplified the intensity of their encounters. Each corner turned, each room cleared, was a perilous venture into the unknown.

The bursts of gunfire echoed off the cracked and pockmarked walls, reverberating through the shattered cityscape. The acrid scent of gunpowder hung in the air, intermingling with the metallic tang of fear and determination.

Bill and Marcel's faces were etched with sweat, dirt, and the grim resolve that marked soldiers in the thick of battle. Their movements were precise, and their communication was honed by shared experience and unspoken trust. As they pressed forward through the treacherous streets, they knew that survival meant outmaneuvering the enemy while navigating a city that had become a deadly labyrinth of destruction and despair.

The once-peaceful town's narrow streets now reverberated with the relentless rattle of gunfire and the desperate shouts of men engaged in a deadly dance of survival. Bill's heart pounded in his chest like a war drum as he rounded a corner, his senses on high alert.

In that fateful moment, he came face to face with a German soldier, their eyes locking on a transient but profound connection. Time seemed to slow as adrenaline surged through Bill's veins, and instinct took over. With a swift, practiced motion, he raised his rifle, the weight of the weapon familiar and comforting in his hands. The burst of gunfire shattered the tense silence, and in an instant, the enemy soldier fell, crumpling to the ground before he could react.

The grim reality of war settled upon Bill once more, like a heavy shroud that clung to his soul. The stark contrast between the peaceful streets he had once known and the brutal chaos of battle was a harsh reminder of the sacrifices and choices that wartime demanded. Bill couldn't afford to dwell on the morality of his actions; survival in this unforgiving urban battlefield demanded unwavering resolve and split-second decisions.

Marcel fought shoulder to shoulder with Bill, their friendship and trust having been forged in the crucible of relentless battle. Amid the harshness of war, they exchanged quick nods and subtle gestures, their unspoken communication a testament to the deep bond between them.

Amid the chaos that enveloped the narrow streets of Dieppe, their aim remained unwaveringly clear—to penetrate the heart of the town and achieve their mission, even if it meant paying the ultimate price. Every step they took, every corner they turned, was evidence of their unwavering grit to press forward, no matter the overwhelming odds stacked against them.

Despite the unwavering German resistance, the Allied forces made painstaking progress. They engaged in brutal house-to-house combat, their advance measured in buildings seized and streets cleared. During this relentless struggle, Bill couldn't help but think of his baby brother, Brian, and the memories of their shared childhood flooded his mind.

With each step deeper into Dieppe's heart, he carried the weight of his brother's memory and the ghosts of fallen comrades who had fought alongside them in past battles. Bill's determination remained unshakable; he was resolute in his commitment to see this mission through to the end. It was a mission fueled by the need to honor the sacrifices of his brothers-in-arms and to bring a sense of closure to their grieving families, who had waited far too long for answers and justice.

Amid the relentless battle, the soldiers of the 2nd Canadian Infantry Division and their comrades from various Allied forces pressed forward with unyielding determination. The once-quiet streets of Dieppe had transformed into a battleground, where every step forward came at a high price.

The echoes of gunfire and the shouts of men filled the air, creating a deafening cacophony that reverberated through the war-torn town. Buildings lay in ruins, reduced to piles of rubble by the unforgiving artillery fire. The narrow streets, once bustling with civilian life, had become deadly traps for the advancing troops.

Bill and Marcel, like so many others, navigated this brutal struggle. They moved from one shattered building to another, seeking cover, and engaging in close-quarters combat with the determined enemy. Every corner turned, every alley crossed, brought the potential for deadly confrontations.

Despite the chaos and devastation surrounding them, the soldiers advanced, resolute in their mission. The streets of Dieppe would indeed bear witness to their sacrifice, courage, and unwavering determination on that fateful day in August 1942.

Amidst the harrowing chaos and devastating scenes that engulfed Dieppe, the Allied soldiers pushed onward with unwavering purpose. Bill and Marcel, side by side with their comrades, fought valiantly in the face of overwhelming odds. Their hearts bore the heavy burden of the mission's gravity and the haunting memories of friends who had made the ultimate sacrifice.

The streets of Dieppe had become a nightmarish battleground, where the deafening roar of battle and the acrid scent of destruction hung thick in the air. Buildings lay in ruins, their once-familiar facades reduced to heaps of rubble and twisted metal. The narrow streets, once lined with quaint houses and bustling shops, were now treacherous corridors of conflict.

Bill and Marcel, driven by their shared purpose and the memory of comrades lost in earlier battles, navigated this grim landscape. They sought refuge in the remnants of shattered buildings, engaging in fierce close-quarters combat with the resolute enemy. Every step forward brought them closer to their aim, but it also brought them face-to-face with the harsh realities of war.

Amid the chaos and devastation, their determination to see the mission through burned brighter than ever, a beacon of hope amidst the darkness of Dieppe's desperate struggle.

In the heart of the battle-scarred streets of Dieppe, the cacophony of war enveloped them completely. The relentless symphony of combat played out in every direction—the ceaseless chatter of machine guns, the thunderous explosions of artillery, the anguished screams of the wounded, and the authoritative shouts of officers directing their troops.

A thick veil of smoke and swirling dust hung in the air, shrouding the battlefield in an eerie haze. It clung to their uniforms, stinging their eyes, and making every breath a gritty, acrid ordeal. The once-familiar streets of Dieppe had transformed into a nightmarish labyrinth of chaos and confusion, where danger lurked around every corner.

Through this maelstrom of destruction and despair, Bill and Marcel pressed forward, their purpose unwavering. The urban warfare had become a relentless test of their courage and resolve, and they faced it with unwavering grit.

During the urban warfare that had turned Dieppe into a hellish battleground, the symphony of war played on with relentless intensity. The rhythm of machine gun fire echoed off shattered buildings, creating a deafening backdrop. Each explosion from artillery rounds sent shockwaves through the city, toppling already crumbling structures, and filling the air with acrid smoke and dust.

Amid the chaos, the cries of wounded soldiers merged with the shouts of orders from officers desperately trying to maintain control. Smoke hung thick in the air, casting an eerie, almost surreal pallor over the scene. The narrow, debris-strewn streets had become deadly traps where every corner held the potential for a deadly ambush.

Bill and Marcel, their faces smeared with sweat and dirt, fought their way through the nightmarish labyrinth that Dieppe had become. They navigated through the rubble-strewn streets, seeking whatever cover they could find in the shattered buildings, and engaging in fierce close-quarters combat with the enemy.

The weight of their rifles felt heavier with each step, and the rapid thudding of their hearts was a constant reminder of the perilous dance they engaged in. Brian's mind drifted momentarily to his baby brother, a reminder of the mission's purpose. They fought on, determined to honor the memories of their fallen comrades and to bring closure to their grieving families.

As the battle raged on around him, Marcel couldn't help but be haunted by thoughts of his family back in Quebec. The weight of worry pressed upon him like a heavy burden, and he longed for their safety. War had an insidious way of reaching into the lives of every individual, no matter how far they might be from the front lines.

With each step he took through the chaotic streets of Dieppe, Marcel's mind also flickered back to memories of his loved ones. He thought of his parents, his siblings, and the countless moments they had shared. The laughter, the warmth of their embraces, and the sense of security that now felt like a distant dream.

The risks of war were all too real, and Marcel understood the fragility of life in these tumultuous times. Yet he couldn't afford to let his worries overwhelm him. With determination etched into his features, he fought alongside Bill and their comrades, driven not only by duty but also by the hope that they could create a better world for their families, far from the horrors of battle.

The intensity of the battle reached a fever pitch as they neared their aim—a nondescript building rumored to house valuable intelligence. The once-hushed whispers among the soldiers had now become urgent, and their hearts pounded in anticipation of the impending clash with the enemy.

Amidst the disharmony of war, the shouts and orders of German soldiers emanated from within the building, sending shivers down their spines. The tension in the air was palpable, and Bill felt the weight of the moment pressing upon him.

With a determined grimace, Bill exchanged a glance with Marcel. Their eyes conveyed a silent understanding—their mission was at a critical juncture, and they needed to seize the opportunity. Every second counted, and the success of their entire operation rested on their ability to breach the enemy's defenses and extract the valuable intelligence rumored to be within those walls.

The fate of their comrades, their fallen friends, and their families hung in the balance, and Bill steeled himself for what lay ahead, ready to confront the enemy with unwavering firmness.

With a swift, silent nod exchanged between Bill and Marcel, they sprang into action. They stormed through the shattered remnants of the door, their rifles raised and ready. The room they entered was a chaotic scene, filled with startled enemy soldiers who had been surprised by the sudden, audacious assault.

The dimly lit space was a maze of overturned furniture and debris, a testament to the violence that had unfolded within. The air was thick with the scent of gunpowder, mingling with the musty odor of old wood and dust.

German soldiers, frozen amid their activities, stared wide-eyed at the sudden intruders. Some were reaching for their weapons, while others scrambled for cover. The room echoed with shouts and yells, the language barrier creating a symphony of confusion and panic.

Bill and Marcel, guided by their training and determination, moved with calculated precision. Their fingers tightened on the triggers of their rifles, and with a burst of gunfire, they aimed to turn the tide of the battle in their favor. In that critical moment, the outcome of the entire operation teetered on the edge of uncertainty, and Brian knew every shot counted.

A relentless firefight erupted in the dimly lit room. The faltering bursts of gunfire filled the air as bullets whizzed past, finding their marks with deadly accuracy. Men on both sides dropped to the floor, casualties of the chaotic clash.

Bill and Marcel, their faces etched with fortitude, engaged the enemy with all the strength and training they could muster. The room became a battleground, illuminated by the sporadic flashes of muzzle fire. The concussive blasts of the rifles reverberated through the space, adding to the disorienting chaos.

Amidst the deafening harshness, Bill and Marcel moved with deadly grace, their combat instincts taking over. They aimed their weapons with precision, targeting the enemy threat and squeezing the triggers with a steady hand.

The exchange of gunfire was relentless, a grim reminder of the brutality of war. The room bore witness to the struggle, with fallen soldiers from both sides lying amidst overturned furniture and shattered debris. Bill and Marcel knew they had come too far to turn back now, that the mission and the memories of their fallen comrades demanded their unwavering resolve.

Amidst the relentless battle, the destiny of Dieppe teetered on a knife's edge. The sacrifices of these valiant soldiers would leave an indelible mark on history. The very streets of the town bore witness to their unwavering courage and determination.

The clash of war continued to echo through Dieppe's war-torn streets, where every alleyway and building had become a battleground. The fate of the town, and indeed the entire operation, hinged on the soldiers' ability to push forward against the overwhelming odds.

The sound of gunfire and the thunderous detonations of explosives filled the air, creating a nightmarish symphony of destruction. Men on both sides fought with an intensity born of desperation and duty. The outcome of this battle would shape not only the course of the war, but also the collective memory of those who had fought and fallen in its fiery crucible.

The battle for Dieppe continued its relentless onslaught, transforming the town's streets into a gruesome theater of war. Each cobblestone thoroughfare bore witness to the grim sacrifices of brave men, their blood mingling with the earth beneath their feet. Bill, Marcel, and their fellow soldiers pressed onward, their willpower unyielding despite the harrowing circumstances.

The town's once-charming streets now lay strewn with debris and the lifeless bodies of the fallen. Every step was a perilous journey, taken amidst a ceaseless storm of enemy gunfire. The soldiers of the 2nd Canadian Infantry Division, alongside their allies, epitomized unwavering resolve as they advanced, inch by agonizing inch, toward their crucial objectives. The battle for Dieppe had become a test of courage, endurance, and the human spirit, one that would leave an indomitable mark on the annals of history.

Navigating through the labyrinthine streets, every step of an arduous journey, Bill felt the weight of his mission pressing upon him. It was more than just gathering intelligence or achieving a strategic goal; it was a solemn quest for justice, a way to honor the memories of the fallen soldiers of the 2nd Canadian Infantry Division.

As he moved forward, the faces of his comrades haunted his thoughts. The camaraderie, the laughter, the shared hardships—all etched in Bill's mind as a solemn promise to remember and seek justice for every one of them. The cacophony of war surrounded him, but his resolve remained unshaken amidst the chaos and danger that encircled him. This mission was his solemn duty, a tribute to those who had given them all for a cause greater than themselves.

Marcel, his heart pounding with the intensity of battle, couldn't help but carry the weight of personal history into the fierce firefight. Amidst the discord of war, his thoughts drifted to his beloved family back in Quebec City. Each step he took through the war-torn streets, each shot he fired at the enemy, was driven not only by a sense of duty to his country but also by a profound determination to protect the people he held dear.

The images of his family, their faces etched with warmth and love, played like a cherished film in his mind, spurring him onward through the perilous urban battleground. The thought of reuniting with them, safe and sound, became a beacon of hope amidst the chaos of war, and Marcel was determined to ensure that hope became a reality.

Amid the debris-strewn streets of Dieppe, Bill's heart was heavy with the memories of his comrades from the 2nd Canadian Infantry Division. Each step forward, each trigger pull, was not just a part of their mission to gather intelligence or achieve a strategic aim; it was a solemn quest for justice.

The faces of his comrades, young and full of life, were etched vividly in Bill's mind. Their friendship, their laughter, and the sacrifices they had made together were an indelible part of his soul. During the chaos and danger surrounding him, their memory served as a relentless driving force, urging him onward through the treacherous streets of Dieppe.

As bullets whizzed by and explosions rocked the town, Bill held onto their memory, determined to ensure that their sacrifice was not in vain. The mission was not just about gathering information; it was a solemn vow to bring closure to the families of his fallen comrades and to seek justice for their untimely deaths.

As Bill and Marcel neared their primary objective, the already fierce intensity of the fighting surged to a new level. German forces had fortified their positions, turning the narrow streets and buildings into formidable strongholds. Every inch of ground was bitterly contested, and the cacophony of battle echoed through the war-torn town.

The building that held the potential intelligence they sought was a veritable fortress bristling with enemy soldiers. Barbed wire barricades and sandbags barricaded its entrances, and machine-gun nests guarded it from above. Bill and Marcel exchanged a determined look, understanding that this would be the most challenging and perilous part of their mission.

With the memories of their fallen comrades fueling their resolve, they knew there was no turning back now. They had come too far and sacrificed too much to be deterred by the formidable defenses that lay ahead.

With an unspoken exchange of determined glances, they steeled themselves for the formidable challenges that loomed on the horizon. In the dimly lit rendezvous point, each member of the covert team understood that the fate of their mission teetered precariously on their shoulders. Their collective success relied heavily on their exceptional skills, teamwork, and the audacious plan they were about to execute.

The daunting task ahead was clear: infiltrate the heavily fortified enemy defenses in Dieppe, extract critical information vital to their cause, and then, against all odds, safely escape from the perilous heart of enemy territory. They knew acutely that failure was not an option; the consequences of being discovered could be catastrophic for both them and the overarching mission.

In that charged moment of silent resolve, their shared determination fueled their spirits, forging an unbreakable bond among them. The mission's success depended not only on their capabilities, but on their ability to synchronize their efforts seamlessly. They knew that the hours ahead would test their mettle, courage, and cunning to their limits. Each step they took, each obstacle they overcame, would inch them closer to their aim, and they were determined to face whatever challenges lay ahead with unwavering determination and unity.

In the heart of the relentless chaos and unrelenting carnage that surrounded them, Bill and Marcel stood resolute, their unwavering willpower etched into every line on their battle-worn faces. The tempest of war raged around them, the deafening noise of artillery fire and the stench of burning rubble serving as a grim backdrop to their unwavering commitment. In their eyes, they carried the weight of fallen comrades, and sacrifices driving them forward with a profound sense of purpose.

The battlefield was a nightmarish tableau of destruction, with shattered buildings looming like skeletal remnants and the scorched earth bearing the scars of countless battles. But amid this apocalyptic scene, Bill and Marcel were beacons of purpose, their footsteps resounding with the echo of their shared pledge. They bore the names and faces of their fallen friends in their hearts, their spirits hardened by the loss of those who had fought by their side.

Though the battle raged on with an intensity that defied reason, Bill and Marcel harbored an unyielding resolution. They knew that the road ahead was fraught with danger and uncertainty and that the cost of their persistence might be steep, but they were undeterred.

The war may have been far from its conclusion, but Bill and Marcel were unswerving in their determination to see it through to the bitter end. In that moment of silent camaraderie, they made a solemn promise to each other and their fallen brethren: they would press on, regardless of the obstacles, the sacrifices, or the horrors they might yet face. Their pursuit of justice and the profound duty they felt to honor their comrades' memory would serve as an unyielding compass guiding them through the relentless storm of war, toward a resolution that would bring closure to their quests for justice, no matter the ultimate cost.

The labyrinthine streets of Dieppe had transformed into a crucible of unrelenting chaos and conflict. The once-quaint town had become a nightmarish battleground, with narrow streets that seemed to constrict the area around the combatants like a vise. The air was thick with the acrid stench of gunpowder, and the ground shook beneath the boots of soldiers as they pressed forward. The haunting echoes of gunfire and thunderous explosions resounded off the centuries-old buildings, enveloping the town in a cacophonous symphony of destruction.

Bill and Marcel, two warriors among many, were unflinchingly resolved in their mission. They fought shoulder to shoulder, their faces grim and determined, as they moved through the perilous maze of Dieppe's streets. The desperation in their eyes was mirrored by the chaos that surrounded them, yet their purpose remained unshaken.

As they advanced deeper into the fray, their target came into view: a building that held the potential intelligence they so desperately sought. The structure loomed ahead; its facade was marred by the scars of battle. It was a symbol of hope amid the chaos, the potential key to unraveling the enemy's secrets. With every step closer to their objective, Bill and Marcel's determination burned brighter, fueled by the knowledge that the fate of their mission hinged on their success. In the relentless combat, their unwavering steadfastness served as a beacon of hope, a testament to the human spirit's ability to endure and strive for victory, even in the darkest of hours.

As Bill and Marcel drew closer to the formidable, heavily guarded structure, they found themselves confronted by a formidable wall of German resistance. The enemy had transformed the area into a veritable fortress, with strategically placed machine-gun nests and fortified positions that turned their advance into a treacherous, inch-by-inch struggle. Each step forward was fraught with peril as they navigated the lethal gauntlet of enemy fire.

The rattle of machine guns and the sharp crack of rifles formed a relentless symphony of danger. The fortified positions provided the enemy with a significant advantage, making it imperative for Bill and Marcel to rely on their extensive training and innate instincts. With bullets whizzing dangerously close, they saw many of their comrades collapse into a pool of death as Bill and Marcel sought cover wherever it could be found, whether behind crumbling walls or overturned carts, their hearts pounding with adrenaline.

Their discipline and combat skills came to the forefront as they returned fire with calculated precision. All shots were a measured response to the relentless onslaught, an effort to neutralize the well-entrenched enemy forces. Each trigger pull was a testament to their courage and unwavering firmness to overcome the seemingly insurmountable odds.

In this perilous dance of gunfire and evasion, Bill and Marcel pressed on, their tenacity unbroken. They understood that their mission's success hung in the balance, and they would risk it all to gather the vital intelligence that could shift the tide of the battle. Amidst the chaos and danger, they remained steadfast, evidence of the resilience of the human spirit in the face of overwhelming adversity.

The weight of their mission's urgency bore down upon Bill and Marcel like an insurmountable burden. With every passing moment, the pressure intensified, and the knowledge that time was their most precious resource gnawed at their minds. They knew acutely that the lives of their comrades hung in the balance, and the success of their entire operation hinged on their capacity to infiltrate the enemy's formidable defenses and secure the crucial intelligence they sought.

Every heartbeat echoed like a thunderous drumbeat in their ears, a constant reminder that passing time could make the difference between victory and failure. As they navigated the treacherous terrain of Dieppe, their thoughts were consumed by the gravity of their task. They knew that the information they were racing to retrieve held the key to a strategic advantage that could change the course of the entire conflict.

Their determination burned brighter with each step, each obstacle they encountered on their perilous journey. The narrow streets, teeming with danger, felt like a labyrinth designed to thwart their progress. But Bill and Marcel pressed on, their resolve unwavering, driven by the knowledge that their life's and the lives of their comrades were at stake and that their success was imperative.

In the crucible of that moment, as they inched closer to their aim, their unwavering commitment to the mission served as their guiding light. They were warriors on a mission of paramount importance, fully aware of the immense responsibility resting on their shoulders. Every ounce of their strength, every ounce of their determination, was dedicated to breaching the enemy's defenses, retrieving critical information, and ensuring the safety of their comrades.

During the chaotic battleground, Marcel, like Bill, bore not only the burden of their mission but also the heavy weight of his motivations. Amidst the relentless fury of the battle, his thoughts frequently drifted to his family and loved one's back in the City of Montreal, thousands of miles away. Their faces and memories were a source of both solace and resolution, fueling his tenacity to press forward in the face of danger.

As he fought alongside Bill, the vivid images of his family back home provided an unwavering source of inspiration. In the flickering moments of respite between bursts of gunfire, he could picture the warm smiles of his parents and the laughter of his children. Their well-being, and by extension, the safety and security of his homeland, rested heavily on his shoulders.

Marcel's commitment to the mission was inextricably intertwined with his love for his family and his profound sense of duty. With each step he took, and each obstacle he overcame, he was driven by the knowledge that his actions on this chaotic battlefield had far-reaching implications for those he held dear. He was not just fighting for a cause; he was fighting to protect the lives and happiness of those he cherished most.

In the crucible of battle, Marcel's determination was a fusion of the mission's imperative and the deeply personal connection he had to his family and homeland. The weight of his motivations propelled him forward through the chaos, giving him the strength to endure and press on, no matter the adversity.

With every step forward, they carried not only the burden of the present moment but also the weight of history, for they were on a quest.

Within the confines of the building, the very heart of their mission, an aura of uncertainty prevailed. The intelligence they sought, rumored to be housed within those walls, remained tantalizingly out of reach. The Germans had entrenched themselves, fortifying their position with grim tenacity, turning the ultimate confrontation into a crucible of uncertainty and danger.

Amid the dimly lit corridors and rooms, Bill and Marcel ventured deeper into the heart of the enemy's lair. The oppressive atmosphere weighed heavily upon them, but they pressed forward with unshakable firmness. Their advance was marked by the physical and mental exhaustion that gripped them, yet it was precisely this relentless determination that propelled them onward.

Their unwavering commitment to the mission, a fire that burned brightly within their souls, served as a beacon of hope amidst the shadows of doubt. It was a dedication born of a shared purpose that transcended the bounds of their limitations. With each step they took, the memories of their fallen comrades stood as a testament to the sacrifices made in the name of duty, a solemn reminder that fueled their relentless pursuit of the truth.

Amid the uncertain and perilous situation that surrounded them, Bill and Marcel remained steadfast. Their quest for justice and pursuit of vital intelligence were not just tasks; they were sacred obligations. The building, with all its secrets and dangers, was the crucible in which their resolve would be tested to the limits, and they were determined to uncover the truth, no matter the cost.

The Dieppe Raid, a pivotal event etched indelibly into their hearts and their nation's history, had cast a long, haunting shadow over Bill and Marcel's lives. The echoes of that fateful day reverberated deep within their souls, serving as an eternal source of motivation. They carried the heavy burden of that tragic chapter, an unforgettable scar that marked not only their personal histories but also the collective memory of their nation.

As they pressed forward in the face of exhaustion and formidable odds, the weight of that harrowing memory bore down upon them like an anchor. It was a memory of bravery and sacrifice, but also one of profound loss and suffering. The faces of comrades lost in the crucible of Dieppe remained vivid in their minds, their names etched in solemn tribute to the enduring camaraderie forged in the crucible of battle.

This shared history was the furnace that stoked the flames of their unyielding tenacity. With every step they took, every obstacle they overcame, they were driven by a sense of duty to honor the memory of those who had fallen that day. The Dieppe Raid was not just a distant memory; it was a living presence that spurred them on, an unrelenting tenacity fueled by the need to uncover the truth and find closure for the wounds of the past.

During their relentless pursuit, Bill and Marcel knew they carried not only their aspirations, but also the collective hopes and sorrows of a nation. The echoes of that fateful day, the scars it had left, and the resilience it had inspired, all converged in their unwavering commitment to their mission, as they sought to bring clarity and justice to the enduring legacy of the Dieppe Raid.

The battlefield stretched before them, an apocalyptic tableau of devastation and disarray that appeared utterly indifferent to their unwavering resolve. It was as though the very fabric of reality had been torn asunder, leaving behind a nightmarish wasteland of shattered buildings. Amid this surreal and harrowing landscape, Bill and Marcel soldiered on, in their footsteps, a defiant march against the relentless chaos that sought to engulf them.

Faced with such desolation, they were bound by an unbreakable bond—a love for their fallen comrades that transcended the horrors of war. Each explosion, each burst of gunfire, seemed but a fleeting specter compared to the enduring memory of those who had sacrificed everything on this very battlefield. Their love for their brethren was a beacon of light amidst the darkness, a source of strength that fueled their every step.

With every shot fired and every obstacle overcome, Bill and Marcel etched a testament to their shared commitment in the annals of history. Their determination was not merely a personal quest; it was a collective mission to uncover hidden truths, to shine a light into the darkest corners of the past that had remained obscured for far too long. The weight of their responsibility was immense, but it was matched by the gravity of their resolve.

Amid this nightmarish theater of war, they pressed forward, determined to unearth the hidden truths that lay buried beneath the rubble of time. Their journey was marked by sacrifice, by the relentless pursuit of justice, and by a love for their fallen comrades that remained an unquenchable flame in their hearts, guiding them through the chaos and chaos of war.

Their advance into the heart of the battlefield was not a mere act of soldiers executing orders; it was a profound mission imbued with a solemn purpose. Bill and Marcel, now guardians of the past, moved forward as sentinels of history, each step a testament to their unquenchable thirst for justice and closure. Their journey was far more than a military maneuver; it was a pilgrimage to the heart of a dark and haunting chapter in their nation's history.

The weight of their mission bore down upon them like an unrelenting burden, a burden they willingly carried in their hearts. Their love for their fallen comrades, those valiant souls who had given their lives on this very battlefield, was an undying flame that illuminated their path. It was a love that transcended the boundaries of life and death, a bond that compelled them to bear witness and seek answers.

In the crucible of their purpose, their spirits burned with an unyielding determination that was forged through hardship and sacrifice. They understood that the road ahead would be fraught with danger, challenges, and sacrifices yet to be made. But in that crucible, their commitment to see the mission through remained unwavering. The sacrifices they had made and the hardships they had endured paled compared to the greater cause they served.

As they pressed on, their footsteps echoed with the weight of history and the echoes of fallen comrades. With every stride, they advanced with a singular purpose—to unearth the hidden truths, to bring justice to those who had suffered, and to find closure for the wounds of the past. Theirs was a journey marked not only by their love for their comrades but by a profound quest for the facts, a quest that would see them through the darkest and most challenging moments, no matter the sacrifices they would face.

Bill and Marcel harbored an unwavering firmness, understanding that they had journeyed too far to contemplate retreat. In that pivotal moment, victory or defeat held little sway over their determination; what mattered was their unyielding commitment to bring their mission to its conclusion, no matter the trials and tribulations they encountered.

As they advanced, each step they took brought them incrementally closer to the elusive answers they sought and the long-sought justice they yearned to dispense. The mission had become a relentless pursuit, with Dieppe serving as both a crucible of challenge and a crucible of revelation. It was here, amidst the tumultuous battlefield, that they were determined to unveil the hidden actualities and untangle the web of mysteries that had shrouded their cause for too long.

The Dieppe Raid, a baptism of fire that had tested their resolve beyond measure, had also given rise to an unbreakable bond between Bill and Marcel. Their shared experiences, the sacrifices made in the crucible of battle, had forged a connection that transcended the horrors of war. Faced with adversity, they stood shoulder to shoulder, their unity a source of strength that would illuminate even the darkest hours of their wartime journey.

With each passing moment, they moved forward, propelled not only by a desire for closure and justice but also by the profound connection they shared. In the battlefield's heart, amidst the cacophony of war, their resolve remained steadfast, a testament to their unwavering commitment to see their mission through to the very end, no matter the hardships and uncertainties that lay ahead.

Amidst the relentless and intense firefight that raged within the narrow, claustrophobic streets of Dieppe, Bill and Marcel showcased a remarkable display of valor. Their mission, fraught with danger, drove them forward as they courageously navigated the urban battlefield toward the elusive building rumored to house the vital intelligence they sought.

The chaos surrounding them was overwhelming. The deafening exchange of gunfire, punctuated by the staccato bursts of machine guns and the sharp crack of rifles, created a cacophonous symphony of war. The very air was thick with the acrid scent of gunpowder, a suffocating reminder of the unyielding violence that engulfed them. Their ears were assailed by the haunting wails of the wounded and the anguished cries of those caught in the crossfire, forming an agonizing backdrop to their relentless advance.

Bill and Marcel pressed forward, their unwavering determination illuminated by the flickering flames and the shattered remnants of the once-picturesque town. They knew that amidst the chaos and destruction, the answers they sought lay within the walls of the rumored building. Each step they took, each obstacle they overcame, was evidence of their unyielding commitment to the mission, to uncover the hidden truths that could alter the course of the battle.

In the crucible of Dieppe's urban warfare, Bill and Marcel forged a path with unwavering valor and purpose. Their journey through the tumultuous streets was marked by the stark realities of combat, where courage was their most prized weapon and the pursuit of critical intelligence was the beacon guiding them through the relentless storm of war.

As Bill and Marcel neared their critical aim, a formidable obstacle emerged before them like an impenetrable fortress. This was no ordinary barricade; it was a heavily fortified German position, standing as the vanguard of the building they sought to breach. The entrance was fiercely guarded, and the enemy soldiers manning it were a force to be reckoned with. Their training had honed them into formidable adversaries, and their resolute determination to defend their ground was palpable.

The Germans, standing shoulder to shoulder, their weaponry gleaming ominously in the dim light, formed a formidable defensive line. Each soldier seemed to embody a testament to their unwavering commitment to protect their stronghold. Their eyes burned with the fire of conviction; their faces etched with the marks of battle-hardened resolve.

Bill and Marcel, confronted with this formidable obstacle, knew that their path was fraught with peril. The odds were stacked high against them, and the enemy's defenses appeared impenetrable. Faced with such formidable opposition, they understood that their training, their instinct, and their unbreakable resolution would be tested to their limits.

As they took in the sight of their adversaries, the gravity of the situation weighed heavily upon them. This was a moment that would define their mission's success or failure, a battle of wills against a determined and well-prepared enemy. It was a clash of forces, where the stakes were nothing less than the pursuit of critical intelligence and fulfillment in their mission.

Bill and Marcel locked eyes in a silent exchange that spoke volumes, their unspoken communication a testament to their shared doggedness. In that fleeting moment, they understood the gravity of the situation and the urgency of the task ahead. They needed not just courage, but also a meticulous plan to shatter the enemy's formidable defenses and gain access to the inner sanctum of the building.

Time, that relentless adversary, was slipping through their fingers, and the fate of their comrades dangled precariously in the balance. The weight of their mission bore heavily upon them, a burden that pressed down upon their shoulders. Every passing second heightened the stakes, intensified the danger, and underscored the crucial nature of their endeavor.

In the shadows of Dieppe's war-ravaged streets, Bill and Marcel knew they were the last line of defense for their comrades, the vanguard of justice, and the harbingers of truth. Their shared commitment to the mission was unwavering, but they also recognized that their determination had to be complemented by a brilliant strategy. They needed a plan to outmaneuver the well-prepared enemy and pierce the armor that guarded the secrets they sought.

As they huddled together amid chaos, their minds raced, concocting a plan that would be their beacon through the darkness of uncertainty. Their bond, forged in the crucible of battle, would be their strength as they embarked on this perilous journey to breach the enemy's defenses and uncover the information that could change the course of their mission.

Bill and Marcel exchanged a nod of understanding, their silent communication a symphony of shared purpose. In that pivotal moment, Bill signaled for Marcel to provide covering fire, a critical diversion that would create the opportunity for his audacious maneuver. The weight of their mission hung in the balance, and their unspoken trust in each other was intense.

With a deep breath, Bill steeled himself for the daring act he was about to undertake. Time seemed to slow as he dashed from one piece of cover to the next, his every movement a testament to his training and instincts. Enemy bullets whizzed perilously close, the shrill snap of near misses echoing in his ears.

The cacophony of gunfire and the thundering heartbeats was a stark contrast to the calculated precision of Bill's advance. He moved with the grace of a predator, skillfully evading the enemy's relentless barrage. The world around him blurred as adrenaline surged through his veins, his focus unwavering on the fortified position he was determined to breach.

Each step brought him closer to his aim, the gap between himself and the enemy's stronghold narrowing with each heartbeat. His heart raced, not with fear, but with a fierce fortitude that surged within him. Bill's audacious move was a testament to his unwavering commitment to their mission, a mission that had brought them to the very brink of danger and discovery.

Marcel became the orchestra conductor of chaos, unleashing a relentless hail of bullets that thundered through the air. His weapon roared in a calculated rhythm, sending a storm of suppressive fire toward the enemy's entrenched position. The enemy, momentarily disoriented and forced to seek cover, had their fire stifled by the relentless onslaught.

Bill seized this critical diversion as his opportunity to take a daring gamble. With nerves of steel, he retrieved a smoke grenade from his belt and hurled it forward. The grenade burst on impact, instantly engulfing their surroundings in a thick, concealing fog. Visibility plummeted to near zero, and the battlefield became an eerie realm of obscurity.

It was a calculated risk, one that could tip the scales in their favor or expose them to unforeseen dangers. But during the swirling smoke, Bill and Marcel pushed forward, their hearts pounding in rhythm with their shared determination. The concealing fog became their shroud, obscuring their advance from prying eyes and providing a vital moment of respite from the relentless enemy fire.

Bill's audacious move was a calculated gamble, born of necessity and fueled by their unyielding commitment to the mission. As the fog thickened around them, the battlefield transformed into a surreal dreamscape, where their pursuit of justice and truth pressed on, shrouded in the uncertain embrace of concealing fog.

The dense smoke descended like a curtain, plunging the battlefield into disorienting chaos. Amidst the foggy obscurity, confusion reigned supreme among the German soldiers. The sudden onset of this concealing shroud left them startled and scrambling to regain their bearings, their shouts of alarm lost in the swirling haze.

Taking full advantage of the disarray he had caused; Bill seized the opportunity for his daring dash toward the heavily fortified position. His heart raced with a fierce determination, and every pounding step was a resounding declaration of his unwavering commitment to the mission. Amid the smoke-choked battlefield, he became a spectral figure, a shadowy harbinger of justice.

As he reached the sandbag barricade, his breath came in ragged gasps, and his senses were heightened to a razor's edge. Startled enemy soldiers, surprised by the sudden intrusion, fumbled in confusion. Bill's training and resolve proved invaluable as he reacted swiftly, disposing of the stunned adversaries who had never seen his approach coming.

With each well-aimed shot and precise movement, Bill exhibited a blend of skill and tenacity that was nothing short of awe-inspiring. The sandbag barricade, once a formidable obstacle, now lay breached and abandoned, a testament to the daring and determination of a soldier driven by a profound mission and fueled by the chaotic cover of smoke.

Marcel, keenly observing the breach they had created in the enemy's defenses, wasted no time. He swiftly joined Bill at the newly gained position, their synchronized movements a testament to their shared resolve and unwavering commitment. Together, they stood at the entrance of the building, their eyes fixed on the elusive prize that lay within, determined to see their mission through to its conclusion.

Their presence at the fortified entrance marked a turning point in their relentless pursuit of justice. The once-imposing stronghold was now under their control, a testament to their strategic prowess and indomitable spirit. Their comrades' lives hung precariously in the balance, and the burden of responsibility weighed heavily upon them.

With determination etched on their faces, Bill and Marcel knew they couldn't afford to falter now. The mission, a crucible of danger and uncertainty, had brought them to this pivotal juncture, where the fate of their comrades and the pursuit of crucial intelligence converged. It was a moment that held the power to shift the tides of battle and reveal the hidden truths that had remained shrouded in darkness for far too long.

Their hearts beat in unison, echoing the shared determination that had brought them to this point. In that crucial moment, as they stood guard at the entrance of the building, their unyielding commitment was a beacon of hope for their comrades and a testament to the resilience of the human spirit in the face of insurmountable odds.

Inside the building, they searched for any critical intelligence and took on an air of solemn urgency. Bill and Marcel plunged headlong into their search, their movements marked by caution and meticulous care. The dimly lit corridors stretched before them like a maze of secrets waiting to be unraveled, and room after room beckoned, holding the potential to reveal the vital documents they sought.

As they advanced, their every step seemed to resonate with the weight of their mission. The gravity of their task bore down on them, a intense presence that filled the air with a sense of purpose and determination. It was a mission that carried the hopes of their comrades and the fate of their operation, and they knew keenly that time was of the essence.

Each room they entered was a realm of anticipation and uncertainty. The walls, adorned with remnants of a once-normal life, seemed to close in around them as they meticulously scoured every corner for any signs of the elusive documents. The tension in the air was deep, as if the very walls held the secrets they sought, and the silence of the building was broken only by the hushed rustling of paper and the occasional creak of a floorboard beneath their boots.

Bill and Marcel's determination to uncover the truth was stanch, their senses attuned to every detail, every potential clue that might lead them to the sought-after intelligence. Amid the dimly lit and foreboding interior, they pressed on, their resolve undiminished, knowing that the success of their mission depended on their ability to uncover the hidden facts that lay within those walls.

As Bill and Marcel delved deeper into the building's interior, their hands trembled with a potent mixture of anticipation and anxiety. Each drawer they opened, every paper they sifted through, and each document they examined held the promise of answers that could change the course of their mission. The atmosphere was thick with an electrifying sense of possibility, and their hearts quickened with every rustle of paper.

With each piece of parchment they scrutinized, their hopes soared, only to plummet when the contents failed to yield the critical information they sought. The room seemed to echo with the rustling of pages, each turn of a document a fleeting moment of expectation followed by the crushing weight of disappointment. The walls, bearing witness to their search, felt like silent observers of their relentless pursuit.

Time, ever unforgiving, continued its inexorable march forward, and the nagging sensation of frustration clawed at their determination. The urgency of their mission weighed heavily on their shoulders, and the elusive intelligence they sought remained maddeningly out of reach. Their shared commitment to the cause was unwavering, but the room's dim light and the persistent absence of answers conspired to test their patience and resolve.

Bill and Marcel persevered, their trembling hands a testament to their determination, as they continued their painstaking search through the documents that held the potential to change the course of their mission. In that quiet, tense space, they battled not only time but also their mounting frustration, driven by the knowledge that the answers they sought could hide in the next piece of paper they examined.

During mounting foiling and as the weight of despair threatened to engulf them, Marcel's keen eye proved to be a beacon of hope. He meticulously combed through a pile of seemingly insignificant papers; his determination unwavering. The dim light in the room cast eerie shadows as he continued his search, his hands trembling with both fatigue and anticipation.

And then, as if guided by fate, Marcel's eagle-eyed gaze caught a glint of something hidden beneath the nondescript layers of paper. His heart quickened with a surge of anticipation as he recognized the potential significance of the concealed object. With a steadying breath, he extended his trembling hand, reaching for the enigmatic glimmer in the dimly lit room.

As his fingers closed around the concealed object, Marcel's heart pounded with a mixture of trepidation and hope. The room seemed to hold its breath in anticipation as he slowly pulled the hidden item into the dim light, revealing it to both him and Bill. In that pivotal moment, the object remained shrouded in mystery, its true nature and importance yet to be unveiled.

Marcel's discovery was a poignant reminder that even in the darkest hours of their search, a glimmer of hope could still shine through, waiting to be uncovered. The dimly lit room bore witness to this pivotal turn of events, as the concealed object held the potential to change the course of their mission, and perhaps even the fate of their comrades.

Hidden beneath the pile of seemingly unimportant papers lay a folder, its edges faded with the passing of time, but its contents brimming with the potential to unlock the answers they had been tirelessly seeking. With trembling hands and bated breath, Marcel carefully withdrew the aged folder from its clandestine resting place, revealing it to the dim light of the room.

The folder itself bore the marks of history, its cover aged and worn, yet the documents within remained remarkably preserved. As Bill and Marcel gingerly paged through the contents, a sense of elation slowly washed over them, like a wave of relief breaking upon their weary souls. The critical intelligence they had relentlessly pursued, the very heart of their mission, had been found.

Each document they perused seemed to hold a piece of the puzzle, shedding light on the secrets that had eluded them for so long. The significance of their discovery resonated deeply within them, as if the room itself bore witness to their triumph. The dim light that had cast shadows of uncertainty now seemed to glow with newfound clarity.

In that moment of revelation, the weight of their mission's purpose became palpable. The folder, faded and unassuming, had become a repository of truth and justice. Bill and Marcel's elation reflected the monumental importance of their find, a discovery that held the potential to change the course of their operation.

Their shared commitment to the mission had finally borne fruit, and as they pored over the contents of the folder, the answers they sought emerged from the shadows of uncertainty into the light of revelation. In the dimly lit room, their sense of triumph was a testament to the resilience of the human spirit and the power of relentless determination.

With a sense of urgency, Bill and Marcel secured the precious documents, fully aware that their mission was only half complete. The critical intelligence they had uncovered was a fragile treasure, and the weight of their responsibility pressed heavily upon them. They understood their journey had entered a perilous new phase.

Time was not their ally, and the relentless German forces that surrounded them were a constant threat. The room, once a haven of discovery, now felt like a vulnerable sanctuary amidst the chaos of war. The dim light bore witness to their purpose as they carefully collected the documents, ensuring each piece was safely tucked away.

The documents, cradled in their hands, were the embodiment of truth, and they held the potential to change the course of their operation and reveal the hidden realities of Dieppe. With the weight of their newfound knowledge, Bill and Marcel were now tasked with the daunting challenge of evading the relentless pursuit of the enemy.

Their mission was far from over, and their journey had become a race against time. Every step they took had to be deliberate and calculated, as they navigated the treacherous path back to their comrades, the bearers of the truth about Dieppe. In the shadowy confines of the building, they knew that their unwavering commitment would be tested once more when they ventured into the heart of danger, determined to see their mission through to its ultimate conclusion.

Clutching the precious cargo tightly, Bill and Marcel retraced their steps through the labyrinthine corridors of the building. Each passage was a winding maze fraught with uncertainty, and the weight of their mission hung heavy on their shoulders. The documents, a silent testament to the truths they carried, were their sole focus.

Beyond the confines of the building, the battle raged on with a ferocity that underscored the immense sacrifice of their fellow soldiers. The loudness of warfare, the relentless exchange of gunfire, and the echoing explosions reverberated through the walls, serving as a constant reminder of the chaos and danger that enveloped them.

With each step they took, Bill and Marcel were acutely aware of the valor displayed by their comrades in the face of adversity. The building, though a temporary respite from the battlefield, was but a fragile sanctuary amidst the tempest of war. Their mission was not only a quest for facts, but also a solemn tribute to the sacrifices made by those who had fought alongside them.

As they navigated the labyrinthine passageways, they understood that the documents they carried were not just pieces of paper; they were a testament to the courage and dedication of their fallen comrades. The echoes of the battle outside were a stark reminder of the perilous journey that lay ahead, but Bill and Marcel remained steadfast, determined to honor the memory of their fellow soldiers, and bring the reality about Dieppe to light.

Stepping out from the building's shelter, Bill and Marcel were met with a scene of profound transformation. The once-veiling shroud of smoke had dissipated, unveiling the full scope of the devastation that had befallen Dieppe. The town, now laid bare, bore the unmistakable scars of a fierce and unforgiving battle. It was as though the very landscape had been reshaped by the ferocity of conflict.

The destruction was all-encompassing, with buildings reduced to rubble, streets marred by the remnants of war, and a haunting silence that hung heavily in the air. The toll of battle had been staggering, and the signs of loss and sacrifice were clear on both sides of the conflict. The indomitable spirit and unwavering bravery of those who had fought and fallen were etched into the very fabric of the town, leaving an indelible mark on history.

As Bill and Marcel surveyed the aftermath, their hearts swelled with a mixture of emotions. Their mission had been a quest for facts, but it was also a tribute to the courage and dedication of the soldiers who had stood their ground in the face of unimaginable adversity. The echoes of battle now subsided, carrying with them the weight of sacrifice, a solemn reminder of the human cost of war.

In that moment, amidst the devastation of Dieppe, Bill and Marcel recognized the profound impact of their mission. The truths they carried were not only revelations. but also a testament to the resilience of the human spirit and the enduring legacy of those who had given them all in the name of duty.

With the invaluable documents safely secured in their possession, Bill and Marcel embarked on a perilous journey that would carry them through the heart of danger and uncertainty. The truth about Dieppe, the very answers they had tirelessly pursued, and the legacy of those who had made the ultimate sacrifice in the name of justice, was their precious cargo.

Each step they took was a testament to their unwavering commitment and indomitable spirit. The weight of their mission bore down upon them, a responsibility that resonated deeply with the honor and duty they felt towards their comrades and their nation. Every footfall seemed to echo with the solemnity of their task.

Their journey was fraught with danger as they navigated through the war-torn landscape, where peril lurked around every corner. Yet, Bill and Marcel pressed on, driven by the knowledge that their mission was far greater than themselves. They were not merely bearers of documents; they were custodians of truth and justice, entrusted with a legacy that demanded unwavering dedication.

Faced with adversity, they carried the hopes of their comrades and the collective memory of those who had given them all. Theirs was a journey that transcended the physical and ventured into the realm of the profound. As they ventured forth, the facts about Dieppe, the answers to long-standing questions, and the enduring legacy of their fallen brethren were held close to their hearts, a beacon guiding them through the darkness of uncertainty and danger.

On that fateful and chaotic day, as the battle raged around them and the relentless roar of gunfire filled the air, the unbreakable bond that had tethered Bill and Marcel reached a poignant and heart-wrenching climax. In the crucible of war, the inevitable had finally come to pass, and Marcel, struck by a deadly hail of bullets, was aware that his time had arrived.

The battlefield, a nightmarish landscape of destruction, bore witness to their unwavering friendship. Bill, his heart heavy with the realization of his comrade's impending fate, refused to abandon his friend, even as danger encircled them like a relentless predator. The cacophony of war faded into the background as Bill stood steadfast by Marcel's side, determined to face the storm of battle together, just as they had always done.

Amidst the chaos and violence that surrounded them, their shared history flashed before their eyes—a journey marked by camaraderie, loyalty, and an unspoken understanding. The bond between them had been forged in the crucible of adversity, and now, in the throes of tragedy, it would be tested like never before.

Bill's unwavering commitment to Marcel was a testament to the depths of their friendship, a bond that had transcended the horrors of war. As they faced the unforgiving reality of the battlefield, they clung to each other, their hearts heavy, knowing that their shared journey was reaching its heart-wrenching conclusion.

In that harrowing moment, Bill's unwavering loyalty and the deep well of love he held for his brother-in-arms blazed like a beacon in the chaos of battle. With a heart heavy with determination and the weight of their shared history, he swung his machine gun toward the approaching enemy forces, a resolute guardian of Marcel's life, determined to protect his friend at all costs.

Each round fired from Bill's weapon was a testament to his unwavering commitment, his finger on the trigger, a pledge to fulfill the promise they had made long ago—to leave the battlefield together, side by side. The staccato bursts of gunfire were his battle cry, a fervent declaration that he would not forsake Marcel, even in the face of insurmountable odds.

The battlefield bore witness to Bill's valiant stand, as he fought desperately to create a barrier of lead and fire between Marcel and the encroaching peril. The deafening roar of his machine gun merged with the chorus of war, his every shot a resounding refusal to let his brother-in-arms face the darkness alone.

During the relentless conflict, Bill's unwavering resolve was a testament to the unbreakable bond they shared—a bond that transcended the horrors of battle and stood as a testament to the depth of their friendship. With every bullet fired, he etched their promise into the annals of history, a promise that he would fight to the bitter end to ensure Marcel's survival, their destinies forever intertwined on the battlefield they knew all too well.

Yet, as if written by the hand of fate itself, another lethal flurry of bullets pierced the air, casting an eerie pall over the battlefield. In that heart-wrenching instant, Bill, the embodiment of unwavering loyalty and love for his brother-in-arms, was struck down, his life snuffed out with brutal swiftness. He crumpled to the ground beside Marcel, his sacrifice etching their destiny together in the unyielding embrace of death.

The battlefield, a theater of tragedy and loss, bore witness to the tragic culmination of their journey. Marcel, who had been fighting valiantly against the relentless tide of adversity, now lay wounded and vulnerable beside his fallen comrade. The cacophony of battle, once a deafening symphony, seemed to hush in the wake of this solemn moment.

Bill's life had been extinguished, his body a stark reminder of the cruel toll that war had exacted. His ultimate act, to protect Marcel at all costs, was a poignant testament to the depth of their friendship and the unbreakable bond that had defined their journey. In death, their destinies had become forever intertwined, their sacrifice an enduring symbol of the price paid in the name of brotherhood and duty.

As Marcel grieved for his fallen friend and brother-in-arms, the battlefield stood as a somber tableau of their shared history, a testament to the sacrifices made and the love that had bound them together. In that moment, their legacy was etched into the very earth on which they had fought and fallen, a legacy that would endure long after the echoes of war had faded away.

In those heart-wrenching last moments, as life slowly ebbed away from Marcel, he clung to the memories of their shared camaraderie and love. Beside the lifeless body of his fallen friend, he whispered words that bore the weight of a lifetime of friendship and shared experiences. Their dreams of returning to Montreal together, the echoes of their laughter, and the tapestry of shared moments were now frozen in time, forever intertwined in the sands of Dieppe.

Marcel's voice, barely more than a frail whisper, carried the essence of their unbreakable bond. With each word, he paid tribute to the profound connection that had defined their journey. The weight of their collective experiences—the battles they had fought, the trials they had endured, and the dreams they had nurtured—rested heavily on his shoulders.

In those poignant moments, as life's embers flickered, the surrounding battlefield seemed to fall away, and their world narrowed to the space between them. Marcel's whispered confidences were a bittersweet farewell, a last testament to the love and friendship they had shared throughout their lives, especially on the battlefield.

Their dreams of returning to Montreal together, once filled with hope and anticipation, now became a poignant reminder of the price they had paid. The echoes of their laughter, once a soundtrack of joy, now resonated with the weight of their sacrifice. Their shared experiences, etched in the sands of Dieppe, became an enduring testament to the indomitable spirit of camaraderie and the enduring power of love that transcended even the darkest moments of war.

In Marcel's last moments, his weakening grip on life loosened, and he, too, succumbed to the wounds that had ravaged his body. As the battle raged on around them, he closed his eyes, leaving behind a world deeply scarred by the ravages of war and a friendship that had been immortalized by the ultimate act of sacrifice.

The battlefield, an unforgiving canvas marred by destruction and chaos, bore witness to their shared destiny. Marcel's life ebbed away during turmoil, and as the world continued to spin with violence, he slipped into the quiet embrace of eternity. His final breaths were a poignant testament to the profound bond that had defined their journey—a bond that had transcended the brutality of war and had found its apotheosis in the ultimate act of selflessness.

In those somber moments, the legacy of their friendship became etched into the very soul of the battlefield. Their sacrifices, their dreams, and the love that had bound them together would forever be remembered as an enduring testament to the resilience of the human spirit in the face of adversity. As the world moved forward, scarred by the horrors of war, their memory endured a poignant reminder of the unbreakable bonds forged in the crucible of battle and the profound impact of their shared sacrifice.

In the end, the two friends from Montreal, their connection fortified by an unbreakable bond forged through trials and tribulations, had reached their shared destiny on the haunting shores of Dieppe. Their memories, intertwined inextricably with the sands and echoes of that fateful battlefield, would eternally persist as a poignant testament to the indomitable spirit of individuals who had given their all for a cause larger than their own lives.

Their lives had converged in the crucible of war, a testament to the unpredictable twists of fate that had brought them together. Through the trials and tribulations they had faced, their friendship had deepened and blossomed, becoming a beacon of strength in the darkest of times.

Their last moments, side by side in the throes of battle, symbolized the culmination of their journey. Their unyielding commitment to each other, to their comrades, and the pursuit of justice had led them to that pivotal juncture on the shores of Dieppe. In that somber yet powerful ending, their story became a part of the tapestry of history, a narrative of sacrifice and unwavering dedication.

As the world moved forward, bearing the scars of war, the memories of these two Montreal friends would endure, a testament to the enduring spirit of those who had given their all for a cause that transcended individual aspirations. Their legacy would forever be a reminder of the profound impact that friendship, sacrifice, and unwavering commitment could have on the world, even in the face of its darkest challenges.

Chapter Two

The evening passed as Brian drank until the bartender told him it was time to close the bar. Brian looked at his watch. It was 1:00 a.m. as he walked through the streets and stumbled to his apartment in NDG, a suburb of Montreal. He collapsed on his bed, dead drunk, not knowing about the disastrous events that were happening overseas as the invasion of Dieppe was taking place with his brother. His brother Bill was a proud member of the Royal Hamilton Light Infantry, the unit that captured "White Beach" in the center of Dieppe. Their mission was to secure the Dieppe waterfront and provide covering fire for other units.

The night in NDG was serene, with the quiet suburban streets occasionally disturbed by the distant sound of a passing car or the hooting of an owl. Inside Brian's apartment, the dimly lit room remained still, save for the occasional shift of his unconscious body as he slept off the effects of his alcohol-fueled night.

Throughout the early hours of the morning, Brian's sleep was restless, marked by fragmented dreams and occasional stirrings. As the night wore on, the alcohol in his system continued to metabolize, leading to a drop in his blood sugar levels. This, coupled with dehydration, took its toll, and Brian's sleep grew increasingly fitful.

Around 4:00 a.m., the room was bathed in the pale light of the early dawn. A persistent headache pierced through the fog of Brian's slumber, gradually pulling him toward consciousness. He groaned and shifted on the bed, his eyes fluttering open to reveal a world that seemed to spin around him.

The room, which had been a blur of darkness, slowly came into focus. Brian's clothes from the night before were still crumpled on the floor, mingled with empty beer bottles, and discarded napkins. His mouth felt parched, his throat dry and scratchy, and the relentless throbbing in his head intensified with each passing moment.

With a deep sigh, Brian mustered the strength to sit up, his hands massaging his temples to ease the pain. His memories from the night before were hazy and fragmented, a jumble of laughter, clinking glasses, and blurry faces.

Outside, the world was waking up, with the early morning sun casting a warm glow on the quiet suburban streets of NDG. Birds chirped in the distance, and the world seemed to carry on as usual, blissfully ignorant of the dramatic events that had unfolded overseas during the Dieppe Raid.

For Brian, however, the immediate concern was the pounding headache that seemed to envelop his entire being. With a groan, he swung his legs over the edge of the bed, slowly standing up. The room spun momentarily, causing him to clutch the edge of the bed for support.

Realizing that he needed water, aspirin, and perhaps a strong cup of coffee, Brian stumbled his way into the small kitchenette, his movements still unsteady. The night's events remained a distant blur, overshadowed by the pressing need to nurse his throbbing head back to health.

As Brian fumbled through his disheveled apartment in search of relief, he had no inkling of the fate that had befallen his brother Bill, who was thousands of miles away on the shores of Dieppe, fighting valiantly amid the chaos of war. The contrast between their worlds could not have been starker, with one battling the aftermath of a drunken night and the other enduring the hardships of combat in a foreign land.

Brian headed to the restaurant CG's, where he frequently goes for breakfast. As he walks towards the restaurant, he listens to his Greek neighbors screaming in Greek which he didn't understand a single word. But one thing was for sure: he had a hell of a headache. As he entered CG's, he sat at his typical booth as Lydia; the waitress, came to give him his first cup of coffee. "You're late today Brian, it's almost lunch." Brian nodded affirmatively as he rubbed his forehead. "What the hell are those Greeks screaming about?" asked Brian. The waitress explained they were probably talking about the news of the disaster in Dieppe. "It's all over the newspaper the Montreal Star," said the server as she went to get Brian the special edition.

Brian's head throbbed as he sipped on the steaming cup of coffee that Lydia, the familiar server at CG's, had placed in front of him. He winced as the hot liquid seared his dry throat, hoping it would provide some respite from the persistent headache.

Lydia, with her warm smile and efficient demeanor, had seen Brian through many a morning after like this one. She was well aware of his habits and often served as a friendly ear for his ramblings. "You're late today, Brian. It's almost lunch," as her remarks echo in Brian's head.

Brian, still rubbing his forehead, nodded in acknowledgment. The noise from his Greek neighbors, whose animated conversation in a language he couldn't understand, had been grating that morning. He looked over at the neighboring booth, trying to make sense of their gestures and tone, but it only added to the pounding in his head.

With a furrowed brow, he turned his attention back to Lydia and asked, "What the hell are those Greeks screaming about?" The question escaped his lips more than a reflex than genuine curiosity.

Lydia sighed softly trying to answer again Brian's question about the Greeks screaming, knowing that Brian often asked questions about his neighbors' conversations, despite never really comprehending their language. "Oh, Brian I explained to you a moment ago, it's probably about the news," she replied with a hint of sadness in her voice. "About the disaster in Dieppe."

She reached under the counter and retrieved a special edition of the Montreal Star which she forgot to get him as she served another one of her regulars, here is the front page. As Brian looked over the paper it was adorned with a stark headline that read "Tragedy Strikes Dieppe: Allied Assault Ends in Disaster." The accompanying photographs captured the chaos and the seeming devastation of the ill-fated raid.

Brian took the newspaper and, though squinting through the ache in his head, attempted to read the headlines. As the words came into focus, a knot formed in his stomach. The photographs and accounts of the Dieppe Raid painted a grim picture of what had unfolded on the distant shores.

He lowered the newspaper, his mind racing to connect the dots. Bill, and his brother's infantry, was part of the operation in Dieppe, a fact that had completely slipped his alcohol-soaked memory. Panic welled up within him as he realized the implications of the news. Bill's fate remained a mystery, and a growing sense of dread gnawed at him.

As Brian sat there, nursing his headache, and staring at the newspaper, he contemplated the stark contrast between his mundane morning and the life-and-death struggles that his brother, Bill, and countless others had endured on this fateful day in Dieppe.

Brian's anxiety surged as he sought more information about his brother's fate during the Dieppe Raid. He approached the local military recruitment office with a heavy heart, hoping to learn whether Bill had been with his unit during the operation and whether he was still alive.

Inside the reception area, festooned with posters of courageous soldiers, Brian felt a sense of unease settle over him. Approaching the desk, he spoke to the officer on duty, his voice trembling with concern. "I need information about my brother, Bill. He was part of the Dieppe Raid yesterday, serving with the Royal Hamilton Light Infantry."

The officer, his expression a mix of empathy and gravity, requested Bill's full name and any identifiable details. Brian shared all he could recall, feeling a knot of dread tightening in his chest. The officer retreated to the back office to make inquiries, leaving Brian to wait anxiously.

The minutes dragged on as Brian's thoughts raced through various scenarios. Had Bill survived the chaos of Dieppe, or had he become one of its unfortunate casualties? The uncertainty weighed heavily on him.

Finally, the officer returned, clutching a piece of paper. His expression remained somber as he delivered the news, "I have information about your brother, Bill. I regret to inform you he was killed in the Dieppe Raid."

Brian's world shattered in an instant. The room seemed to spin, and the words hung heavily in the air. The officer continued, offering details about the circumstances of Bill's passing, but Brian struggled to absorb the information. His brother, his flesh and blood, was gone, lost amid the chaos of that ill-fated operation.

Tears welled up in Brian's eyes as he tried to process the devastating news. The weight of grief pressed down on him, and he felt a profound sense of loss. The realization that he would never see his brother again was almost too much to bear.

"Thank you," Brian said, his voice choked with emotion. "Thank you for letting me know." He left the recruitment office with a heavy heart, the world around him suddenly bleak and unforgiving. The news of Bill's death during the invasion of Dieppe marked the beginning of a painful journey through grief and mourning, a journey that would shape the rest of Brian's life.

Overwhelmed by the grief of losing his brother Bill in the disastrous Dieppe Raid, Brian's footsteps felt heavy as he left the military recruitment office. The weight of the news hung like a dark cloud over him, and he couldn't shake the feeling of sorrow and loss that threatened to consume him.

In search of solace and some way to numb the pain, Brian instinctively headed to McKibbin's Irish Pub, a place that had become a refuge during difficult times. The familiar surroundings and the camaraderie of the regular patrons offered a semblance of comfort.

As he walked through the pub's door, the low hum of conversation, the clinking of glasses, and the warm, dimly lit atmosphere greeted him like an old friend. The bartender, Liam, recognized Brian and nodded in acknowledgment. He poured a shot of whiskey and slid it over the bar without a word.

Brian took the glass in trembling hands and downed the fiery liquid in a single gulp. The burn in his throat was a welcome distraction from the overwhelming grief that threatened to drown him. He ordered another, then another, each shot providing a temporary respite from the agony that gnawed at his heart.

His mind whirled with questions, trying to make sense of the senseless tragedy. How could this have happened? Who was responsible for the disaster in Dieppe? Brian knew the answers wouldn't bring Bill back, but he couldn't help but yearn for some understanding, some closure.

As he sat at the bar, Brian's thoughts drifted back to the night before, when he had been blissfully unaware of the events unfolding overseas. He recalled the laughter and conversations at CGs, the

Greek neighbors, and the mundane concerns of daily life. It all felt like a distant memory, a stark contrast to the harsh reality of the present.

Liam, the bartender, approached Brian with a sympathetic look. He had seen many patrons drown their sorrows, but he knew that Brian's pain ran deeper than most. "You've been through a lot, my friend," Liam whispered. "If you need someone to talk to, I'm here."

Brian nodded, appreciating the gesture, but the words caught in his throat. How could he articulate the depth of his grief and the profound sense of loss? Instead, he simply raised his glass in acknowledgment, signaling for another round.

The hours passed in a blur as Brian sought refuge in the numbing embrace of alcohol. McKibbin's Irish Pub provided a temporary escape from the harsh realities of life, a place where he could momentarily forget the pain of losing his brother in the tragedy of Dieppe.

As Brian's mind became clouded with the numbing effects of alcohol, his thoughts kept circling back to the haunting question: Who was responsible for his brother Bill's death in the Dieppe Raid?

In the dimly lit corner of McKibbin's Irish Pub, surrounded by the comforting din of fellow patrons, Brian's mind churned with a mix of anger, grief, and confusion. He couldn't comprehend why the operation had gone so terribly wrong, why Bill and so many others had to pay the ultimate price.

The news of the disaster in Dieppe had been a stark wake-up call, shattering his previously blissful ignorance. Brian was now hearing about the raid's objectives, the plans to gather intelligence and test amphibious assault tactics. But now, those objectives seemed distant and meaningless in the face of the devastating loss.

He couldn't help but wonder about the decisions made by the higher-ups, the generals, and the leaders who had sanctioned the operation. Were they aware of the risks, the formidable German defenses, and the challenges that awaited the soldiers on the beaches of Dieppe?

Brian knew that in the chaos of war, mistakes could happen, and the fog of battle could obscure even the best-laid plans. But the magnitude of the disaster left him searching for answers, for someone to hold accountable. His anger simmered beneath the surface, an ember that threatened to ignite into a blaze of indignation.

As he nursed his drink, Brian reflected on the broader context of the war. He knew the Allies faced immense challenges and that every battle carried its uncertainties. The fight against the Axis powers demanded sacrifice and unwavering determination. But Bill's death felt like an unbearable cost, one that Brian struggled to reconcile with the larger goal of victory.

The hours slipped away, and the patrons of McKibbin gradually dispersed, leaving Brian alone with his thoughts and the dimly lit bar. He knew that in time, he would have to come to terms with the loss of his brother, to honor Bill's memory and make sense of the tragedy.

But for now, in the haze of alcohol and grief, Brian's thoughts remained fixated on the weighty question that had taken hold of his soul: Who handled the death of his brother in the ill-fated invasion of Dieppe? The answer remained elusive, and the pain of not knowing tore at his heart.

Brian's descent into a dark desire for revenge weighed heavily on his depth. The anger and pain stemming from his brother Bill's death in the ill-fated Dieppe Raid had consumed him to where he was contemplating actions he never thought himself capable of. The idea of seeking retribution and making someone pay for Bill's life had taken root in his mind.

One name, in particular, echoed in his thoughts: Brendan Murphy and his mysterious group, which would be known for their underground activities and rumored connections to acts of violence. Their reputation had reached Brian's ears the previous night, and their willingness to exact justice through extralegal means was a tempting proposition.

As Brian grappled with these dark thoughts, he isolated himself from friends and family, consumed by a singular purpose: to find those responsible for Bill's death and make them pay. He became consumed by a relentless pursuit of retribution, believing it was the only way to honor his brother's memory.

He made inquiries, seeking individuals who could put him in touch with Brendan Murphy's group. The more he delved into this dangerous world, the more he distanced himself from the values and principles he had once held dear. The line between right and wrong blurred in his mind as he inched closer to a path that would change him irrevocably.

But as he ventured deeper into this dark territory, a glimmer of doubt and self-reflection emerged. Brian's late-night encounters with shadowy figures and whispered promises of revenge left him increasingly unsettled. He couldn't ignore the moral conflicts that gnawed at his conscience.

One sleepless night, as he contemplated his next move, he recalled the values that Bill had upheld. Bill had been a soldier who believed in the fight against tyranny, but he had also been a brother who had cared deeply for his family. Brian realized that the path of reprisal would tarnish Bill's memory and betray the principles he had fought for.

Brian's internal struggle intensified, torn between the desire for revenge and the realization that it would ultimately bring him down a dark and destructive path. He knew he had a choice to make—one that would define his life.

Brian's call to Brendan Murphy was not driven by a desire for justice or accountability; it was fueled by an unrelenting thirst for revenge. The pain of losing his brother, Bill, in the disastrous Dieppe Raid had consumed him, and he believed that aligning himself with Brendan and his IRA sympathizers was the only way to make someone pay for Bill's death.

As the clock approached eight o'clock, Brian's mind was clouded by thoughts of vengeance. He felt a burning rage and an overwhelming need to act against those he believed were responsible for the tragedy in Dieppe. In his pursuit of revenge, he will cast aside his previous convictions and principles.

When he arrived at McKibbin's Irish Pub to meet Brendan, the atmosphere was tense with the weight of their shared purpose. Brendan, a figure known for his connections and influence within the IRA sympathizer community, was ready to discuss their plans. Brian's determination to seek revenge had drawn him into a dangerous world of covert actions and subversion.

As they sat at a corner table, their voices lowered in a conspiratorial tone, Brian and Brendan discussed their intentions. Brian clarified he would do whatever it took to undermine Britain's fight against Germany, even if it meant resorting to violence and subterfuge.

Brendan, a seasoned advocate for the IRA's cause, understood the depth of Brian's anger and thirst for revenge. He saw in Brian a potential ally, someone who could be used to further their goals. The prospect of having someone as driven and motivated as Brian on their side was enticing.

Their conversation delved into plans for sabotage, espionage, and acts of defiance against the British. Brian's heart pounded with a newfound sense of purpose, even as he knew that the path he had chosen was fraught with danger and moral complexity.

As the night wore on, Brian's commitment to his vengeful cause deepened, and he felt he was finally taking action to avenge his brother's death. However, he was also stepping into a world of secrecy and violence, where the consequences of his actions would be far-reaching and unpredictable.

Brian had chosen a new path that would forever alter the course of his life, leading him into a dangerous alliance with those who sought to undermine Britain's fight against Nazi Germany. The pursuit of payback had driven him to a dark place, where the lines between right and wrong blurred, and the consequences of his choices remained uncertain.

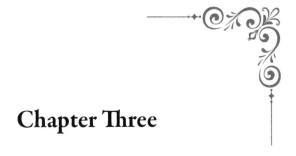

Chapter Three

As Brian sat at the table in McKibbin's Irish Pub, surrounded by Brendan Murphy and his group of IRA sympathizers, he couldn't help but feel a sense of unease. The atmosphere in the pub had shifted from conspiratorial whispers to an open discussion, and the tension in the air was palpable.

Brendan re-introduced Brian to the rest of the group, each member's name a mix of curiosity and suspicion. Brian Kelly, however, greeted Brian with hostility, immediately questioning his presence and motives. The accusation that Brian might be a spy hung in the air, causing a collective murmur of concern among the group.

Brendan quickly intervened, attempting to quell the rising tension. He informed the group of Brian's motivation for joining their cause—the tragic loss of his brother at Dieppe. The revelation caught the attention of the group, and Brian's presence made more sense.

Brian Kelly, though initially hostile, softened slightly upon hearing the connection to Dieppe. "Your brother was at Dieppe?" he asked, his tone no longer accusatory but tinged with empathy.

Brian nodded somberly. "Yes, he was," he replied, his voice heavy with grief and determination. "And I want those responsible for what happened there to pay."

The group fell silent, the weight of Brian's words sinking in. They had all been drawn together by a common cause—to undermine British efforts in the war—but Brian's personal tragedy added an extra dimension to their mission. He was not merely seeking revenge for revenge's sake, but was driven by a deep desire for justice.

As the group continued their discussion, they saw Brian as a potential asset, someone who could bring a unique perspective and motivation to their efforts. The tragic loss of his brother had transformed him into a passionate advocate for their cause, and it was a level of commitment that resonated with the group.

Brian's journey had taken an unexpected turn, plunging him into a world of clandestine activities and subversion. The group had its reservations, but they also recognized the value of having someone as dedicated and determined as Brian on their side. As they discussed their plans and strategies, they couldn't help but wonder how his presence might change the course of their mission to undermine Britain's fight against Nazi Germany.

The meeting at McKibbin's Irish Pub continued, with Brendan Murphy and his group engaging in a candid discussion with Brian about their objectives and strategies. Brian, driven by his desire for revenge and justice in the wake of his brother's death at Dieppe, focused as they shared their plans to undermine Britain's efforts in the war.

Over time, the initial suspicion surrounding Brian's presence dissipated. The group saw in him not only a fervent advocate but also a potential asset who could bring a fresh perspective to their mission. Brian's determination to ensure that those responsible for the tragedy in Dieppe were held accountable resonated deeply with them.

Brian Kelly, who had been initially hostile, became more understanding as he realized the personal stakes involved for Brian. "I get it now," he said, his tone no longer confrontational. "You're not here to play games; you want justice for your brother. We can respect that."

Brendan Murphy, the group's de facto leader, continued to outline their plans, which included acts of sabotage, espionage, and subterfuge aimed at undermining British efforts in various ways. Brian, while still focused on revenge, appreciated the broader implications of their actions. He saw the potential to make a significant impact on the war effort, not just for his satisfaction, but also for the greater cause he had joined.

As the night wore on, Brian's determination grew. He had found a new sense of purpose in aligning himself with Brendan and his group. It was a path fraught with danger and moral ambiguity, but he will accept the risks in pursuit of his goals.

In the weeks and months that followed, Brian became an integral part of Brendan's team. He contributed his passion, determination, and knowledge to their efforts, while they helped him channel his thirst for revenge into strategic actions aimed at undermining the British war machine.

Brian's journey had taken an unexpected turn, from a grieving brother seeking vengeance to a dedicated member of an underground organization with a mission to alter the course of history. The consequences of his choices remained uncertain, but he was committed to ensuring that his brother's death would not be in vain and that those responsible would face the penalties.

As the discussion continued at McKibbin's Irish Pub, the group's plans for subversion and resistance against British efforts in the war grew increasingly detailed. Brendan Murphy, with his commanding presence and strategic mind, laid out a series of actions they intended to take in the coming weeks.

Brian, who had joined the group focusing singularly on revenge, became more deeply involved in their mission. He saw that their actions, while aimed at undermining the British war effort, could also serve a broader purpose—a purpose that would honor the memory of his brother and prevent future tragedies like Dieppe.

Throughout the evening, the atmosphere in the pub shifted from suspicion to a sense of camaraderie. The group members shared their personal stories and motivations for joining the cause. Each one had been touched by the ravages of war in their way, whether through family losses, political convictions, or a desire for a better future.

Brian Kelly, who had initially been confrontational, became an ally rather than an adversary. "We're all here for a reason," he said, his voice filled with determination. "And we can't afford to let our personal vendettas blind us to the bigger picture."

Gráinne O'Connor, one of the group's members, shared her experiences of growing up in an Ireland divided by political strife. Her passionate recounting of her family's history and her longing for a united and independent Ireland struck a chord with Brian, reinforcing the idea that their actions had far-reaching implications beyond their grievances.

As the night wore on, the group's resolve solidified. They discussed logistics, contacts, and the importance of discretion in their operations. They were a diverse but dedicated team, each member contributing their unique skills and perspectives to the cause.

Brian, still carrying the weight of his brother's death, felt a sense of purpose and belonging among this group of like-minded individuals. He knew that the path he had chosen was fraught with danger, but he would accept the risks in the pursuit of justice and the hope of preventing future tragedies of war.

The meeting at McKibbin's Irish Pub marked the beginning of a new chapter in Brian's life, one in which his desire for revenge was transformed into a broader mission of resistance and change. As the group continued to plan their actions, they became a formidable force, determined to make a lasting impact on history.

In the days and weeks that followed their meeting at McKibbin's Irish Pub, Brian became increasingly integrated into Brendan Murphy's group of IRA sympathizers. As they honed their plans for subversion and resistance against British efforts in the war, Brian's role grew more defined, and he forged deep bonds with his newfound comrades.

The group's actions ranged from acts of sabotage to intelligence gathering, all aimed at undermining British operations and support for the war. Brian, once consumed by his thirst for revenge, now viewed these activities through a broader lens. He saw them to prevent further tragedies like Dieppe and to honor his brother's memory by making a tangible impact on the war effort.

Brian Kelly, who had initially been skeptical of Brian's intentions, had become a trusted ally and confidant. The two shared their personal stories and motivations, finding common ground in their determination to bring about change. They became a formidable team, each contributing their unique skills to the group's operations.

Gráinne O'Connor's unwavering commitment to the cause continued to inspire Brian. Her dream of a united and independent Ireland, free from the shackles of British rule, resonated deeply with him. He saw their actions as not only a means of seeking justice for his brother, but also as a step toward achieving a better future for all.

As Brian's involvement deepened, so did his sense of responsibility. He understood that the consequences of their actions could be severe, and he was determined to ensure that their efforts remained focused on their goals rather than descending into chaos and violence.

The group's activities took them to various locations, and they operated with meticulous planning and precision. Their actions were discreet, and they left a few traces behind. It was a high-stakes game, and the stakes grew higher with each successful operation.

Brian's journey, from a grieving brother seeking revenge to a dedicated member of an underground organization with a broader mission, continued to develop. He had found a new purpose among his comrades, and he was committed to seeing their cause through to the end.

As they worked tirelessly to undermine British efforts in the war, Brian's brother Bill remained a constant presence in his thoughts and memories. He knew that every action he took was in pursuit of justice for Bill and hoped to prevent more lives from being lost to the ravages of war.

Chapter Four

As the group of IRA sympathizers gathered at Brian's apartment, their discussions turned to the pressing issue of acquiring weapons for their subversive activities. Brendan Murphy had expressed frustration at their lack of firepower, which was hampering their ability to effectively undermine the Allies' fight against the Axis powers.

Brian Kelly, who had initially been skeptical of Brian's involvement, now presented an idea that captured the group's attention. He proposed raiding the Westmount Armory, a nearby location where they might find a cache of weapons.

Gráinne, always eager for action, asked, "Why don't we hit one of the armories? They are always full of weapons, right?" Her suggestion resonated with the group, and they nodded in agreement.

Brian, wanting to ensure clarity on their plan, asked, "Which one?" Brian Kelly, who seemed to have some knowledge of the area, quickly responded, "How about the Westmount Armory? It's on Ste-Catherine Street West." He pointed out that it was conveniently close to his residence, which would make it easier to coordinate the operation.

The group pondered the suggestion and agreed that the Westmount Armory was a viable target. Brian Kelly added, "We can hit it tonight. There is usually not more than one watchman guarding the whole place."

Brian, ever mindful of their actions, emphasized a crucial point. "Just one thing I want to be understood. I don't want the old watchman hurt." The group members exchanged solemn glances and nodded in agreement, understanding the importance of minimizing harm to innocent individuals.

Their plan was set in motion, and a sense of purpose filled the room. As the hours passed, they made preparations for their mission to the Westmount Armory, fully aware of the risks and potential consequences that lay ahead. It was a pivotal moment for the group, as they took a step closer to gaining the weapons they believed would further their cause and ultimately bring about the change they sought.

The group hit the armory after midnight. The old watchman was situated in his office listening to a hockey game on the CBC radio station as the sounds from the radio filled the building. Brian and the group gathered the weapons and headed to the back door. "Damm that old man must be deaf as a doornail. You can hear the game all over the building," uttered Brian. Everyone agreed as they exited the building.

The group's sense of relief was short-lived as the night air was pierced by the sound of approaching police sirens. Panic gripped them, and they quickly realized that they were not out of danger.

As they tried to make their way to a safer location, the situation took a dire turn. The sound of barking canines filled the air, sending a chill down their spines. The police had deployed dogs to aid in their search, and the animals' keen senses threatened to give away their position.

Desperation fueled their actions as they attempted to evade both the police officers and their relentless canine companions. The group members scattered in different directions, hoping to confuse their pursuers and create an opportunity to regroup later.

Brian, carrying the weight of the weapons they had gained, knew that their chances of escaping capture were dwindling. The darkness of the night provided some cover, but the police dogs were closing in, their barks growing louder and more insistent.

Each member of the group faced a moment of reckoning, torn between the urgency of escape and the commitment to their cause. The pursuit was relentless, and their options were limited.

In the chaos and uncertainty of the moment, they made split-second decisions that would determine their fate. The night air was filled with tension and fear as they raced against time and the relentless pursuit of the police and their canine companions. The consequences of their actions were closing in, and the group members knew their journey had taken a dangerous turn, one that would test their resolve and determination to the limit.

Brian's heart pounded in his chest as he sprinted up Westmount Street, desperate to escape the relentless pursuit of the police and their canine companions. Every step was a painful reminder of the risks he had taken and the commitment he had made to his cause.

With each breath he took, the distance between him and his pursuers grew, but he knew he couldn't stop until he was certain he had evaded capture. The chase had taken him to the back of St. Joseph Oratory, a towering basilica that loomed in the darkness.

Out of breath and with adrenaline coursing through his veins, Brian quickly assessed his surroundings. He needed a place to hide, to catch his breath, and to plan his next move. The oratory offered a potential refuge.

Moving swiftly, Brian scoured the exterior of the building, looking for any point of entry. His heart sank as he realized that the main doors were securely locked. The police were likely not far behind, and he couldn't afford to waste time.

Just as panic threatened to set in, Brian spotted an open window on the lower level. Without hesitation, he scrambled to reach it, his hands and clothes catching on the rough exterior of the building. With a last burst of effort, he squeezed through the window and into the oratory.

The interior of St. Joseph Oratory was a stark contrast to the chaos outside. It was quiet and dimly lit, with a sense of serenity that provided a stark difference to the events of the night. Brian took a moment to catch his breath and gather his thoughts.

He knew he couldn't stay in the oratory for long, but it offered him a temporary break and a chance to plan his next steps. The consequences of their daring mission weighed heavily on him, but his determination remained unshaken. Brian was prepared to do whatever it took to continue his journey down the perilous road of resistance and subversion, even if it meant seeking refuge within the hallowed walls of St. Joseph Oratory.

Brian finally, after some time and the quietness of the surroundings, with no sounds of canines, Brian figured it was his chance to leave.

Brian's cautious journey continued as he walked through the streets of Westmount, his senses on high alert for any signs of danger. The Westmount lookout provided a momentary pause in his escape, allowing him to survey the southern end of Montreal for any signs of pursuit. He strained his ears for the telltale sound of sirens but heard nothing. For the moment, the police were not closing in on his location.

With a measure of relief, Brian continued his trek toward his apartment. Every step was deliberate, and he maintained a watchful eye on his surroundings, scanning for any signs of a police presence. The weight of the weapons he carried served as a constant reminder of the risks he had taken and the importance of his mission.

As he neared the street of his apartment, Brian's anxiety heightened. He knew he was not in the clear yet and that the danger was far from over. He moved slowly, his senses finely tuned to detect any hidden officers of the law or potential threats.

The streets were eerily quiet, and the darkness of the night added to the sense of uncertainty. Brian remained vigilant, knowing that he needed to reach his apartment safely to regroup and plan his next steps.

As he finally approached his apartment building, he couldn't help but feel a sense of relief that he had made it this far without incident. However, he also understood that the consequences of their daring mission would continue to hang over him and his comrades.

With cautious steps, Brian entered his apartment building and made his way to his unit. He knew acutely that the night's events had changed the course of his life, and the challenges that lay ahead were far from over. The commitment he had made to seek justice for his brother and make a lasting impact on history remained unwavering, and he knew that the path he had chosen was filled with uncertainty and danger.

As Brian settled into the armchair next to his apartment's window, his exhaustion and the events of the night weighed heavily on his mind. He gazed out, scanning the quiet streets for any signs of movement or potential threats. With each puff of his newly lit Rothman cigarette, he tried to calm his racing thoughts.

The night had been long and fraught with danger, and he had done his best to navigate the challenges that came his way. The dim light of dawn crept over the horizon, casting a pale glow over the city of Montreal. It was a new day, and Brian couldn't help but wonder about the safety and whereabouts of his comrades.

As he took another drag from his cigarette, fatigue overcame him. The adrenaline that had fueled his escape and evasion slowly waned, leaving him physically and mentally drained. The armchair was comfortable, and the warmth of the early morning sun on his face provided a sense of reassurance.

Slowly, as the cigarette burned down to the filter, Brian's eyelids grew heavy. The thoughts of his comrades, the weapons they had gained, and the daring mission they had undertaken swirled in his mind. With each passing moment, his body succumbed to exhaustion.

Unbeknownst to him, the sun continued its ascent in the sky, filling the apartment with gentle morning light. Brian's weariness finally overcame him, and he drifted into a deep and much-needed sleep.

Hours later, he awoke to the bright rays of the sun streaming through the window, warming his face. Disoriented and unsure of the time, he rubbed his eyes and tried to regain his bearings. The events of the previous night came flooding back, and he knew he had much to contemplate and plan for in the wake of their daring mission.

As Brian sat up in the armchair, he realized that the journey he had embarked upon had only just begun. The consequences of their actions were still uncertain, and the challenges ahead remained daunting.

Brian got up and went to his bathroom so he could wash his face. He changed his shirt and after contemplating where he should hide the stolen weapons decided to place them in a small opening in the ceiling of his closet.

Brian sat in his favorite booth at CG's, hunger gnawing at him, he contemplated his next steps. He knew he needed to eat and gather his thoughts, but the events of the previous night still weighed heavily on his mind.

Lydia, the familiar server, brought him his order, providing a small but welcome distraction. The aroma of the food filled the air, and Brian ate, finding some solace in the simple act of nourishing himself. A full stomach had always helped him think more clearly, and he hoped it would provide some clarity now.

However, as he savored his meal, his sense of unease returned. Two young Montreal police officers entered the restaurant and took seats at the counter. Panic surged through Brian as he realized there was no immediate escape. He had been living in the shadow of the events of the previous night, knowing that capture was a constant threat.

The officers engaged in conversation with Lydia, discussing the events of the night. Brian's heart raced as he strained to listen, the weight of their words hanging in the air. The officers revealed that the Westmount Armory had been broken into, and a group had made off with weapons. Brian knew they were referring to his comrades and their daring mission.

Lydia, ever the inquisitive server, asked if the police had caught any of them. Brian held his breath, waiting for the officers' response. To his immense relief, one officer replied, "Not yet, but we will."

A wave of relief washed over Brian, though he knew that the danger had not completely passed. He continued to eat, trying to maintain an air of nonchalance, while his mind raced with thoughts of what to do next. The events of the previous night had left an indelible mark on his life, and he understood that the path he had chosen was fraught with uncertainty and danger.

As Brian continued to eat his meal, the weight of his recent escape and the ongoing pursuit of his comrades lingered in the background of his thoughts. The conversation between the two young police officers at the counter carried on, but Brian's attention remained divided.

The officers, unaware of his presence, discussed the ongoing investigation into the break-in at the Westmount Armory. Brian couldn't help but feel a mixture of relief and anxiety. While he had evaded capture for now, the danger still loomed, and he knew he couldn't let his guard down.

Lydia, serving the officers' coffee, continued to inquire about the situation. "Have you got any leads on who did it?" she asked.

The officers exchanged a glance before one of them replied, "We're following up on some leads, but it's a tricky situation. These guys seem to know what they're doing."

Brian's heart raced as he considered the implications of their words. He knew that the group he had joined was determined and resourceful, but their actions had certainly attracted the attention of law enforcement. The officers' acknowledgment of the group's competence only added to the weight of the situation.

As he was finishing his meal, Brian contemplated his next moves. He had to reconnect with his comrades, assess the situation, and determine the best course of action. The events of the past night had left an indelible mark on his life, and he was determined to see their mission through to its conclusion, whatever that may entail.

With his meal finished and his thoughts racing, Brian paid his bill and left the restaurant, the knowledge that he was still on the run a constant reminder of the perilous path he had chosen.

Brian stepped out of CG's restaurant, the bright Montreal sun contrasting with the tension that still gripped him. While he had narrowly avoided capture, he knew that the danger was far from over. The police were actively investigating the break-in at the Westmount Armory, and his comrades remained in the crosshairs of law enforcement.

As he walked the streets of Montreal, Brian considered his next steps. He needed to regroup with his comrades, assess the situation, and decide on their next move. Aware that the police would be closely monitoring their usual haunts and hideouts, Brian knew that reuniting with his fellow IRA sympathizers would be a challenging task. He would have to rely on their network of contacts and their ability to maintain secrecy.

Brian's mind raced with thoughts of the weapons they had gained, the mission they had undertaken, and the risks they faced. He had ventured deep into the world of resistance and subversion, and there was no turning back.

As he moved through the bustling streets of Montreal, Brian couldn't help but feel a profound sense of purpose. The events of the past night had thrust him into a world of intrigue, danger, and uncertainty.

With every step, he contemplated the road ahead, knowing that the path he had chosen was fraught with challenges and consequences. Brian was resolute in his commitment to his cause and his determination to bring about the change he sought, no matter the sacrifices or risks involved. The journey continued, and the fate of his comrades and the impact they would make on history remained uncertain but unwavering in their resolve.

In the days that followed, Brian embarked on a series of clandestine meetings with his fellow IRA sympathizers. Their network of contacts allowed them to communicate discreetly and arrange rendezvous points away from prying eyes. Each meeting was filled with hushed conversations and careful planning as they assessed the situation and discussed their next moves.

The break-in at the Westmount Armory had sent shockwaves through the city, and the police were intensifying their efforts to apprehend the group responsible. Brian's comrades, like him, were acutely aware of the risks they faced, but their fortitude to undermine Britain's war effort remained steadfast.

One evening, at a dimly lit pub far from their usual haunts, Brian and his fellow IRA sympathizers gathered to discuss their plans. Brendan Murphy, the group's leader, outlined their objectives and the importance of the weapons they had acquired. They knew their actions had brought them to the attention of law enforcement, but they were undeterred.

Brian felt a renewed sense of purpose as he sat among his comrades. The memory of his brother Bill, who had given his life in the invasion of Dieppe, blazed in his mind. He was no longer the same man who had stumbled home drunk on that fateful night. His commitment to seeking justice for his brother and holding those responsible to account had transformed him. As the group discussed their strategies and considered potential targets, Brian's determination to make those who had caused his brother's death pay with their lives grew stronger.

The path ahead remained fraught with danger and uncertainty, but Brian and his fellow IRA sympathizers were resolute about their commitment to their cause. With each meeting and each clandestine operation, they moved one step closer to their objectives, fully aware of the sacrifices and risks involved.

The events of the past night had marked the beginning of a journey that would test their resolve, challenge their principles, and shape the course of their lives. Brian, now fully immersed in their mission, knew that their actions would have far-reaching consequences, and he was prepared to face whatever came their way on the perilous road they had chosen.

The covert meetings and surreptitious operations continued, each one executed with precision and secrecy. Brian and his fellow IRA sympathizers operated in the shadows, driven by their unwavering commitment to their cause and their willpower to bring about change.

Their activities took them to various parts of Montreal and beyond, always staying one step ahead of law enforcement's efforts to apprehend them. The weapons they had gained from the Westmount Armory became instrumental in their plans, as they handpicked targets that would weaken Britain's war effort and send a powerful message.

Brian's transformation from a dispirited man burdened by grief to a determined agent of change was clear to all who knew him. The memory of his brother Bill remained a driving force, propelling him forward with an unshakable determination.

With each operation, the group grew bolder, and their actions garnered attention. Their acts of sabotage and disruption made headlines, sending shockwaves through the city. The police intensified their efforts to apprehend the group, but Brian and his comrades continued to operate with a level of cunning and secrecy that kept them one step ahead.

As the months passed, Brian couldn't help but reflect on the events that had led him to this point. His journey from a grief-stricken man to a dedicated agent of change had been filled with challenges and dangers, but he remained steadfast in his commitment. He was prepared to see their mission through to its conclusion, no matter the cost.

The fate of Brian and his fellow IRA sympathizers remained uncertain, and the consequences of their actions weighed heavily on their shoulders. But they knew they were making a difference, and that the sacrifices they were making were in pursuit of a greater goal.

The road ahead was still fraught with peril, but Brian and his comrades continued to move forward, guided by their unyielding determination to bring about the change they sought and to make those responsible for their grievances pay with their lives. The battle they had embarked upon was far from over, and they were prepared to face whatever challenges lay ahead on the perilous path of resistance and subversion.

The news from Brendan about the involvement of a crack investigative team from the RCMP sent a ripple of unease through the group gathered at their customary table in McKibbin's Irish Pub.

The tension in the room was palpable as they absorbed the implications of this development.

Doyle O'Reilly's question hung in the air as they awaited Brendan's explanation of the potential threat posed by Inspector Robert McAllister and his team. Brendan's expression grew serious as he continued to speak.

Inspector McAllister's reputation as the best that the RCMP offered was well known, and his involvement in their case elevated the stakes considerably. If anyone could track them down and bring them to justice, it would be him.

Brian, who had been through so much since that fateful night in Dieppe, couldn't help but feel a sense of frustration and anxiety at this recent development. The pressure they were already under had intensified, and the consequences of their actions were growing more severe.

As the group contemplated the challenges ahead, the determination in their eyes remained unwavering. They knew they had chosen a path fraught with danger, and they were prepared to face whatever obstacles came their way.

The battle they had embarked upon was far from over, and the involvement of Inspector McAlister only added to the urgency of their mission. They would need to be more careful, more strategic, and more resolute than ever before as they continued their journey down the perilous road of resistance and subversion.

The news of Inspector Robert McAllister's involvement weighed heavily on the minds of Brian and his comrades as they gathered at their table in McKibbin's Irish Pub. The atmosphere was tense, and the sense of urgency in the room was intense.

Brendan Murphy, their leader and the one with connections to the police station, continued to explain the gravity of the situation. Inspector McAllister was not just any law enforcement officer; he was renowned for his investigative prowess and determination. His reputation had earned him the nickname "the best," and he posed a significant threat to their activities.

Brian couldn't help but feel a mixture of frustration and anxiety. The pressure they were already under had intensified, and their mission had become even more perilous. Every move they made would now be scrutinized by an elite team of investigators, making their operations even riskier.

Despite the challenges and the increasing danger, Brian and his comrades remained resolute. The memory of his brother Bill and their commitment to seeking justice fueled his determination. They knew they couldn't back down now; the stakes were too high.

As they sat at their table, they discussed how they would need to adapt their tactics, become even more discreet, and stay one step ahead of Inspector McAllister and his team. The battle they had embarked upon was far from over, and they were prepared to face the heightened pressure with the same unwavering resolve that had brought them this far.

With each passing day, their journey down the perilous road of resistance and subversion became more treacherous, but Brian and his comrades were determined to see it through, no matter the obstacles they encountered. The fight for justice and their quest for vengeance continued, and they were ready to face whatever challenges lay ahead.

In the days that followed, Brian and his fellow IRA sympathizers adhered to a new level of caution and secrecy in their operations. Inspector Robert McAllister's involvement had elevated the danger they faced to a whole new level, and they knew acutely that their every move was under scrutiny.

Their meetings became even more discreet, held in remote locations and with heightened security measures in place to avoid detection. Communication was conducted through encrypted channels, and they employed a web of contacts to relay messages and coordinate their activities.

Each operation was carefully planned and executed with meticulous attention to detail. The group had to be more strategic than ever before, avoiding patterns that could be tracked and leaving no trace behind. The weapons they had gained remained instrumental in their efforts, and they used them with precision and restraint.

Brian, driven by the memory of his brother Bill and the desire for vengeance, became a key player in their operations. His determination to see their mission through to its conclusion burned brighter than ever. He understood that the involvement of Inspector McAllister meant they were in a race against time and a battle of wits.

As the group continued to carry out acts of sabotage and disruption against British interests, they remained vigilant for any signs of Inspector McAllister and his team closing in. The tension and uncertainty of their situation were ever-present, but their commitment to their cause remained unshaken.

The battle they had embarked upon was a perilous one, and the stakes had never been higher. Brian and his comrades were prepared to face whatever challenges lay ahead, driven by their unwavering resolve to bring about the change they sought and to make those responsible for their grievances pay with their lives. The road ahead remained treacherous, but they were determined to navigate it with courage and determination.

Chapter Five

B rian's battle against the biting winter winds left him chilled to the bone as he sought refuge inside CG's. He shivered as he sat down and rubbed his hands vigorously, trying to coax some warmth back into his frozen fingers. The cold was a stark reminder of the harsh reality of their operations, where they had to contend not only with danger but also with the elements.

A cup of hot coffee offered some respite from the cold, and Brian gratefully accepted it. His concern for Lydia, the friendly server who had become a familiar face in his daily routine, was clear in his question. He couldn't help but worry about her well-being.

The news of Lydia's injury, sustained during the explosion at the recruitment center the previous night, sent a pang of concern to him. While he was relieved to hear that her injuries weren't severe, he couldn't shake the feeling that their activities were affecting the lives of innocent bystanders.

As he sipped his coffee, Brian reflected on the unintended consequences of their actions. Their mission had always been driven by a sense of justice and a desire for vengeance, but it was becoming increasingly clear that the collateral damage was a harsh reality they had to confront.

The personal connection he felt with Lydia made the situation even more poignant. She had been a source of comfort in his turbulent life, and the thought that she had been injured because of their activities weighed heavily on him.

Brian understood that the path they had chosen was fraught with complexity and moral ambiguity. Their fight for justice came at a cost, not only to themselves but to those who were in the wrong place at the wrong time. It was a sobering reminder of the sacrifices and challenges they faced on their perilous journey of resistance and subversion.

Brian knew that their mission had always been driven by a deep desire for vengeance and justice for his brother Bill, who had paid the ultimate price during the invasion of Dieppe. But as he sat there, he couldn't help but question the path they had chosen.

The unintended consequences were gnawing at him, and he wondered whether their actions were truly making a difference or if they were simply perpetuating a cycle of violence and suffering. He contemplated the moral complexities of their situation and the ethical implications of their choices.

Yet, despite these doubts and concerns, Brian's resolve remained unshaken. He knew he couldn't turn back now. The memory of his brother's sacrifice and the injustices he had witnessed compelled him to see their mission through to its conclusion.

The road ahead remained treacherous and fraught with moral uncertainty, but Brian and his comrades were determined to navigate it with courage and conviction. The battle they had embarked upon was far from over, and they were prepared to face whatever challenges and ethical dilemmas lay ahead on their perilous journey of resistance and subversion.

In the days that followed, Brian found himself grappling with the moral complexities of their actions more than ever before. The injury to Lydia, someone he cared for during their tumultuous activities, weighed heavily on his conscience.

He couldn't escape the fact that their pursuit of justice and revenge was exacting a toll not only on themselves but also on innocent individuals like Lydia. Their covert operations had consequences that rippled beyond their intended targets, and Brian was increasingly troubled by the ethical implications of their choices.

The memory of his brother Bill, who had given his life in the invasion of Dieppe, remained a driving force in Brian's life. It was the foundation of his unwavering commitment to their cause. However, he couldn't ignore the growing doubts that festered in his mind.

Brian knew that the path they had chosen was a treacherous one, fraught with moral obscurity and hard decisions. He grappled with whether their actions were truly making a difference or if they were perpetuating a cycle of violence and suffering.

Yet, even in the face of these doubts, Brian couldn't turn away from the mission he had undertaken. His comrades, equally committed to their cause, looked to him for leadership and guidance. The stakes had never been higher, and the battle they had embarked upon was far from over.

As Brian continued to navigate the challenges and ethical dilemmas of their perilous journey of resistance and sedition, he did so with a heavy heart and a deep sense of responsibility. The road ahead remained uncertain, but he was resolved to see their mission through to its conclusion, no matter the sacrifices or moral complexities they encountered along the way.

Brian's inner turmoil continued to simmer as he grappled with the moral complexities of their actions. The injury to Lydia had been a stark reminder of the unintended consequences of their covert operations. It was increasingly difficult for him to reconcile the desire for justice and revenge with the collateral damage their actions caused. He wondered whether Bill would have approved of the path they had chosen and the consequences it entailed.

Brian found solace in the camaraderie of his fellow IRA sympathizers, who shared his dedication and resolve. They were all bound by a common purpose, yet they too grappled with their moral dilemmas and doubts.

As they continued to navigate the treacherous road of resistance and insurrection. The involvement of Inspector Robert McAllister had heightened the danger they faced, but it had also strengthened their resolve to see their cause through.

Brian knew that the path ahead was uncertain, fraught with ethical challenges and hard decisions. He couldn't predict the outcome, but he remained committed to doing everything in his power to make those responsible for his brother's death pay with their lives. The battle they had embarked upon was a complex and perilous one, and the road ahead was filled with uncertainty. Their journey continued, driven by the memories of their fallen comrades.

Brian headed to his meeting when he turned the corner. Brian's heart raced as he approached McKibbin's Irish Pub and found it surrounded by police cars and ambulances. A sinking feeling settled in his stomach, and he knew that something significant had occurred. The scene before him was chaotic, and he couldn't help but fear the worst.

Instinctively, he stepped back, realizing that approaching the pub at that moment was not a wise move. He needed to wait and gather more information before he could determine the nature of the incident and whether it had any connection to his activities.

Brian's mind raced with possibilities, and a sense of foreboding hung in the air. The pressure they had been under had already taken a toll on their operations, and this unexpected turn of events only added to the uncertainty and danger they faced.

He knew that he would have to exercise caution and patience as he awaited more information. The road ahead remained fraught with peril, and Brian couldn't help but wonder if their decision to stand down from subversive attacks had come too late to prevent further tragedy.

Brian stood at a distance, hidden in the shadows of a nearby building, as he observed the unfolding scene outside McKibbin's

Irish Pub. The flashing lights of police cars and the sound of sirens created a chaotic atmosphere that sent shivers down his spine.

There was a knot in his stomach as he anxiously watched paramedics rushing in and out of the pub, carrying stretchers and attending to the injured. The presence of ambulances showed that whatever had transpired inside the pub had led to casualties, and Brian couldn't help but feel a deep sense of unease.

Questions raced through his mind. What had happened inside the pub? Were any of his comrades involved? Had their decision to stand down come too late to prevent this tragedy?

Brian's heart pounded in his chest as he waited for more information. He knew that jumping to conclusions could be dangerous, but he couldn't shake the feeling that the incident might have been connected to their activities, directly or indirectly.

As he continued to watch and wait, the weight of the situation pressed down on him. The pressure they had been under had escalated, and the consequences of their actions were becoming increasingly apparent. Brian braced himself for the inevitable reckoning that lay ahead, praying that none of his comrades were among the casualties and fearing that their world of resistance and subversion was spiraling out of control.

Hours passed as Brian maintained his vigil, hidden from view, watching the scene unfold outside McKibbin's Irish Pub. The presence of emergency responders and the continuous activity at the scene only heightened his anxiety and sense of foreboding.

As time wore on, Brian couldn't help but wonder about the fate of his comrades. The decision to stand down from subversive attacks on military establishments had been a difficult one, born out of the realization that their activities were causing unintended harm to innocent bystanders. But had their withdrawal come too late? Had this incident, with its police presence and ambulances, directly resulted from their previous actions?

The weight of responsibility pressed down on Brian's shoulders. He knew that the line between their pursuit of justice and the unintended consequences of their actions was a fine one. Their mission had been driven by a deep desire for vengeance and justice, but it had also led to chaos and tragedy.

As he continued to wait for more information, Brian couldn't escape the fear that their world was unraveling before his eyes. The pressure they had been under had escalated to an unbearable level, and the consequences were now undeniable.

The road ahead remained uncertain, and Brian was filled with a sense of trepidation. The choices they had made, the battles they had fought, and the sacrifices they had endured were all coming to a head in this moment of crisis. It was a sobering reminder of the high cost of their mission, and Brian could only hope that he would soon learn more about the incident and its implications for their cause.

Brian's decision to leave the scene outside McKibbin's Irish Pub was a cautious one, driven by the realization that staying hidden any longer could jeopardize his safety. The uncertainty surrounding the incident had left him on edge, and his thoughts were consumed by concerns for the safety of his comrades.

As he made his way back home, Brian couldn't help but replay the events of the day in his mind. The pressure they had been under, the decision to stand down from subversive attacks, and the crisis outside the pub had all converged to create an atmosphere of anxiety and tension.

Upon reaching his apartment, Brian took refuge in his armchair, which sat beside the window overlooking the street below. It was a vantage point that allowed him to monitor any movement that might warrant a quick escape through the fire escape at the back of his building.

The minutes ticked by, and Brian's senses remained on high alert. The world outside was fraught with uncertainty, and he knew he had to be prepared for whatever might come next. The safety of his comrades, the consequences of their actions, and the future of their mission hung in the balance.

As he sat in his dimly lit apartment, Brian braced himself for the unknown, ready to face whatever challenges and dangers lay ahead on the perilous road. The path they had chosen was fraught with peril, and he couldn't afford to let his guard down, even for a moment.

Brian's apartment was shrouded in a hushed stillness, the only sound the occasional distant hum of the city outside. He remained seated in his armchair by the window, his eyes fixed on the dimly lit street below.

Outside, the city's nighttime activities continued, oblivious to the turmoil in Brian's mind. He strained to detect any unusual movements or sounds that might signal a need for a hasty retreat. The fire escape, a potential lifeline, beckoned him as a silent promise of escape should danger draw nearer.

Thoughts raced through his mind like shadows in the night. What had transpired at the pub? Were his comrades safe? Had their withdrawal from subversive activities come too late to prevent this crisis?

Brian's sense of responsibility weighed heavily on him. He knew that the decisions they had made collectively had led to this point, and he couldn't shake the feeling that the consequences of their actions were now catching up with them.

As minutes turned into hours, Brian remained vigilant, unable to shake the sense of foreboding that had settled over him. The future of their mission hung in the balance, and the safety of his comrades was a constant source of concern.

The room was shrouded in darkness, illuminated only by the faint glow of the city's lights outside. Brian's eyes remained fixed on

the window, a solitary figure on the edge of uncertainty, ready to face
whatever challenges and dangers lay ahead on his perilous road.

The night wore on, and Brian's vigil from his apartment
continued. The city's bustling sounds gradually gave way to a deeper
quiet as the hours passed, but Brian's senses remained finely tuned to
any signs of trouble.

His thoughts circled back to his comrades, the ones he had
shared so much with on this journey of resistance and subversion.
The decision to stand down from their subversive attacks on military
establishments had been difficult but necessary, and he couldn't help
but wonder if it had come too late to prevent the crisis outside the
pub.

Each passing moment was laden with uncertainty, and Brian's
sense of responsibility weighed heavily on his shoulders. The choices
they had collectively made had led them to this point, and he
couldn't escape the feeling that the consequences of their actions
were closing in on them.

The fire escape, a potential escape route, remained a constant
presence at the back of his mind. Brian knew that should the need
arise; he would have to rely on it to make a swift exit and evade any
danger that might threaten him.

As the night slowly surrendered to the first hints of dawn, Brian
remained seated in his dimly lit apartment, a solitary figure on the
precipice of an uncertain future. The safety of his comrades and the
fate of their mission were still hanging in the balance, and the road
ahead remained treacherous and fraught with danger.

As the first rays of dawn filtered through the window of Brian's
apartment, casting a pale, grayish light into the room, he felt a
strange mix of relief and exhaustion wash over him. The long night
of vigilance had taken its toll, both physically and emotionally.

Brian's eyes, heavy with fatigue, continued to scan the street
below, although the urgency of the situation had diminished with

the coming of daylight. The city outside had slowly awakened, with people starting their daily routines, unaware of the turmoil that had gripped Brian's mind throughout the night.

The sense of menacing still lingered, but Brian knew he had to take some respite. He had been prepared for danger, but the hours of waiting had tested his endurance. The fire escape, once a symbol of escape and evasion, now seemed more like a lifeline to rest and recuperation.

With great effort, Brian pushed himself up from the armchair and made his way to the small kitchencttc. He poured himself a glass of water and felt the cool liquid soothe his parched throat. It was a slight comfort, but it was something.

As he returned to the window, he couldn't shake the feeling that the road ahead was going to become even more treacherous. The incident outside McKibbin's Irish Pub had been a stark reminder of the dangers they faced, and Brian knew that he and his comrades would have to be even more cautious in the days to come.

The memory of his brother Bill and his commitment to their cause remained his driving force. Brian was determined to see their mission through, no matter the sacrifices and challenges that lay ahead. The city below was waking up to a new day, but for Brian, the road of resistance and destabilization remained as uncertain as ever.

Brian's decision to head to CG's was motivated by the restaurant's reputation as a hub of gossip and information. He quickly prepared himself for the cold weather, donning his parka, and made his way to the familiar establishment.

As he entered CG's, he was greeted by the welcome sight of Lydia, the server he had grown fond of. Her absence had been keenly felt, and Brian couldn't help but feel a sense of relief and warmth as he saw her again. He approached her and enveloped her in a big hug, expressing his delight at her return and how much her presence meant to the restaurant.

Lydia reciprocated the sentiment and led Brian to his customary booth, where she promptly poured him a cup of coffee. It was a small but comforting gesture, and Brian appreciated the sense of normalcy it brought to his day.

With a curious glint in his eye, Brian leaned in and asked Lydia about the gossip and news making the rounds. It was a way to stay informed about the city's events, especially given their recent involvement with the RCMP inspector.

Lydia recounted the information she had gathered since her early shift, sharing tidbits about a shooting at the Astor Bar on St. Catherine Street. However, it was her mention of a significant shootout at McKibbin's Irish Pub on Bishop Street that piqued Brian's interest.

He leaned in, eager for more details. "What happened at the pub?" he inquired; his voice laced with curiosity.

Lydia, ever the reliable source of information, relayed the account she had heard. A confrontation had taken place between the group responsible for the recent bombings and an RCMP inspector. Brian listened intently, his heart racing as he processed the implications of what she was saying.

The news of the shootout and its casualties weighed heavily on his mind, and Brian couldn't help but wonder if this was the beginning of the reckoning he had feared. The road ahead remained fraught with uncertainty, and the challenges they faced were becoming increasingly complex and dangerous.

As Lydia continued to share the details of the shootout at McKibbin's Irish Pub, Brian's sense of unease deepened. The implications of what she was describing were significant, and he couldn't help but feel a growing sense of dread.

Listening intently, Brian learned that the confrontation had involved the group responsible for the recent bombings—the very group he and his comrades were connected to. That an RCMP inspector had been involved in the altercation made it even more ominous.

Lydia's words painted a grim picture: four individuals killed, three wounded. The toll was substantial, and Brian couldn't help but wonder if any of his comrades had been among the casualties. The news hung heavily in the air, and he knew that their world had just taken a perilous turn.

Brian's thoughts raced as he considered the potential consequences of this violent encounter. The involvement of law enforcement, and an inspector from the RCMP, no less, meant that their actions were under even greater scrutiny. The pressure was mounting, and the group's ability to continue their mission was becoming increasingly jeopardized.

Yet, even in the face of these challenges, Brian's determination remained unshaken. The memory of his brother Bill and justice for his death were driving forces that compelled him to continue down this perilous path.

As Lydia continued to share the latest gossip and news, Brian's mind was consumed by the implications of the shootout. The road ahead was more uncertain than ever, and the challenges they faced were growing in both complexity and danger. The fate of his comrades and the future of their mission hung in the balance, and Brian knew that the decisions he and his group made in the coming days would be critical.

Brian's breakfast was a somber affair as he contemplated the grim reality of their situation. The shootout at McKibbin's Irish Pub and the involvement of law enforcement had raised the stakes to a dangerous level. It was becoming increasingly clear to him that staying in Montreal was no longer a viable option.

With a heavy heart, Brian made a tough decision—he needed to leave town, at least temporarily, to evade the growing law enforcement presence and the potential threats to his safety. He knew that in their world of confrontation and sedition, betrayal was always a lurking danger.

Chapter Six

The destination he settled on was Quebec City, a place where he was an unknown entity. It was a choice made of necessity, driven by the need for anonymity and safety. Brian understood he was facing an uncertain future, and he needed to take action quickly.

Finishing his breakfast, he settled the bill and left CG's, knowing that it might be the last time he walked its familiar streets for a while. Heading back to his apartment, Brian moved with a sense of urgency. He wasted no time packing what he needed, mindful of the fact that every minute counted.

As he walked out of his apartment, and onto the street, a chilling sight unfolded before him. Police cars and a SWAT van raced by, coming to a screeching halt in front of his building. The realization hit him like a ton of bricks—someone had turned him in.

Brian's heart raced as he realized how narrowly he had escaped capture. It was a close call that served as a stark reminder of the dangers he faced. With each step he took away from his apartment and the chaos that had erupted there, Brian knew he was venturing into an uncertain and perilous world.

The road ahead was fraught with danger, but he was determined to navigate it with caution and resilience. Quebec City beckoned as a place of refuge, a temporary sanctuary where he could regroup and plan his next moves in his high-stakes game of resistance and subversion.

Brian's journey to Quebec City had been marked by tension and uncertainty, but he found himself incredibly fortunate as he hitched a ride with the first truck heading east on Highway 40. The truck driver, despite the language barrier, had provided him with safe passage and dropped him off at Galeries de la Capitale, a shopping center in the city.

Inside the bustling mall, Brian took a moment to gather himself and satisfy his hunger at one of the food court kiosks. As he meandered through the mall, he noticed a sign in one restaurant, which was Greek, showing that they needed help.

Brian, ever resourceful and eager to establish himself in his new surroundings, approached the manager and explained his situation—that he had just arrived in town and was seeking employment and a place to stay. To his surprise, fortune favored him once more.

The owner, Bill Destounis, offered him a job on the spot, and the owner's wife, Stella, informed Brian that they had a vacant basement apartment available if he was interested. Brian wasted no time in accepting both offers. His stroke of luck seemed almost miraculous, considering the circumstances that had led him to Quebec City.

Brian started his new job as an assistant cook and dishwasher, ready to immerse himself in his work and his newfound life. When the restaurant closed, they took him to their house to show him the basement apartment, which he found to be perfect for his needs.

The turn of events had been unexpected, but Brian couldn't help but feel a glimmer of hope in this new chapter of his life. As he settled into his job and his new living quarters, he knew that the road ahead remained uncertain, but for the time being, he had found a safe haven in Quebec City—a place where he could regroup, plan, and, hopefully, continue pursuing justice for his brother's death while navigating his complex world.

The apartment was a welcome surprise, and Brian couldn't have asked for a better place to settle into his new life in Quebec City. As he entered the furnished apartment, he took in the details of his additional living space.

The living area was comfortable, adorned with tasteful furnishings that made it feel like home. A sofa and coffee table provided a spot to relax, while a dining area offered a place to enjoy meals. The walls were decorated with artwork and photographs, giving the space a personal touch.

The kitchen was equipped with modern appliances, making it easy for Brian to prepare his meals. The bedroom featured a comfortable bed, a dresser, and ample storage space for his belongings. The apartment even had its own bathroom, ensuring privacy and convenience.

The basement apartment was well-lit, with windows allowing in natural light and offering views of the surrounding area. It was a far cry from the dimly lit and sparsely furnished accommodations he had grown accustomed to in Montreal.

As Brian settled into his new surroundings, he felt a sense of gratitude for the kindness and generosity of the restaurant owners who had offered him this opportunity. It was a chance for a fresh start, a place where he could rebuild his life and continue his pursuit of justice for his brother's death.

With a roof over his head and a job to sustain him, Brian knew he was in a much better position than he had been in Montreal. Yet, the challenges and uncertainties of his mission still lay ahead, and he was determined to face them head-on, no matter the sacrifices required.

Brian settled into his new routine, working diligently at the restaurant six days a week. Sundays were his sole day off, coinciding with the restaurant's closure. It was a day he often spent catching up on the news and trying to find any updates about the events in Montreal, although his efforts had been mostly in vain.

One Sunday morning, as he perused the newspaper in his furnished apartment, Brian was abruptly interrupted by a knock at the front door. His heart raced as he opened the door to reveal a vision of beauty—a young woman named Anastasia, who introduced herself as the daughter of the restaurant owners and his new employers.

Stunned by her presence and momentarily at a loss for words, Brian greeted her with a warm but somewhat awkward smile. Anastasia, undeniably charming, explained that her parents, who lived upstairs, had sent her to extend an invitation. They wanted to host him for supper that evening at six o'clock.

Brian's initial surprise quickly gave way to a sense of delight, and he readily accepted the invitation with a wide smile. As Anastasia turned to leave, Brian couldn't help but watch her graceful departure with a mixture of fascination and gratitude. It was an unexpected and pleasant turn of events, offering a welcome reprieve from the challenges and uncertainties of his new life in Quebec City.

The hours leading up to the dinner invitation passed slowly for Brian. He found himself nervous about the prospect of dining with Anastasia's family, who also were his employers. The small apartment, where he had been living for a short time, suddenly felt like it needed tidying up.

With anticipation bubbling inside him, Brian used his free time to freshen up, ensuring that he looked presentable for the evening ahead. He changed into a clean shirt, combed his hair, and tried to put his best foot forward. The prospect of dinner with Anastasia's family was not just an opportunity for a good meal; it felt like a chance to establish rapport and build connections in this new city.

As the clock inched closer to six o'clock, Brian left his apartment and made his way upstairs to Anastasia's family's home. He knocked on the door, a hint of nervousness still lingering, but his excitement overshadowed any anxiety he might have felt.

The door swung open, revealing Anastasia, who greeted him with a welcoming smile. She led him into their home which was filled with friends of the family, and Brian couldn't help but be struck by the warmth and hospitality of her family. Their graciousness made him feel at ease as if he were a welcomed guest, not just an employee.

The dinner passed with pleasant conversation and delicious food, and Brian couldn't help but feel a sense of gratitude for the unexpected turn his life had taken. Anastasia's family had not only provided him with a job and a place to stay, but had also extended their hospitality, which made him feel like he was becoming a part of their community.

The dinner at Anastasia's family home turned out to be a delightful and memorable Greek feast. Brian, their honored guest, was treated to a culinary experience that showcased the richness of Greek cuisine and the warmth of their hospitality.

The meal began with a selection of traditional Greek appetizers, known as "mezedes." On a beautifully set table, they served dishes like tzatziki, which was a creamy yogurt-based dip with cucumbers, garlic, and dill, served with warm pita bread. Some Dolmades grape leaves stuffed with a flavorful mixture of rice, herbs, and ground meat, then simmered in a lemony sauce. Spanakopita, a flaky layer of phyllo pastry filled with a savory blend of spinach, feta cheese, and herbs, and some Kalamata Olives that Brian didn't like but ate, anyway. They were plump and briny, these olives provided a burst of bold flavor.

The main course was a hearty and aromatic affair, with several dishes to choose from. They had Moussaka, which was a layer of eggplant, ground lamb or beef, and creamy béchamel sauce, baked to perfection. Souvlaki skewers of marinated and grilled chicken or pork served with lemon wedges and pita bread, which Brian found delicious. A refreshing combination of crisp lettuce, ripe tomatoes, cucumbers, red onions, Kalamata olives, and crumbled feta cheese, drizzled with olive oil and sprinkled with oregano. A Rice Pilaf, a fragrant rice cooked with onions, garlic, and herbs, offers a flavorful side dish. Also, some Roasted Vegetables, a medley of seasonal vegetables, are roasted to bring out their natural sweetness.

Brian's favorite part was the Desserts. He took one of everything. Greek desserts are known for their sweet indulgence, and this meal was no exception. Baklava is a layer of flaky phyllo pastry filled with a mixture of chopped nuts and sweetened with honey or syrup. Loukoumades, which was a small, airy doughnut drizzled with honey and sprinkled with cinnamon and crushed walnuts. Galaktoboureko, a creamy custard dessert encased in layers of phyllo pastry and soaked in a sweet syrup, was Brian's favorite. He wanted to ask for another piece, but held back. He didn't want to look like a pig.

Throughout the meal, guests sipped on traditional Greek beverages, including a glass of Retsina, a Greek white wine with a unique pine resin flavor. After the meal was finished, they poured everyone a small glass of Ouzo, a potent anise-flavored liquor often served with a splash of water, turning it cloudy white.

The dinner was filled with laughter, conversation, and the joy of sharing delicious food. Brian was not only treated to a culinary journey through Greece but also embraced as an integral part of Anastasia's family, who had opened their hearts and their home to him.

As the evening ended, Brian left with a full stomach and a heart filled with gratitude for the warmth and generosity of his hosts. It was a meal that had not only satisfied his hunger but also nourished his soul, reminding him of the bonds of friendship and the potential for new beginnings in this city that was

As he bid farewell to Anastasia and her family and their guess that evening, Brian carried with him a renewed sense of hope and purpose. Despite the challenges and uncertainties that lay ahead, he was reminded that in this new city; he had found not only refuge but also the potential for new friendships and connections. It was a small but significant step forward in his journey to seek justice for his brother's death and navigate the complex world of resistance and subversion.

In the frigid months that followed, Brian's life had settled into a comfortable routine. He found solacc and purpose in working at the Destounis restaurant, where he was not only treated as an employee but as a member of the family. The restaurant owners, Mr., and Mrs. Destounis had shown unwavering kindness and generosity toward him, and Brian had grown close to their daughter, Anastasia, whose beauty continued to captivate him.

Under the guidance of the seasoned Mr. Destounis, Brian honed his skills in the culinary trade. He had progressed to where he could run the restaurant during the evenings by himself, allowing older adult couples to enjoy much-deserved nights off. It was a testament to the trust they had in Brian and the bond that had formed between them.

One particularly busy night, on July 1st, as Canada celebrated Dominion Day, the restaurant was bustling with patrons. Brian and the staff worked tirelessly to serve the enthusiastic crowd. Eventually, as the night wore on, the last customer departed, and the restaurant closed down.

As the crew began the routine cleaning and closing procedures, Brian was mopping the floor when the door unexpectedly swung open. Without looking up, he instinctively uttered, "Sorry, we're closed."

However, the voice that responded was one Brian had never expected to hear again. He stopped in his tracks and turned to face the newcomer, his mop in hand. "Brendan? What are you doing here? I thought you were in prison."

Brendan, Brian's once-closest friend and confidant, seemed untroubled by the situation. He casually replied, "I thought you'd be happy to see your best pal."

Brian's eyes bore into Brendan as he questioned, "How did you get out of jail?" The implications of Brendan's presence and his unexpected freedom were deeply troubling.

Brendan, maintaining his nonchalant demeanor, offered a somewhat cryptic explanation. "Let's just say I'm a nice guy. We worked out an arrangement—some information for my release."

Brian couldn't hide his disbelief and dismay. "You turned on the others?"

Brendan's response was chillingly pragmatic. "Every man for himself."

Brian's anger and disappointment were palpable as he recounted his narrow escape that fateful day. "By the way, how the hell did you find me?"

Brendan leaned in; his expression was serious. "I have my ways, Brian."

The unexpected reunion with his friend-turned-traitor had thrown Brian's world into disarray once more. The questions about Brendan's motives and the true nature of his release lingered, casting a shadow over the fragile stability he had found in Quebec City.

The night felt longer than usual for Brian as he grappled with the complex emotions stirred up by Brendan's unexpected appearance. He couldn't help but replay the events of their past and wonder how their paths had diverged so dramatically.

The following day, Brian woke up early, his thoughts still consumed by the impending meeting with Brendan. He dressed quickly, choosing a spotless shirt, and a worn but well-fitting jacket that had become his trademark attire. Before leaving his furnished apartment, he took a moment to glance at the photograph of his late brother, Bill, which sat on a small table by the window. Bill's memory served as a constant reminder of the purpose that had driven Brian to this point.

As he walked to the designated meeting spot near the St. Lawrence River, Brian's mind raced with questions. He needed answers, not just about Brendan's release and actions, but about the bigger picture. He was determined to find out if there was any truth to the rumors that had circulated about the disastrous events in Dieppe, events that had claimed his brother's life.

When Brian arrived at the old pier, the midday sun cast shimmering reflections on the water, creating an idyllic yet incongruous backdrop for their clandestine meeting. He scanned the area, alert for any signs of surveillance, though his instincts told him that Brendan wouldn't put him at risk.

Moments later, Brendan arrived, his expression betraying little emotion. They exchanged a curt nod as they spoke, mindful of the importance of their words. Brendan was the first to break the silence.

"You want answers, Brian. I get it. But I need you to understand that things have changed. Loyalties shifted. And I had to make a choice."

Brian, his voice tinged with a mix of anger and frustration, retorted, "A choice that put our comrades in danger? A choice that could have destroyed everything we believed in?"

Brendan's gaze didn't waver as he replied, "Sometimes survival means making tough decisions. You weren't there, Brian. You didn't see what I saw."

Their conversation continued, marked by moments of heated argument and tense silences. Brian pressed for details about Brendan's agreement with the authorities and the extent of his betrayal. He needed to know whether Brendan had truly severed all ties with their former group or if he was still playing a dangerous double game.

As they talked, it became apparent that there was more to Brendan's actions than met the eye. His motives were complex, driven by a mixture of self-preservation, disillusionment, and a desire for a fresh start. The past had become a tangled web of secrets and regrets, and their friendship, once unbreakable, had been irrevocably altered.

By the time the conversation concluded, Brian had gained a semblance of understanding, though many questions remained unanswered. Brendan had offered a measure of transparency, though he remained a mysterious figure with uncertain loyalties.

As they parted ways, the old pier bore witness to a fractured bond, a testament to the harsh realities of their tumultuous journey. Brian was left to grapple with the complexities of his friend's actions, unsure of what the future held and whether trust could ever be fully restored between them.

In the days that followed their tense reunion at the old pier, Brian couldn't shake the feeling of unease that had settled over him. His meeting with Brendan had yielded some answers, but it had also raised more questions about the path they had both taken and the diverging allegiances that had torn their once-close friendship asunder.

Brian had always been a man driven by a sense of justice, fueled by the memory of his brother Bill and the desire to make those responsible for the disaster at Dieppe pay for their actions. Brendan's actions had muddied the waters of that pursuit, leaving Brian to wonder if they could ever fully reconcile their differences.

At the Destounis restaurant, where Brian continued to work and had found a semblance of stability and family, life went on. Anastasia and her family remained a source of support and warmth, offering a counterbalance to the turmoil that seemed to follow Brian like a shadow.

Yet Brian knew he couldn't ignore the larger forces at play. Rumors of war and conflict continued to swirl around him, and he couldn't help but feel that he was on the precipice of a new chapter in his life, one that would demand tough choices and unwavering resolve.

Chapter Seven

The city of Quebec, with its winding streets and centuries-old architecture, provided a backdrop to Brian's contemplations. It was a place of history and change, a city that had seen the rise and fall of empires. And in that city, Brian was just one man, grappling with his past and uncertain future.

As he walked along the cobblestone streets of Old Quebec, his thoughts turned to the larger world beyond the city's walls. The war raged on, and the events in Europe were casting a long shadow over Canada and its people. Brian couldn't help but wonder if his quest for justice would ever find its resolution or if the world's turmoil would forever keep him in its grip.

One thing was certain: Brian's journey was far from over. The choices he made, the alliances he formed, and the secrets he uncovered would shape his destiny and lead him down a path fraught with danger and uncertainty. But he was determined to press forward, driven by a sense of duty and a deep-seated need to honor his brother's memory.

The future remained uncertain, but one thing was clear: Brian's resolve had never been stronger, and he was prepared to face whatever challenges lay ahead in his pursuit of justice and truth.

As Brian waited at the haunted Irish pub, L'Oncle Antoine, the anticipation of the evening's events swirled within him. He couldn't help but feel a mixture of excitement and nervousness as he glanced at the small package in his jacket pocket. Inside lay a delicate diamond ring, a symbol of the future he hoped to build with Anastasia.

The old pub, with its rustic charm and stories of hauntings, added an element of intrigue to their dinner date. Brian had chosen it, hoping the unique atmosphere would make the occasion even more memorable for both of them.

As the evening approached, Brian's thoughts drifted to the conversation he had with Mr. Destounis, Anastasia's father. Brian had sought the old man's permission to ask for his daughter's hand in marriage, a gesture rooted in tradition and respect. Mr. Destounis had been delighted by the proposal, readily giving his blessing. The idea of having Brian as a son-in-law was met with warmth and approval.

As the clock ticked closer to 7 p.m., the pub filled with patrons, some seeking a taste of the supernatural, others simply enjoying the cozy ambiance. Brian's heart raced with both the nerves of his impending proposal and the eagerness to see Anastasia.

Finally, Anastasia arrived, her smile lighting up the dimly lit pub. She greeted Brian with a warm hug, her dark eyes reflecting the anticipation of the evening ahead. They found a quiet corner in the pub, where they could enjoy their dinner and the haunted atmosphere.

Throughout the evening, Brian and Anastasia shared stories and laughter, their connection deepening with each passing moment. Brian couldn't have asked for a more perfect setting for this special occasion.

As the night wore on, Brian's nervousness resurfaced. He knew that the time broached the subject that weighed heavily on his mind. Taking a deep breath, he reached into his pocket and produced the small diamond ring. With trembling hands, he slid the ring across the table toward Anastasia.

Anastasia's eyes widened in surprise as she picked up the ring, her fingers delicately tracing its contours. She turned to Brian, her gaze filled with a mix of emotions, and asked softly, "What's this, Brian?"

Brian took a steadying breath and looked deeply into her eyes. "Anastasia, we've shared so much, and you've become an integral part of my life. I love you more than words can express, and I want to spend the rest of my life with you. Will you marry me?"

The pub, with its whispered legends of lost souls, seemed to hold its breath as Anastasia's answer hung in the air, and the fate of their future together rested on her response.

Time seemed to stand still as Brian awaited Anastasia's response, his heart pounding in his chest. The hushed atmosphere of the haunted pub lent an air of anticipation to the moment, as though the spirits of L'Oncle Antoine were silently watching the scene unfold.

Anastasia held the delicate diamond ring in her hand, her fingers trembling slightly. Her gaze shifted from the ring to Brian's eyes, and there was a vulnerability in her expression that Brian had never seen before. It was as though the weight of their shared history and the promise of their future hung in the balance.

Finally, Anastasia's lips curled into a warm, radiant smile. The tension in the air dissipated, replaced by an overwhelming sense of relief and joy. She nodded, her eyes glistening with tears of happiness. "Yes, Brian, a thousand times, yes. I love you too, and I want nothing more than to spend my life with you."

As Brian slipped the ring onto Anastasia's finger, their hands briefly touched, sending a shiver of electricity down his spine. The haunted pub, known for its ghostly apparitions and eerie tales, seemed to come alive with their shared moment of happiness.

Their dinner continued with a newfound sense of excitement and anticipation of the future. They talked about their dreams, their hopes, and the life they wanted to build together. It was a night filled with laughter, whispered promises, and stolen glances across the table.

By the time they left L'Oncle Antoine, the pub's ghosts, if they indeed existed, might have witnessed a love story of their own. Brian and Anastasia walked hand in hand through the historic streets of Quebec City, their hearts full of love and the promise of a life filled with adventure, happiness, and the enduring bond of their shared commitment.

The haunted pub, with its mysteries and legends, had become the backdrop for a new chapter in their lives, one that was sure to be filled with love, laughter, and the echoes of their shared history.

After their enchanting supper at L'Oncle Antoine, Brian, and Anastasia were filled with excitement and a shared sense of destiny. The haunted pub had been the backdrop to a significant moment in their lives, and the memory of the evening would forever hold a special place in their hearts.

As they left the pub, the cool night air of Quebec City wrapped around them, and the cobblestone streets seemed to echo with their laughter and whispered promises. Brian and Anastasia walked hand in hand, their steps light and purposeful, toward Anastasia's family home.

The Destounis residence was a charming house with an inviting warmth that extended beyond its doors. Anastasia's parents, Mr., and Mrs. Destounis, had welcomed Brian into their lives with open arms, recognizing the genuine love and connection between their daughter and the young man from Montreal.

With each step they took, the anticipation of sharing their engagement news with Anastasia's parents mounted. Brian and Anastasia's hearts raced in unison, their love for each other and the promise of a shared future propelling them forward.

Upon arriving at the Destounis home, they exchanged meaningful glances that conveyed their readiness for this significant moment. Anastasia's hand trembled slightly as she reached for the door handle, and Brian's reassuring smile bolstered her confidence.

As the door swung open, they were greeted by the comforting aroma of Greek cuisine, a testament to the Destounis family's culinary expertise. The warm, inviting ambiance of the house immediately enveloped them, making them feel like cherished guests in their own love story.

Anastasia's parents, sitting in the cozy living room, looked up with expressions of curiosity and warmth. The Destounis had long suspected that their daughter and Brian would be together, and the sight of the two of them entering the room hand in hand confirmed their hopes.

With a beaming smile, Anastasia spoke, her voice filled with a mixture of excitement and reverence. "Mom, Dad, we have something incredible to share with you." Her eyes sparkled with emotion as she held up her left hand, the delicate diamond ring catching the soft glow of the room's lighting.

Mr. and Mrs. Destounis exchanged knowing glances; their hearts filled with joy. They had been waiting for this moment, and their anticipation was met with elation as Brian and Anastasia shared their engagement news.

Brian, his voice filled with sincerity, addressed Anastasia's parents directly. "Mr. and Mrs. Destounis, I love your daughter with all my heart, and I have asked her to marry me. We want your blessings and your love as we embark on this journey together."

Tears of happiness welled up in Mrs. Destounis' eyes as she embraced her daughter, and Mr. Destounis extended a welcoming hand to Brian. Their blessings were offered with genuine warmth and enthusiasm, affirming their belief in the love that Brian and Anastasia shared.

The room seemed to glow with the collective joy of the moment, a celebration of love, family, and the promise of a bright future. Brian and Anastasia's engagement not only deepened their commitment to each other, but also strengthened their connection with Anastasia's family.

As they sat together in the living room, sharing stories and laughter, the evening felt like a chapter from a fairy tale—a love story that had overcome obstacles and adversity to find its perfect moment of happiness.

The engagement marked the beginning of a new chapter in their lives, one filled with anticipation, dreams, and the unwavering support of their families. In the warm embrace of the Destounis home, Brian and Anastasia knew that their love was not only a force of nature, but also a testament to the power of love and destiny.

In the days and weeks that followed their memorable night at L'Oncle Antoine, Brian and Anastasia's love story continued to flourish. The haunted pub had become a cherished memory, a place where their journey toward a shared future had begun.

Brian's bond with Anastasia's family, the Destounis, grew stronger with each passing day. He was not only a valued member of their restaurant team, but also a beloved addition to their close-knit circle. The acceptance and warmth he received from Anastasia's family reaffirmed the depth of their commitment to each other.

As Brian and Anastasia started planning their future together, they dreamed of a life filled with love, adventure, and the promise of new horizons. Brian's proposal had marked the beginning of their engagement, and the anticipation of their wedding day was a constant source of joy.

Together, they explored the historic streets of Quebec City, immersing themselves in the rich culture and traditions of the city. From romantic walks along the cobblestone roads to visits to local art galleries and cozy cafes, every moment they shared deepened their connection.

Brian had found not only a loving partner in Anastasia but also a confidante, a source of strength, and a kindred spirit. They talked about their dreams, their passions, and the values that would shape their life together. Anastasia's unwavering support for Brian's quest for justice and truth only strengthened their bond.

One evening, as they strolled along the banks of the St. Lawrence River, their fingers intertwined, Brian couldn't help but reflect on the twists and turns of his life's journey. From the alleys of Montreal to the haunted pub in Quebec City, his path had been marked by challenges, friendships, and the enduring memory of his brother, Bill.

Their love story was a testament to resilience, forgiveness, and the power of second chances. It was a reminder that even in the face of adversity, new beginnings were possible.

As Brian and Anastasia gazed at the shimmering river under the starlit sky, they felt a sense of peace and contentment. The future remained uncertain, but their love was a steady anchor, guiding them through the uncharted waters that lay ahead.

Their engagement was not just a promise of marriage, but a commitment to facing whatever challenges life might bring with unwavering love and unwavering faith in each other. Together, they were ready to embark on the next chapter of their journey, hand in hand, with hearts full of hope and a shared dream of a life filled with love and adventure.

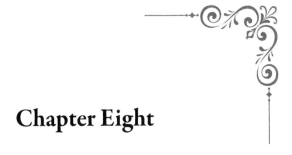

Chapter Eight

One night, as Brian was preparing to close the restaurant, Anastasia came in and sat at the booth at the back of the restaurant. Brian spotted her and smiled as he walked towards her and sat down in front of her. "What a surprise that you came here tonight. I didn't expect you to be here tonight. You doing all right?" "Yeah, I'm okay. I just needed to talk to you. I've been thinking about this for a while and I've decided that you had to know what I did." "You did?" "Yes, I didn't want you not to know what kind of work I was doing." "Okay, I'm listening." Before she started, someone walked in and caught her attention. Anastasia seemed to be speechless as she stared at the intruder. Brian turned to see who or what Anastasia was staring at. It was Brendan. Brian stood up and went to speak to him. "What the hell are you doing here?" "We've got to talk."

Brian's surprise and confusion intensified as he confronted Brendan, the unexpected guest who had walked into the restaurant. The tension in the air was palpable as Brian and Brendan exchanged a series of terse words.

Anastasia, who had initially planned to share something important with Brian, watched the exchange between the two men with growing concern. She couldn't help but wonder what connection Brian had with this unexpected visitor.

Brendan's presence was like a sudden storm disrupting the tranquil evening. He appeared both determined and apprehensive, as if he had urgent news to convey, yet was wary of Brian's reaction.

Brian had mixed emotions upon seeing Brendan. Part of him felt a sense of betrayal because of their past, while another part couldn't deny the history they shared as friends. Brendan's arrival had thrown a wrench into Anastasia's attempt to confide in Brian.

As the other patrons in the restaurant continued with their meals, unaware of the brewing tension, Brian decided they should step outside for a private conversation. He gestured for Brendan to follow him, leading him to a secluded spot away from the prying eyes and ears of others.

Anastasia left alone at her booth, watched their departure with a sense of unease. She knew that whatever had brought Brendan here must be significant, and she hoped it wouldn't disrupt the life she was building with Brian.

Outside, Brian and Brendan engaged in a conversation that was both intense and complicated. The weight of their shared history hung heavily in the air as they confronted the past and the choices that had led them down different paths.

As the minutes passed, Brian couldn't help but wonder how this unexpected meeting would affect his future with Anastasia. The revelation Anastasia had wanted to share remained unspoken, overshadowed by Brendan's arrival and the secrets he carried.

Anastasia, still seated inside the restaurant, watched the night sky through the window, her thoughts filled with uncertainty. She had hoped to confide in Brian, to share her past with him as he had shared his with her. But now, as she waited for their return, she couldn't escape the feeling that the future had become even more uncertain than before.

Brian and Brendan stood in the quiet alley outside the restaurant, their conversation shrouded in a mix of nostalgia and tension. It had been almost a year since they last spoke face to face, and the weight of their shared history hung between them like an unspoken truth.

Brendan, his voice laced with a sense of urgency, finally broke the silence. "Brian, I know you must be wondering why I'm here, especially after everything that's happened."

Brian nodded; his gaze fixed on his old friend. "Yeah, I can't say I expected to see you again, Brendan. What brings you back into my life?"

Brendan hesitated for a moment, his eyes flickering with a mixture of guilt and determination. "I've been living with regret, Brian. Regret what happened that day in Montreal, for the choices I made. I needed to find you, to make amends."

Brian's brow furrowed as he recalled the events of that fateful day in Montreal—the day Brendan had betrayed their group. "Regrets won't change the past, Brendan. What's done is done."

Brendan's expression grew somber. "I know, and I can't change what happened. But I need to make things right, not just for myself, but for all of us who were involved."

Brian's curiosity was piqued. "What do you mean, 'make things right'?"

Brendan took a deep breath, his words measured. "There's something I've discovered, Brian. Something that could bring closure to the past, to the pain and loss we've all endured."

Brian regarded Brendan with skepticism. "Closure? After all this time?"

Brendan nodded; his gaze was steady. "I've been in touch with someone who has information—information about that mission in Montreal, about what really happened, and who was responsible."

Brian's heart quickened as he processed Brendan's words. The mission in Montreal, and the disastrous events of that day, had haunted him for a long time. He had lost his brother, Bill, and had carried the burden of unanswered questions. That there might be answers, even after all this time, was both tantalizing and unsettling.

Brendan continued; his voice was unwavering. "I need your help, Brian. I can't do this alone. Together, we can uncover the truth, expose those who orchestrated it all, and finally find the closure we've been searching for."

Brian contemplated Brendan's proposal. It was a lot to take in—the prospect of revisiting the past, the potential dangers that lay ahead, and the uncertainty of what they might uncover. But the desire for answers, for justice, burned within him, and he couldn't deny the opportunity to make sense of the painful past.

With a sigh, Brian finally spoke. "All right, Brendan. I'll help you. But understand this: it won't change what happened, and it won't bring back those we've lost. But if there's a chance to uncover the truth and hold those responsible, accountable, then I'm in."

Brendan's eyes shone with gratitude, and for a moment, it was as though the weight of their shared history had lifted slightly. They had embarked on a new journey, one that would lead them back into the shadows of their past and, perhaps, toward the closure they both sought.

Brian and Brendan had stood in the quiet alley outside the restaurant, their conversation shrouded in a mix of nostalgia and tension. It had been nearly a year

As they returned to the restaurant, Anastasia watched them closely, her heart heavy with unanswered questions. The revelation she had intended to share with Brian remained unspoken, overshadowed by the unexpected reunion of old friends and the mysteries of their shared history.

Back inside the restaurant, Anastasia's gaze followed Brian and Brendan as they returned from their intense conversation. Their expressions held a mixture of resolve and uncertainty, leaving her curious and anxious about the implications of Brendan's unexpected visit.

Brian retook his seat across from Anastasia, his mind now divided between the past and the future. He realized that his involvement with Brendan's quest for closure might complicate his relationship with Anastasia, but he also knew that the truth was something he had long sought.

Anastasia couldn't contain her curiosity any longer. "Brian, who is he, and what was that all about?"

Brian paused for a moment, choosing his words carefully. "Anastasia, that's Brendan. He's an old friend from my past, someone I thought I'd never see again."

Anastasia's brow furrowed in concern. "But what brought him here? And what were you two talking about?"

Brian leaned in closer, his eyes locking onto Anastasia's. "He claims to have information about an event in Montreal, something that's haunted me for a long time. It was a mission that went wrong, and I lost my brother in it."

Anastasia's eyes widened, and her voice was filled with empathy. "Brian, I did not know. I'm so sorry."

Brian offered a faint smile, touched by her understanding. "Thank you, Anastasia. It's something I've carried with me for a long time. Brendan believes he can shed light on what happened that day."

Anastasia's curiosity deepened. "And what do you think?"

Brian sighed; his gaze distant. "I don't know, Anastasia. It's a lot to take in, and it could be dangerous. But if there's a chance to uncover the truth and find closure, I have to explore it."

Anastasia placed her hand on Brian's, offering support and understanding. "Brian, I'm here for you, no matter what. If this is something you need to do, I'll stand by your side."

Brian's heart warmed at her words, and he squeezed her hand affectionately. "Thank you, Anastasia. Your support means the world to me."

As they sat together, the weight of their conversation hung in the air—a mixture of uncertainty, hope, and the shared acknowledgment that their lives were about to become entwined with the mysteries of the past. Anastasia's revelation, postponed by the unexpected reunion with Brendan, still loomed, and the path ahead remained uncertain.

Brian couldn't help but wonder if the truth Brendan sought would ultimately lead to answers about the past and, in doing so, help them all find the closure they desperately needed.

Anastasia gazed into Brian's eyes, her expression earnest as she continued, "By the way, you were going to tell me something important to you, about us before we got interrupted by Brendan. What was it?"

Brian, still processing the unexpected reunion with Brendan, took a moment to refocus on their conversation. He realized that the revelation Anastasia had intended to share earlier was still hanging in the air, waiting to be unveiled.

Anastasia hesitated for a moment before responding, "Do you know what the Canadian Left is?"

Brian furrowed his brow, admitting, "I'm afraid I don't, Anastasia. What is it?"

Anastasia nodded, understanding that this was not a familiar topic for Brian. She took a deep breath, preparing to shed light on her involvement in a complex world. "Let me try to explain a bit about it."

With a sense of purpose, Anastasia explained the historical context. "At the beginning of World War II, the Canadian intelligence gathering apparatus underwent a massive expansion of scope. The Royal Canadian Mounted Police, formally known as the RCMP, began investigating people and organizations based on their race, religion, political affiliation, or nationalist beliefs. The Canadian left wing became a major priority for intelligence services in the RCMP during the period between the two world wars, particularly focusing on the Communist Party of Canada or the CPC. As the likelihood of a second world war increased in 1938, some attention shifted to fascist movements in Canada."

Brian listened intently, trying to grasp the significance of Anastasia's revelation. Her words hinted at a complex web of political and intelligence activities that he had never been directly involved with.

"Okay," Brian replied, a little confused about where this conversation was heading. He wondered what this had to do with their relationship and the secrets she had hinted at.

Anastasia took a deep breath, her eyes locking onto Brian's as she continued, "Well, Brian, I've been part of the Left Wing since the beginning of the war."

Brian's expression shifted from confusion to astonishment as the implications of Anastasia's revelation sank in. Anastasia was part of the government of Canada, which he had been trying not only to undermine but also desperately trying to distance himself from.

The weight of this revelation hung in the air, its implications reverberating through Brian's mind. Anastasia had shared a significant part of her life with him, a part that was deeply intertwined with the political landscape of wartime Canada.

As Brian processed this new layer of Anastasia's identity, he couldn't help but wonder how it would affect their relationship and the path they were now embarking on—one that led toward the shadows of their shared past and, potentially, toward answers that had eluded them for far too long.

Anastasia sensed Brian needed more clarity and context to understand her role in the intricate world of Canadian intelligence during the war. She continued her explanation, delving deeper into her experience.

"As the war intensified and the threat of espionage loomed larger, the RCMP underwent a significant transformation. They formed specialized divisions, and I worked in the Left Division. Our primary aim was to monitor, infiltrate, and gather intelligence on individuals or groups with leftist or communist leanings, particularly those who might have ties to international communist organizations."

Brian, though taken aback by the revelation, nodded in understanding. He had heard of similar intelligence operations in other countries during the war, where national security concerns led to extensive surveillance.

Anastasia continued, her voice tinged with a sense of duty and responsibility, "My role within the Left Division was not to suppress dissent or persecute individuals based on their beliefs. Instead, it was to ensure that any potential threats to national security were assessed and addressed appropriately."

Brian could see the complexity of Anastasia's position. She had been part of an intelligence apparatus that had to make tough decisions during a tumultuous time, walking a fine line between protecting the nation and safeguarding civil liberties.

"Anastasia," Brian whispered, "I understand you were doing what you believed was right for your country during those challenging times. It must have been a difficult position to be in."

Anastasia's gratitude for Brian's understanding was clear in her eyes. "Thank you for seeing it that way, Brian. I never wanted to keep this from you, but I also knew it wasn't a simple story to tell. I hope we can move forward together, with honesty and trust."

Brian smiled, his heart feeling lighter. "Absolutely, Anastasia. We'll face whatever challenges come our way together."

As they sat together, hand in hand, they realized that their relationship had taken on a new depth—one that embraced their shared past, even the shadows, and offered the promise of a brighter future built on trust and understanding.

Brian looks into Anastasia's eyes with love, compassion, and trepidation. Brian knew Anastasia was in love with him. But would her nationalistic love for her country be stronger than her love for Brian? He loved Anastasia more than life itself. He was scared that it would all fall apart. Could he find a way around this predicament, or was he too far involved with Brendan and the life he created? He had to take revenge on his brother, he just had to.

As Brian gazed into Anastasia's eyes, he couldn't deny the depth of his feelings for her. Love, compassion, and trepidation swirled within him. He knew Anastasia loved him, but he also understood the complexities of her commitment to her country, which had entangled her in the world of intelligence and surveillance.

Questions weighed heavily on Brian's mind. Would Anastasia's loyalty to her country outweigh her love for him? Could their love withstand the challenges posed by their differing allegiances and past secrets? These uncertainties gnawed at his heart.

Brian's love for Anastasia was profound, and he couldn't imagine a life without her. Yet, he was also burdened by the promise he had made to himself—to seek revenge for his brother's death. The life he had become embroiled in, alongside Brendan and their clandestine activities, had taken on a life of its own.

The choices before him seemed daunting. Could he reconcile his love for Anastasia with his quest for vengeance? Or was he too deeply enmeshed in a world that threatened to tear apart everything he held dear?

Anastasia, sensing Brian's inner turmoil, gently squeezed his hand. "Brian," she whispered, "I want you to know that my love for you is unwavering. Yes, I have commitments for my country, but that doesn't diminish what we share. We can find a way to navigate these challenges together."

Brian's heart skipped a beat at her words. The glimmer of hope they held was a beacon in the darkness. He knew their journey would be fraught with obstacles, but with Anastasia by his side, he felt a renewed determination to seek the truth about his brother's fate while preserving the love they shared.

As they faced an uncertain future, their love became a source of strength—a force that could conquer the shadows of the past and illuminate the path ahead.

Brian's love for Anastasia was unwavering, and her reassurance provided a glimmer of hope in the midst of their uncertainties. He cherished their bond and believed that together they could confront the challenges that lay ahead.

Anastasia, perceptive as ever, could sense the weight of Brian's desire for revenge. She understood the pain that drove him, the need for justice, and the haunting memory of his brother's sacrifice on the shores of Dieppe. While she was committed to her duty, she also knew that love had the power to transform, bridge, divide, and guide their actions.

As they sat together, their intertwined hands symbolized their shared journey—a path that would lead them to uncover the truth about Bill's death while navigating the complexities of their respective allegiances.

Anastasia spoke softly, her voice filled with empathy. "Brian, I can't erase the past or the pain you've endured, but together we can seek the truth and ensure that justice is served. It won't be easy, and there will be challenges, but we have each other."

Brian nodded; his eyes locked onto Anastasia's. "I don't know what the future holds, Anastasia, but I know I love you, and I'm willing to face whatever comes our way with you by my side."

Anastasia smiled; her heart warmed by Brian's unwavering commitment. "And I love you, Brian. We'll navigate this journey together, step by step."

Their love, born amid secrets and shadows, had grown stronger through honesty, and understanding. It was a love that could conquer the darkest of challenges and light the way toward the truth they both sought—a truth that would bring closure to Brian's quest for justice and allow them to build a future together, hand in hand.

"Oh, I almost forgot the most important thing I wanted to tell you."

"What could be more important than hearing that you love me, my darling?" answered Brian.

"I have some sort of bad news to tell you."

"And what possible bad news can you ever tell me, Anastasia?"

"We have to postpone our marriage a couple of weeks."

"A couple of weeks. Why?"

"I'm afraid that we have some very important dignitaries that will visit us that week, August 17–24."

"Dignitaries really, are Churchill and FDR coming to Quebec City for some poutine?"

"How did you know it was them coming? It was top secret."

"I didn't know Anastasia; I was trying to be a smart ass, that's all."

"Oh my god, I cannot believe that overreacted that way. I was a bundle of nerves after I heard about it. Please, don't tell anyone or even talk about it."

"Promise me, Brian."

"I promise."

Brian couldn't believe the luck that was placed in his lap. The actual men who were responsible for his brother's death were going to be here in a couple of weeks. He had to contact Brendan right away. This news changed everything!

The revelation that Anastasia had to postpone their marriage for a couple of weeks because of the visit of important dignitaries left Brian both surprised and intrigued. His initial jest about Churchill and FDR visiting Quebec City had inadvertently hit the mark, though Anastasia's reaction had confirmed that it was a top-secret matter.

Anastasia's plea for secrecy and her evident nervousness left Brian with a sense of curiosity. He promised not to speak of it and agreed to keep the matter entirely confidential.

As Anastasia left, Brian's mind raced with possibilities. The timing of the dignitaries' visit was significant—August 17-24. The same week that held painful memories of his brother Bill's death in Dieppe.

The realization struck Brian like a lightning bolt. The dignitaries included the leaders of the Allied forces responsible for the Dieppe Raid—Winston Churchill and Franklin D. Roosevelt. This news was a game-changer.

Brian needed to contact Brendan immediately. The opportunity to confront those responsible for Bill's death was too important to pass up. He knew this news could alter the course of their plans and bring them closer to the truth.

Chapter Nine

The upcoming visit of Churchill and Roosevelt had added a layer of complexity to Brian and Anastasia's lives, one that would test their loyalties, convictions, and commitment to each other as they ventured into uncharted territory.

Brian wasted no time and immediately reached out to Brendan. They had to seize this opportunity, a chance to confront the very individuals responsible for Bill's death in Dieppe. His fingers danced across the phone's keypad as he dialed Brendan's number.

After a few rings, Brendan's voice crackled through the line. "Hello?"

"Brendan, it's Brian. I've got some news that'll change everything."

"What's going on, Brian?"

Brian proceeded to explain the situation, starting with Anastasia's revelation about the upcoming visit of Churchill and Roosevelt to Quebec City. Brendan listened intently, his sense of urgency growing with each word.

"So, you're saying they'll be in Quebec City the same week Bill died in Dieppe?" Brendan asked, his voice low and serious.

"That's right, Brendan. It's too much of a coincidence to ignore. We have a chance to finally confront them, to find out the truth."

Brendan took a moment to think it over. "This could be our shot, Brian. The timing is eerie, but it might just be the sign we've been waiting for. We'll need a solid plan, though."

Brian nodded, even though Brendan couldn't see him through the phone. "I'm willing to do whatever it takes to make this happen. We need to meet in person, Brendan, and figure out the details."

"Agreed. Let's meet at L'Oncle Antoine Pub in an hour. I'll gather the others."

"What others?" asked Brian.

"Fellow sympathizers to our cause."

"Okay, fine. I see you then."

As they hung up, Brian felt a mix of emotions—hope, determination, and the weight of the revenge he had sought for so long. The upcoming meeting with Brendan would set in motion a series of events that could change their lives forever, leading them closer to the payback for Dieppe and the ultimate reckoning with those responsible.

As Brian and the group continued to plan their operation to confront Churchill and Roosevelt during their visit to Quebec City, a heavy weight tugged at Brian's conscience. He couldn't shake the feeling that he was betraying Anastasia by using the information she had shared with him.

Anastasia had inadvertently revealed her involvement with the RCMP's Left Division, a secret she had kept from him. Brian knew that her allegiance to her country and the government's interests might conflict with their plans for revenge. He struggled with the realization that he was pitting himself against the woman he loved.

Late at night, as he lay in bed, Brian's thoughts swirled in a maelstrom of conflicting emotions. He knew he needed to talk to Anastasia, to explain the situation and his motivations. But he also feared that doing so, might jeopardize their relationship.

The next morning, he took a walk along the picturesque streets of Quebec City to clear his mind. As he strolled through the historic district, he couldn't help but marvel at the beauty of the city, the same city where he had found solace and love with Anastasia.

Brian knew he had to make a choice. He could pursue his quest for revenge, potentially at the cost of his relationship with Anastasia, or he could walk away from his past and forge a new future with the woman he loved. It was a decision that weighed heavily on his heart and one that he knew he could not delay much longer.

As he gazed out at the majestic St. Lawrence River, Brian made a silent promise to himself: he would find a way to reconcile his desire for justice with his love for Anastasia, no matter the challenges that lay ahead.

Brian returned to his apartment with a sense of determination. He knew he needed to have an honest and heartfelt conversation with Anastasia. It was the only way to reconcile his desire for revenge with his love for her.

That evening, as they sat in Anastasia's cozy apartment, Brian took a deep breath and began. "Anastasia, there's something I need to talk to you about. It's important, and I want you to know that it doesn't change how I feel about you."

Anastasia looked at him, her eyes filled with curiosity and concern. "What is it, Brian? You're starting to worry me."

Brian continued, "You told me about your involvement with the RCMP's Left Division, and I need you to know that I understand your commitment to your country. But there's something I haven't told you."

Anastasia listened intently as Brian recounted the story of his brother Bill, the Dieppe Raid, and his burning desire for revenge. He shared the pain of losing Bill and the overwhelming need to hold those responsible accountable for his death.

Tears welled up in Anastasia's eyes as she realized the depth of Brian's anguish. She reached out and gently placed her hand on his. "Brian, I did not know. I'm so sorry for what you've been through."

Brian nodded; his voice filled with emotion. "I know you didn't, and I don't want this to come between us. But I need to be honest about my intentions. I've joined a group that plans to confront Churchill and Roosevelt when they visit Quebec City. It's my way of seeking justice for Bill."

Anastasia was silent for a moment, her mind racing. She knew the risks involved, both for Brian and for her position within the RCMP. But she also understood the pain he carried and the need for closure. Finally, she spoke. "Brian, I love you, and I can't bear to see you hurt like this. I understand your need for justice, and I won't stand in your way. But promise me you'll be careful and that you'll come back to me."

Brian squeezed her hand, his eyes locked onto hers. "I promise, Anastasia. And I want you to know that nothing will ever change how I feel about you. You are the most important person in my life."

As they held each other, they knew that their love would be tested in the coming days. The path ahead was fraught with danger and uncertainty, but they were determined to face it together, united by their love and a shared quest for justice.

In the days that followed, Anastasia couldn't shake the growing unease that had settled in her heart. She had always been a dedicated officer in the RCMP's Left Division, committed to safeguarding her country's interests. But now, she found herself torn between her loyalty to Canada and her love for Brian.

As she contemplated Brian's plan to seek justice, Anastasia realized that the path he was on might not lead to the outcome she had hoped for. The lives of some of the most powerful leaders in the world—Franklin D. Roosevelt, Winston Churchill, Joseph Stalin, and even Canada's own Prime Minister William Lyon Mackenzie King—were potentially in danger. Anastasia knew that her duty was to protect her country and its allies, and she couldn't stand by if she believed that harm might come to these leaders.

Late one night, unable to sleep, Anastasia quietly slipped out of bed and went to her small home office. She turned on her desk lamp and pulled out a classified document from her drawer. It contained information about the group that Brian had joined, their plans, and their potential threat to the visiting dignitaries.

Anastasia knew she had a choice to make—one that would have profound consequences for her relationship with Brian and her commitment to her country. She picked up the phone and dialed a secure line within the RCMP.

"Agent Anastasia reporting in. I have critical information regarding a potential security threat to the upcoming summit," she said with a heavy heart.

The following days were a whirlwind of activity. Anastasia's superiors took her report seriously, and a joint operation with international intelligence agencies was launched to ensure the safety of the visiting leaders. Anastasia's involvement was kept discreet, and she continued to maintain her cover within the Left Division.

But the strain on her relationship with Brian was clear. She couldn't tell him about her actions, and he grew increasingly frustrated with her apparent reluctance to support his quest for justice. Their love remained, but it was strained by the secrets they were forced to keep.

As the days drew closer to the summit, Anastasia couldn't help but wonder about the choices she had made. She hoped her actions would prevent any harm from befalling the visiting dignitaries, but she feared the toll it might take on her relationship with Brian. The path they had chosen was fraught with challenges, and the future remained uncertain.

Chapter Ten

Anastasia was looking out the window of her office at the Left Wing department of the Royal Canadian Mounted Police local office when her secretary knocked on her office door before she entered. "Ms. Destounis Inspector McAlister would like to speak to you if you have a minute?"

"Have a minute? I guess I could find one minute to speak to the inspector."

The secretary went out of the room, and Inspector McAllister walked in and sat in front of Anastasia.

"Good morning Ms. Destounis. I'm following up on the transmission that you sent out on a discussion you overheard at a restaurant."

"Yes, I overheard a discussion that worried me about the security of the meeting next week."

"I see. Were you able to get any names, Ms. Destounis?"

"One name that I overheard was Brendan."

"That is the only name you heard?"

"I'm afraid so."

"How many were there?"

"I'm not sure. They were sitting in a booth behind me. I believe there were five of them."

"Well, we'll have to investigate this location."

"The location I was talking about is my parent's restaurant. I was anxious about what might happen to them if they find out that you are after them."

"Don't worry, Ms. Destounis, we'll protect them. I promise."

"I've heard that before, Inspector. Didn't we promise the Dupuis family? If I'm not mistaken, they all died in a car bomb when they were going to church."

"Well, that was an exception to the rule, Ms. Destounis. We'll be very careful about your family's safety."

"I'm afraid I'm having a hard time believing you, Inspector."

"Now, Ms. Destounis, you must believe me. I will take all the precautions to protect your family."

"Well, I don't inspector, that is why I will lead this investigation."

"Now listen here, Ms. Destounis. I'm head of this investigation and what I say is the law."

"Well, inspector, since I'm head of the Left Wing of the RCMP in the Quebec City area and I rank above you, then I will be in charge of this investigation, understood?"

The inspector sat there, trying to figure out what he was about to say next. The problem was that she was right. Being head of the Left Wing of the RCMP in Quebec City made her the boss. He knew she was right.

"Okay, what do you want us to do?"

Anastasia leaned forward; her determination was evident in her eyes. "I want a thorough investigation into this group. Find out who they are, what their intentions are, and if there's any potential threat to the security of our country. But I also want a guarantee that my family's safety will be a top priority."

Inspector MacAlister nodded, realizing that Anastasia was not only knowledgeable about her position but also deeply concerned about her family. "Very well, Ms. Destounis. We will proceed with the investigation as you've outlined. And I will personally oversee the security of your family."

Anastasia sighed, a mix of relief and worry washing over her. She knew that this investigation could uncover dangerous individuals, and the safety of her loved ones weighed heavily on her mind.

"Thank you, Inspector. Please keep me informed of any developments," Anastasia said, her voice tinged with concern.

The inspector rose from his seat, acknowledging the gravity of the situation. "I will, Ms. Destounis. We'll work together to ensure the safety and security of all involved."

With that, he left Anastasia's office, leaving her to contemplate the complex web of politics, espionage, and personal loyalties that had entangled her life. The investigation had begun, and she could only hope that her actions would protect her family and her country from any potential threats that lay ahead.

As Anastasia delved deeper into the investigation of the mysterious group linked to the IRA sympathizers, her worries grew. She knew Brian was deeply entangled with this group and keeping him away from Inspector McAllister's radar was becoming increasingly challenging.

One evening, after a long day at the RCMP office, Anastasia visited Brian at the restaurant where he worked. She needed to discuss the delicate situation with him and come up with a plan to keep him out of trouble.

As she entered the restaurant, Brian spotted her and waved her over to the booth where he was sitting. Anastasia slid into the seat across from him, her expression serious.

"Brian, we need to talk," she began, her voice low and urgent.

Brian furrowed his brow, concern clear in his eyes. "What's going on, Anastasia? Is something wrong?"

Anastasia took a deep breath, choosing her words carefully. "I've been leading an investigation into that group you're involved with. I overheard something that could pose a threat to national security."

Brian's eyes widened, and he leaned in closer. "Anastasia, you know I'm part of that group. Are you saying they're in trouble?"

Anastasia nodded. "Yes, Brian, they're under investigation by the RCMP. I don't want to see anyone get hurt, especially you."

Brian's face tightened with worry. "What are we going to do?"

Anastasia lowered her voice even further. "I have to protect my family and the country. But I also want to protect you. We need to find a way to keep you out of this investigation, to keep you safe."

Brian sighed, running a hand through his hair. "I don't want to see anyone get hurt either, especially you. But I can't just abandon my friends. They're like family to me."

Anastasia reached across the table, placing her hand on Brian's. "I understand your loyalty, but we need to be careful. Maybe there's a way to help your friends without directly involving yourself. We have to think this through."

Brian nodded; his gaze locked with Anastasia's. "Okay, we'll figure something out together. Just promise me you'll stay safe, too."

Anastasia smiled weakly, relieved that he would work with her on a plan. "I promise, Brian. We'll navigate this together, and I'll do my best to keep you out of harm's way."

As they continued to discuss their strategy, both Anastasia and Brian knew they were facing a precarious situation. Balancing their personal feelings and loyalties with the dangerous world of espionage and political intrigue would not be easy. But they were determined to protect each other and ensure the safety of those they cared about most.

IN THE DIMLY LIT CORNER of L'Oncle Antoine Pub, Brian and his IRA sympathizer deliberated their next steps. The news of Anastasia's involvement and the impending visit of the world leaders hung heavy in the air.

Brendan, always the pragmatic one, broke the silence. "All right, Brian, we appreciate your honesty. Now, let's focus on what this means for us. We can't just abandon our mission, but we also can't underestimate the danger."

The group nodded in agreement, recognizing the complexity of their predicament. They had to carry out their mission without exposing themselves to heightened scrutiny from the authorities.

Brian continued, "I've thought about this. We need to proceed cautiously. Anastasia is important to me, but so is avenging Bill's death. If we act recklessly, we risk everything."

Brendan chimed in, "Brian, we can use this situation to our advantage. Anastasia might have access to valuable information about the security measures in place during the leaders' visit. We need to gather as much intel as possible."

Brian nodded, seeing the potential in Brendan's suggestion. "You're right. If we can learn more about their plans, we might find an opportunity to strike without drawing suspicion."

The group spent hours strategizing, considering various scenarios and how to leverage Anastasia's position within the RCMP. They kept a close eye on her activities without revealing their knowledge of her involvement.

As the meeting concluded, Brendan emphasized, "Brian, we've come this far, and we can't turn back now. Just be careful with Anastasia. We can't afford any missteps."

Brian knew the road ahead would be fraught with danger and uncertainty. He was torn between the woman he loved and the burning desire for vengeance. It was a perilous path they had chosen, one that would test their loyalty, resolve, and the lengths they would go to revenge Brian's brother's death at Dieppe and those who were responsible.

In the shadows of their clandestine meeting, they set their sights on the days to come, where the destinies of Anastasia, the world leaders, and their quest for revenge would inevitably converge in a fateful collision of secrets and revelations.

Chapter Eleven

B rian's footsteps echoed in the empty hallway as he ascended the stairs to his apartment. Thoughts swirled through his mind like a temper, torn between love and vengeance, devotion to Anastasia, and the burning desire to avenge his brother's death.

Inside his apartment, he paced back and forth, the weight of his decision pressing upon him. The memory of Bill's sacrifice haunted his every waking moment, and the shadow of Dieppe loomed large in his life. The desire for justice had consumed him for a long time, but now, a new emotion threatened to derail his plans—love.

Brian knew he couldn't ignore the powerful connection he had with Anastasia. She had become an integral part of his life, her presence a beacon of hope in his darkest hours. But his thirst for revenge was equally relentless, a fire that couldn't be extinguished.

He sat down at the rickety wooden table, wrestling with his internal conflict. It was a pivotal moment, a crossroads where he had to make a choice that would define his future. With a deep sigh, he reached a resolution—a painful one.

His love for Anastasia was undeniable, but the mission was his raison d'être, the purpose that had driven him since Bill's death. Brian knew he had to put his quest for vengeance first. He believed Anastasia would understand, that she was bound by duty to her country.

With newfound determination, Brian picked up his phone and called Brendan. There was no turning back now. His comrades would need to know that he was fully committed to the cause, even if it meant putting love aside.

As the phone rang on the other end, Brian's heart raced, knowing that the path ahead would be fraught with danger and sacrifice. But he had made his choice, and he was ready to face the costs head-on.

Brendan's voice crackled through the phone, breaking the tense silence in Brian's apartment. "Brian, what's the word? Everything okay?"

Brian took a deep breath, his voice steady but laced with resolve. "Listen, we need to talk. There's something you should know."

Brendan sensed the gravity in Brian's tone and replied cautiously, "All right, spill it. What's going on?"

Brian hesitated for a moment, grappling with the weight of his decision. "As you know Anastasia works for the RCMP. She's part of the Left Division, and she's been listening in on our conversations."

Silence hung in the air, pregnant with the implications of Brian's revelation. Brendan finally responded, his voice low and measured. "Are you sure about this?"

"I'm positive," Brian affirmed. "She's deeply involved in this, and I'm afraid she'll come after us. We're closer than ever to getting our mission, and I can't let her jeopardize that."

Brendan understood the gravity of the situation. "All right. We'll need to be extra cautious. We can't afford any loose ends. Keep an eye on her, but don't let her catch on."

"I know," Brian replied, his heart heavy with the realization that his relationship with Anastasia was hanging by a thread. "I never wanted it to come to this, but I can't let anything stand in the way of justice for Bill."

Brendan's voice softened. "We're with you, no matter what. We'll see this through to the end."

As they hung up, Brian couldn't help but feel a profound sense of isolation. The path he had chosen was fraught with danger and heartbreak, and he knew sacrifices lay ahead. But his love for his brother and his unwavering commitment to the cause compelled him to press on, no matter the price.

In the following days, Brian found himself in a precarious position. He continued to see Anastasia, to pretend that everything was normal. He couldn't bear to confront her about her involvement with the RCMP, not yet. He needed more time to figure out how to navigate this treacherous path.

Anastasia, unaware of his knowledge, was as affectionate as ever. She sensed that something was amiss with him, but couldn't put her finger on it. Brian's mind was a whirlwind of conflicting emotions. He loved her deeply, but he couldn't ignore the gnawing desire for revenge that had driven him for so long.

The day of the impending meeting with Churchill, Roosevelt, and the others drew nearer. Brian had been secretly preparing, gathering whatever information he could about their security arrangements. He knew that this was the opportunity he had been waiting for, the chance to confront those who had caused his brother's death.

As the day approached, he kept his distance from Anastasia, claiming that he was overwhelmed with work at the restaurant. She worried about him, but couldn't push him to open up. She had her secrets to protect.

Finally, the day arrived. Brian knew he had to act fast. He reached out to Brendan and their group, arranging a meeting to complete their plan. This was the moment he had been building toward, the culmination of over a year of pain and anger.

As he made his way to the meeting point, Brian couldn't shake the feeling that everything was about to change. His love for Anastasia and his thirst for revenge were on a collision course, and he was caught in the middle, torn between conflicting loyalties. The fate of many hung in the balance, and Brian knew that the decisions he would make in the coming hours would shape the rest of his life.

The meeting with Brendan and their group was held in secret, in a dimly lit basement that smelled of dampness and old bricks. The faces around the table were tense, each person aware of the gravity of the situation. Brian laid out the plan he had devised, leveraging the upcoming visit of the world leaders as their opportunity to strike at those responsible for his brother's death.

Brendan and the others listened intently, weighing the risks and rewards. They all knew that this was a perilous undertaking, one that could have far-reaching consequences. But the desire for justice burned within them, just as it did in Brian's heart.

As they discussed the plan, Brian's thoughts kept drifting back to Anastasia. He knew he had to tell her about what was happening, but he couldn't bring himself to do it just yet. The love they shared was genuine, and he feared that revealing his intentions would shatter their relationship irreparably.

The group agreed to move forward with the plan. They had little time to prepare, and the stakes were incredibly high. Brian couldn't help but feel a sense of purpose and fortitude as they parted ways, each member tasked with their part in the operation.

That evening, as he returned home, Brian sat in the quiet of his apartment, wrestling with his inner demons. He knew that the path he had chosen was fraught with danger and that the consequences could be devastating. But he also believed that he was on the cusp of finally revenging his brother's death.

As he stared out of the window into the night, he made a solemn promise to himself that he would see this mission through, no matter the cost. The love he had for Anastasia and the desire for revenge had collided, and he was caught in the crossfire, but he was determined to reconcile the two and, in doing so, find closure for his brother's death.

Brian's conflicting emotions swirled within him like a turbulent storm as he gazed at the majestic St. Lawrence River. The river, once a source of cherished memories spent with his beloved brother Bill, now served as a reminder of their shared adventures and the innocence of youth, forever lost to the ravages of war.

The warmth of those cherished moments brought a smile to his face, but it quickly faded as his thoughts turned to the looming specter of the Chateau Frontenac. In just two days, the world's most influential leaders, including Winston Churchill and Franklin D. Roosevelt, would gather there to discuss the course of the war. It was an opportunity Brian had longed for, the chance to exact revenge for his brother's death and the countless Canadian lives lost in the battle of Dieppe.

Brian knew the gravity of his mission and the magnitude of the decision he was about to make. His love for Anastasia tugged at his heartstrings, but the burning desire for justice fueled his resolve. The weight of his past and the uncertain future ahead converged, leaving him standing at a crossroads, torn between love and vengeance.

As he continued to gaze at the river's flowing waters, the setting sun cast long shadows across the landscape, mirroring the inner turmoil that raged within him. Brian had a monumental choice to make, one that would shape the destiny of nations and determine the course of his own life.

With the weight of his decision bearing down on him, Brian knew he had to tread carefully. He couldn't let anyone, not even Anastasia, discover his true intentions. His plan for revenge needed to remain concealed, hidden beneath a facade of cooperation and unity.

As he strolled through the park, his thoughts turned to his upcoming meeting with Anastasia. He knew he had to maintain his composure and not reveal any hint of his sinister plot. He couldn't risk Anastasia becoming suspicious or, worse yet, discovering his intentions to harm the Allied leaders.

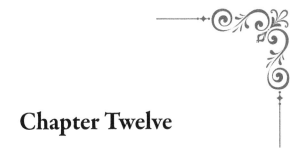

Chapter Twelve

The next two days will be crucial. Brian needed to gather as much information as possible about the security measures in place for the conference. He'd already been discreetly investigating the Chateau Frontenac, trying to identify weak points in the security perimeter. But he also needed to ensure that Anastasia remained unaware of his true motives.

Their love was genuine, but it had become entangled in the web of espionage and revenge. Brian lived a double life, torn between the woman he loved and the mission he felt compelled to fulfill.

As he watched the sun dip below the horizon, casting long shadows that seemed to stretch into eternity, Brian knew that the coming days would test not only his resolve but also the depth of his feelings for Anastasia. It was a perilous path he had chosen, one with no obvious outcome, but he was determined to see it through to the end.

The days leading up to the Allied leaders' arrival were fraught with tension for Brian. He continued to gather information about the security measures at the Chateau Frontenac while maintaining his facade of cooperation and unity with Anastasia and her RCMP colleagues.

Anastasia, unaware of Brian's hidden agenda, became increasingly absorbed in her role as part of the security detail for the conference. She attended briefings, coordinated with other agencies, and ensured that all protocols were in place to protect the visiting leaders.

Brian was working quietly behind the scenes. He infiltrated a group of workers responsible for setting up the conference hall. It gave him access to the layout of the venue, security routines, and even a glimpse of the heavily guarded room where the meetings would take place.

The final days, he balanced his duties at the Greek restaurant with his covert activities, always mindful of the need for secrecy. His interactions with Anastasia became strained as he struggled to keep his true intentions hidden.

As the last days of the conference drew nearer, Brian's heart grew heavier. He loved Anastasia deeply, but he couldn't let go of his burning desire for revenge. It was a battle of conflicting emotions, and he knew that the choices he made in the coming days would define not only his fate, but also that of the leaders about to converge in Quebec City.

Brian couldn't help but wonder if he was walking a path that led to redemption or damnation, and the uncertainty gnawed at him as he continued his dangerous double life.

The eve of the conference was a restless night for Brian. He knew that the next day would be pivotal, a day that could either lead to the realization of his vengeance or the potential loss of everything he held dear.

Anastasia had been busier than ever, coordinating last-minute security details and ensuring that every threat was mitigated. She confided in Brian about her concerns regarding potential security breaches and the need for vigilance. Brian did his best to reassure her and played the role of a supportive fiancé, even as his mind raced with thoughts of the impending mission.

In the early hours of the morning, Brian received a message from Brendan, setting up a clandestine meeting on the outskirts of

Quebec City. He excused himself from Anastasia's apartment, citing a need to pick up a few supplies for the restaurant. She kissed him farewell, unaware of the dangerous rendezvous that awaited him.

The meeting with Brendan and his associates was shrouded in secrecy. They discussed the details of their plan, the layout of the Chateau Frontenac, and the weaknesses of the security measures. Brian once again his thoughts were torn between his loyalty to Anastasia and his commitment to the cause. He knew that if he backed out now, Brendan and the others would go ahead without him, and his chance for revenge would slip away.

As he left the meeting, Brian couldn't help but feel the weight of his choices bearing down on him. He returned to Anastasia's side, determined to see his plan through to the end, but his heart ached knowing that he was betraying the woman he loved.

Chapter Thirteen

Finally, the day of the conference was here, and the Chateau Frontenac bustled with activity. World leaders, military personnel, and security forces filled the historic hotel. Brian and Anastasia both played their parts, concealing their inner turmoil behind masks of duty and dedication.

The moment of truth was fast approaching, and Brian knew that the decisions he made in the hours ahead would have consequences that rippled far beyond his own life. He couldn't escape the realization that the path he had chosen was leading him down a dangerous road, one where loyalty, love, and vengeance clashed in a deadly dance.

The morning sunbathed the historic Chateau Frontenac in a gentle, golden glow as world leaders from various nations gathered within its opulent halls for the high-stakes conference. Brian and Anastasia, two enigmatic figures, stood at a discrete distance from the proceedings, their hearts heavy with the burdens of their respective secrets.

Anastasia, her eyes scanning the crowd with the precision of a seasoned operative, remained vigilant, ever watchful for the faintest signs of potential threats that might lurk amidst the sea of diplomats and dignitaries. Her sharp gaze darted from one face to another, her senses finely tuned to any anomalies or hints of danger that might disrupt the delicate balance of the gathering.

Meanwhile, Brian, a man marked by a simmering resentment that had grown over time, kept a watchful eye on the very leaders who had convened under the ornate roof of the Chateau Frontenac. His gaze, though unobtrusive, bore a weight of disillusionment as he observed those in power, each decision, and policy as a reminder of the world's complexities and the compromises that defined his role.

As the conference unfolded, the Chateau's grandeur provided a stark backdrop to the intricate dance of diplomacy and the undercurrents of secrecy that swirled beneath the surface. In this world of high-stakes negotiations and geopolitical intrigue, Brian and Anastasia stood on the fringes, their hearts heavy, knowing that their truths, concealed behind veils of secrecy, could have far-reaching consequences in the delicate balance of international relations.

The tension in the opulent conference room was so thick it seemed to hang in the air like a heavy, suffocating fog. As the world leaders began their discussions, the weight of the global issues at hand bore down on them all. Brian, among the onlookers at the periphery of the proceedings, couldn't help but feel the intensity of the moment.

For Brian, the rising tide of anger that surged within him was an all-too-familiar sensation, a deep well of emotions stirred by the bitter memories of his past. His thoughts involuntarily drifted back to the horrors of Dieppe, a day that had scarred his soul and taken the lives of his brother and comrades. At that moment, he couldn't suppress the overwhelming sense of loss and grief that washed over him.

As he watched the world leaders gather, Brian's gaze fixated on two figures in particular: Churchill and Roosevelt. To him, they were not just leaders but symbols of a painful truth he had carried with him for what seemed an eternity. He blamed them for the tragedy at Dieppe, holding them accountable for the fate of his brother and fellow soldiers. The grudge he had nursed for so long had festered like an unhealed wound, and today, amidst the high-stakes conference, was the day he had long awaited.

Brian's anger and resentment simmered beneath the surface, like a dormant volcano on the brink of eruption. The room, once a place of decorum and diplomacy, now seemed to bear witness to the tumultuous storm of emotions within him. He knew that today, the weight of his pent-up grievances would find their voice, and the echoes of Dieppe would reverberate in the corridors of power.

As the high-stakes conference continued to unfold, Brian seized a fleeting opportunity to slip away from the gathering, his departure masked by the chaos of the diplomatic discussions. With a tactful excuse about needing to inspect restaurant supplies, he quietly left, careful not to draw any undue attention to his intentions.

Anastasia, deeply engrossed in her crucial role of safeguarding the proceedings, gave a subtle nod in response to his explanation, her focus unwavering on her security duties. Little did she know that with every step he took away from the conference room, Brian was moving further away from her, slipping through her grasp like grains of sand slipping through an open hand.

In the elegant halls of the Chateau Frontenac, amidst the grandeur and gravity of international diplomacy, Brian's discreet departure unfolded as a silent narrative of his intentions. His reasons for leaving were known to him alone, and the distance that grew between him and Anastasia hinted at a chapter of the story that had yet to be written.

Brian convened with Brendan and their trusted allies once more, their faces etched with determination and their resolve unyielding. The culmination of their meticulous preparations had brought them to this pivotal moment. They knew acutely that the opportunity to execute their plan would present itself when the targets were at their most vulnerable, and they had painstakingly readied themselves to seize that moment with unwavering precision.

In the clandestine gathering, their camaraderie was intense, a silent testament to the shared purpose that bound them together. Their final preparations, shrouded in secrecy, had forged a unity of purpose that transcended the risks and uncertainties that lay ahead. They had become a tightly knit team, their trust in each other unbreakable.

As they stood on the height of action, the weight of their mission bore down upon them. Their commitment to the cause, the sacrifices they had made, and the gravity of the decisions they were about to undertake hung heavily in the air. They knew that the path they had chosen was tense with peril, but they were resolute in their determination to see it through to the end.

With their preparations complete, they were poised to seize the moment of weakness that would allow them to enact their plan. Each member of the group understood the significance of their role and the stakes that were involved. At that pivotal juncture, they were not just a team; they were a force of unwavering purpose, ready to change the course of history.

Within the stately confines of the Chateau Frontenac, Anastasia, the sentinel of security, found herself ensnared by a disquieting sense that all was not as it seemed. Her trust in Brian had been steadfast, but a disconcerting doubt clawed at the edges of her consciousness. As she observed the proceedings of the conference, an unshakable unease settled over her.

In a moment of prudence, Anastasia excused herself from her post, her steps measured and her demeanor composed, masking the storm of apprehension raging within her. Discreetly, she reached out to her colleagues in the security division, navigating a web of covert communication channels to voice her mounting concerns.

The burden of responsibility weighed heavily on her shoulders, and the gravity of her actions was not lost on her. In the shadowed corridors of the Chateau, she sought answers, her instincts honed by years of vigilance and training. Her contact with her colleagues was a lifeline, a means to express the disquiet that gnawed at her core and to ensure that no detail, however subtle, went unnoticed in their shared mission to safeguard the conference and its attendees.

As the high-stakes conference reached a pivotal juncture, the world leaders collectively took a much-needed break for lunch, their discussions temporarily suspended. It was precisely during this fragile interlude, a brief respite amidst the gravity of international diplomacy, that Brendan and his team sprang into action.

With meticulous planning and a keen understanding of the Chateau Frontenac's security protocols, Brendan and his operatives recognized that this fleeting moment of reprieve would render the Chateau's security apparatus momentarily distracted, creating the perfect opening for them to execute their audacious plan.

The conference attendees dispersed in search of sustenance, unaware of the impending turmoil that would soon disrupt their carefully structured proceedings. During the bustling activity, Brendan, and his team, shadowed by the cloak of secrecy, readied themselves to strike with decisive precision, fully cognizant of the gravity of the moment and the world-changing consequences that their actions would unleash.

Brian, his soul ablaze with an unquenchable desire for revenge, had willingly placed himself at the epicenter of the clandestine operation. His motivations ran deep, fueled by an insatiable yearning to avenge the death of his beloved brother at Dieppe. The risks loomed ominously on the horizon, casting long shadows over his path, but the singular prospect of retribution was all-consuming, drowning out the cacophony of doubt that whispered at the edges of his consciousness.

As he navigated the labyrinthine corridors of the hotel, every step carried the weight of his convictions. The very air seemed to pulse with anticipation, and the gravity of his mission bore down upon him. Brian couldn't help but reflect on the enormity of the task before him, wondering if this moment—fraught with peril and promise—might be his last chance to set things right.

His determination was a flame that burned within, illuminating his path with an unwavering purpose. The echoes of Dieppe, the memory of his brother, and the haunting specter of betrayal had coalesced into a relentless drive that propelled him forward, despite the treacherous road that lay ahead. In that pivotal moment, Brian was poised to confront his past, seeking justice in the face of adversity, with the fervent hope that retribution would finally bring solace to his wounded soul.

Anastasia's worst fears materialized into a haunting reality as the urgent message of a security breach reached her ears. Her heart thundered in her chest, each beat a resonating drumbeat of alarm, as she swiftly departed from her location, a surge of adrenaline fueling her resolve. Her mind raced; her instincts finely tuned as she hastened her return to the hallowed halls of the Chateau Frontenac. In that critical moment, her unwavering determination was firmly rooted in her mission: to shield the world leaders from imminent danger and avert a potential catastrophe of global proportions.

Unbeknownst to her, Anastasia's path was hurtling toward an inexorable collision with Brian's, two forces destined to converge at the precipice of destiny. The choices they were about to make, in the scant minutes ahead, held the power to shape not only the fate of their love but the destiny of the entire world.

As their footsteps raced toward the inevitable intersection, the clock ticked relentlessly, each second an indelible mark on the canvas of their shared history. In this pivotal juncture, love, duty, and the specter of betrayal hung in a delicate balance, and the choices made in the crucible of their next encounter would resonate far beyond their personal destinies, for the fate of nations and the world itself teetered on the precipice of uncertainty.

Within the grandeur of the Chateau Frontenac, the world leaders savored their midday reprieve, blissfully oblivious to the imminent danger that encroached upon their sanctuary. Brian, concealed beneath the guise of a discreet server, ventured closer to the hallowed conference room, each step a resounding echo of his racing heartbeats. This was the moment he had long expected, the defining juncture where the embers of his vengeance would blaze into a fiery reckoning. The memory of his brother's tragic demise, etched deeply into his soul, fueled the relentless determination that coursed through his veins.

With every move he made, the gravity of his mission weighed heavily on him. Brian knew that this was the culmination of years of pain and plotting, a chance to confront the architects of his torment and exact a reckoning they could not escape. The hallways of the Chateau, once silent witnesses to history, now bore witness to a clandestine act of justice, a clandestine act that would carry profound consequences.

As he neared the conference room, his senses sharpened, his heart a relentless drumbeat of purpose. Brian understood that this moment was not only about avenging his brother's death, but also about the salvation of his soul. In this clandestine operation, he sought to bring closure to a chapter of his life defined by pain and betrayal and to ensure that those responsible would finally pay the price for their actions.

Brian's cautious steps brought him closer to the entrance of the conference room, where an unexpected sight unfolded before him. Anastasia, her countenance a mosaic of concern and determination, engaged in an urgent exchange with the vigilant members of the security team. Their conversation was shrouded in an air of gravity that mirrored the impending danger.

In that fleeting moment, their eyes met, and a profound tension hung in the air, a palpable reflection of the complex conflict that churned within Anastasia's gaze. She had placed her unwavering trust in Brian, her heart entwined with his, and the love they shared had once forged an unbreakable bond. However, her duty as an RCMP officer stood in stark opposition to the clandestine mission that had brought Brian to this precipice.

As their gazes locked, Brian could discern the inner turmoil that raged within Anastasia, a tempest of emotions that mirrored the tempestuous situation at hand. Their love, the very force that had once united them, now found itself ensnared in the crosshairs of duty and vengeance. The choices they were about to make would not only define the outcome of their personal connection, but would reverberate through the corridors of power, potentially altering the course of history itself.

With a careful, almost imperceptible motion, Brian activated the small device given to him by Brendan—a signal that resonated silently among their fellow conspirators, a silent clarion call that the time for action had arrived. In that covert moment, the weight of their mission bore down upon him, a realization that they stood on the precipice of destiny.

As he prepared to slip into the conference room, where history and intrigue converged, a soft yet commanding voice called out to him, shattering the shroud of secrecy that enveloped him. It was Anastasia, her voice a sudden intrusion into the intricate tapestry of their clandestine operation, a testament to the turmoil that swirled within her.

In that pivotal instant, the world teetered on the edge of chaos, and Brian found himself at the crossroads of duty, love, and vendetta. The choices he would make in the breathless moments that followed would echo through time, for they were choices that transcended the personal, choices that could rewrite the annals of history and shape the destinies of nations.

"Brian, what on earth are you doing here?" Anastasia's voice, filled with a mix of surprise and concern, sliced through the charged atmosphere like a blade. Her words carried both the weight of authority and the undercurrent of genuine worry. "You shouldn't be in this area," she added, her tone tinged with a protective urgency, as if attempting to shield him from the perilous path he seemed poised to tread.

Brian pivoted on his heels to face Anastasia, his gaze filled with a potent blend of emotions—heartache, resolve, and the weight of the unspoken. His voice, though steady, carried a subtle undertone of turmoil as he replied, "I was just checking on the guests, making sure they have everything they need." The words, a veil concealing the true nature of his presence, masked the tumultuous conflict raging beneath the surface.

Anastasia's brow knitted in a deep furrow, her eyes betraying a creeping sense of suspicion that cast a shadow over her features. "Something doesn't feel right," she asserted in a resolute tone. "I need you to step away from the conference room," her words, a blend of duty and vigilance, carried the weight of her responsibilities as an RCMP officer, masking the internal turmoil that her unwavering commitment to security concealed.

Brian's mind raced in a frantic flurry of thoughts. Detainment was a luxury he couldn't afford at this crucial juncture. The fates of Churchill and Roosevelt, along with his quest for justice, dangled precipitously in the balance. In that charged moment, he couldn't help but believe that he was their sole chance for the retribution he had sought for so long. The weight of history, vengeance, and the hope for justice converged within him, urging him to press forward despite the ominous shadows of doubt and suspicion that now surrounded him.

"I can't do that," Brian replied, his voice laced with a strained attempt at conviction. His words hung in the air, a feeble shield to protect the secrets he carried. "I have to make sure everything is in order," he added, hoping to deflect her attention and maintain his precarious position in the heart of the unfolding drama.

Anastasia, her eyes now fixed with unwavering resolve, took a measured step closer to Brian. Her hand, moving with a deliberate purpose, inched toward the holster secured at her side. Her voice, carrying an unspoken command, rang out with a steely edge. "Brian, I won't ask again. Step away from the door." The gravity of the situation had escalated, and her stance left no room for negotiation.

In the crucible of that fraught moment, Brian found himself at a precipice of profound consequence. He stood on the cusp of a defining choice, each path fraught with perilous uncertainties. On one hand, he could agree to Anastasia's orders, relinquishing his vengeful mission and bringing an end to the quest that had consumed him for years. On the other, he could choose to press forward, resolute in his determination, yet exposing himself to an abyss of risks—risks that could imperil not only his own life, but also the lives of the world leaders gathered within the conference room.

The gravity of his decision bore down upon him, a heavy mantle that he could not escape. In that agonizing moment of hesitation, the weight of his past, his love for Anastasia, and the fervent pursuit of retribution intertwined in a turbulent maelstrom of emotions. The choices he was about to make would ripple through the tapestry of fate, and Brian grappled with the profound ramifications of his next steps, a choice that would either shackle him to the ghosts of the past or propel him further into the shadows of a dangerous present.

Beyond the imposing walls of the Chateau Frontenac, Brendan and his dedicated team stood poised for action. Each member of the group, their faces obscured by shadows and their resolve unyielding, had their targets squarely within their sights. Their collective breaths were held in anticipation, a taut silence punctuated only by the heartbeat-like rhythm of their synchronized pulse. The world teetered on a precipice, and the impending events hinged on Brian's signal, the linchpin in the meticulously orchestrated operation.

The inexorable march of time bore down upon them, each passing moment a reminder of the stakes that hung perilously in the balance. The destiny of the world, of nations, and generations yet unborn swayed in the balance, awaiting the decisive action that would shape the course of history. The Chateau Frontenac, with its hidden secrets and veiled intentions, was the epicenter of their mission, and the moment of reckoning loomed ominously on the horizon.

In that charged instant, Brian could feel the immensity of the moment pressing down upon him like an unforgiving weight. He stood at the precipice of a profound dilemma, torn between the all-consuming drive for vengeance that had fueled his every step and the profound sense of duty he bore towards the woman he loved.

Deep within, he understood the cost of his actions and the potential consequences that loomed ominously on the horizon. If he pressed forward, to continue on his vengeful path, he would put Anastasia in an impossible and heart-wrenching position. His actions would compel her to make an agonizing choice, a choice that would force her to navigate the treacherous crossroads between her unwavering duty and the intense, genuine feelings she harbored for him.

The gravity of the situation weighed heavily on Brian's soul, the very essence of their relationship at stake. In that turbulent moment, he grappled, knowing that his decisions bore the power to alter irrevocably the course of their lives and to set in motion events that neither of them could fully comprehend.

Anastasia, her hand poised near her holster, locked her gaze onto Brian's eyes with a piercing intensity. Her scrutinizing stare probed for any subtle signs of deceit, for the truth hidden within the depths of his conflicted soul. The tension in the air was intense as she sought to unravel the enigma that was Brian at this moment.

Within those expressive eyes, she sensed the turbulent tempest of his inner turmoil. A complex interplay of emotions flickered across his features, and Anastasia's feelings ran the gamut from deep concern to mounting frustration. She couldn't fully fathom the enigmatic web that Brian was ensnared in, but an indomitable gut feeling gnawed at her, whispering that something was undeniably amiss.

In that charged exchange, neither Brian nor Anastasia could entirely comprehend the complexities of the other's reality. Their connection, once bound by trust and affection, now existed at the nexus of suspicion and uncertainty. The forces that had once united them had given way to an inexorable tension, a testament to the mysteries that swirled around them and the uncharted territories of their future.

Anastasia's voice quivered with a blend of emotional turmoil and unwavering conviction as she implored, "Brian," her words hanging in the charged air, "I don't know what's going on, but you're making a grave mistake. Please, step away from that door." Her plea, laced with a profound concern for his well-being and the potential consequences that loomed, echoed with the weight of her plea for him to reconsider the precipice upon which he stood.

Brian's thoughts raced like a whirlwind, his mind a battlefield of clashing possibilities and dire consequences. The mosaic of choices lay before him, each bearing its weighty burden. In the depths of Anastasia's gaze, he saw the tempest of emotions playing out—a flurry where love for him waged war against the unwavering sense of duty that defined her.

The conflict was a palpable tension, a silent and heart-wrenching duel that painted a poignant portrait of their relationship hanging in the balance. Brian, torn between his insatiable desire for revenge and the woman he cherished, understood the harrowing implications of his actions. He knew that should he press forward with his mission; it could unleash a tempest that would irreparably damage the delicate tapestry of their connection, and the mere thought of losing her was an anguish too profound to bear.

Yet, the burning desire for revenge still raged within him, an inferno that consumed his every thought and action. The past, with its agonizing wounds, held him captive, refusing to relinquish its hold. In that pivotal moment, Brian grappled with the inexorable tug of vengeance and the fragile love that stood in direct opposition, a poignant reminder of the choices that could rend the fabric of their lives asunder.

As Brian teetered on the brink of stepping back, a sudden, distant explosion rocked the very foundations of the Chateau Frontenac. Its ominous reverberations were swiftly followed by the discordant symphony of gunfire, the cacophonous eruption of chaos and danger. Panic surged like wildfire through the hallowed halls of the historic edifice, and the once-steadfast security team, now thrust into a maelstrom of crisis, sprang into frantic action.

In that heart-stopping moment, Brian and Anastasia, their gazes locking with shared dread and haunting realization, understood that the world they knew had irreversibly shifted. The tendrils of peril had woven their way into the very fabric of their existence, and the choices that had once seemed so stark and agonizing paled compared to the unfolding tumult of uncertainty and danger.

Anastasia's finely honed instincts surged to the forefront, a rush of adrenaline guiding her in this moment of crisis. Her unwavering sense of duty crystallized, and she understood with painful clarity that her paramount responsibility was to protect the leaders ensconced within the conference room, shielding them from the gathering storm of chaos.

With a heart heavy with the weight of her decision, she holstered her weapon, the resolute click echoing through the corridor. In that solemn act, she wordlessly acknowledged the gravity of their situation and the urgency of her responsibilities. She turned to Brian, a nod of shared resolve passing between them like a silent pledge—a pledge to navigate the turbulent waters of uncertainty and danger together, bound by duty, love, and the inexorable current of fate.

"Go," Anastasia urged, her voice taut with the strain of the moment, "Do what you have to do." Her words, a somber acceptance of their roles in this unfolding crisis, resonated with a poignant mix of understanding, sacrifice, and the inescapable demands of their respective missions.

Brian didn't hesitate for a heartbeat any longer. Without a word, he turned on his heel and sprinted toward the conference room, his every step echoing with the staccato rhythm of fear and a steely resolve that burned within him. The tumultuous chaos erupting outside, now a pandemonium of sound and fury, would serve as the perfect smokescreen, veiling his covert mission in a cloak of mayhem and disarray.

As Brian approached the hallowed entrance to the conference room, a discord of gunfire and frenzied shouts reverberated through the corridor. The fate of Churchill, Roosevelt, and the very essence of the world's destiny teetered on the precipice of uncertainty. In that harrowing moment, Brian steeled himself, the fire of determination burning fiercely within him. He understood that time seized control of a world in disarray, ready to defy the consequences that loomed ominously over his audacious actions.

Brian's entrance into the conference room was nothing short of explosive. His heart raced like a thundering drum as he crossed the threshold, only to find himself thrust into the heart of an unbridled maelstrom. The leaders of the Allies, whose faces bore the unmistakable marks of fear and bewilderment, were huddled together, their voices muted by the overwhelming disarray that enveloped them.

Around him, the security personnel, dedicated and resolute, were engaged in a bitter firefight with shadowy assailants, their identities shrouded in mystery. The air crackled with the acrid scent of gunpowder and the frenetic urgency of battle, casting an eerie pall over the room that was now the epicenter of a high-stakes struggle between forces unseen.

With unwavering resolve, Brian's gaze darted across the tumultuous tableau of the room until it landed upon two figures—Churchill and Roosevelt. In his heart, he carried the unshakable conviction that these two men bore responsibility for the death of his beloved brother. Emotions surged within him like a tempestuous whirlwind, a volatile mix of anger, grief, and a fierce, unrelenting thirst for revenge.

Their presence was a haunting reminder of the profound loss he had endured, and in that charged moment, the past and the present collided, fueling his determination to confront the shadows that had haunted him for far too long.

Amid the cacophonous chaos that engulfed him, Brian moved with a singular, unwavering purpose. His resolve was a guiding beacon as he navigated the turbulent sea of uncertainty. With deliberate intention, he reached into the concealed recesses of his coat pocket, fingers brushing against the contours of the small, clandestine device he had meticulously prepared for this fateful moment.

Drawing a steadying breath, Brian activated the hidden explosive with a deft, practiced motion. With a surgeon's precision, he discreetly placed the device in a strategic location within the room, the weight of his actions carrying a potent mix of vengeance and resolve. The countdown to reckoning had begun, and Brian was prepared to bear the weight of its consequences, no matter how cataclysmic.

As Brian took a step back, a chilling awareness settled upon him like a shroud. He had only precious moments left before the impending explosion would shatter the room and unleash a whirl of devastation. The gravity of what he was about to bear down on his conscience with an oppressive weight, a haunting specter that threatened to suffocate him.

Yet, even as the enormity of his actions gnawed at his soul, he understood that there was no turning back now. The explosion, imminent, was the catalyst he needed—a tempest of chaos and distraction that would allow him to slip through the clutches of pursuing authorities, to vanish into the obscurity of his mission's shadowy depths. The countdown to his escape was inexorably linked to the detonation that loomed, and Brian steeled himself to bear the consequences, no matter how profound or irreversible they might be.

In the crucible of a heart-wrenching moment, Brian grappled with a revelation that pierced the shadows of his unrelenting desire for revenge. He understood, in a mere split-second, that his perilous journey had veered into a dark and treacherous abyss. The specter of innocent lives hanging in the balance, their very existence teetering on the precipice of destruction, was a stark reminder of the moral crossroads upon which he stood.

With a resolute and swift determination, Brian chose the path of mercy and redemption. His trembling hand, racing against the inexorable countdown, skillfully deactivated the explosive device just as it reached its final, fateful seconds. In that pivotal moment, he reclaimed a fragment of his humanity and spared the room from the cataclysm that had loomed, his actions resonating with a poignant echo of sacrifice and the salvation of countless souls.

As the room braced itself for an impending explosion that never came, a wave of bewildering disarray descended upon the gathered leaders and security personnel. Panic, swift and unrelenting, rippled through the room like wildfire, turning their faces into masks of terror and confusion.

Amid this pandemonium, Brian remained a phantom amid chaos, his presence undetected. Seizing the chaotic distraction that had become his ally, he slipped away from the room, his footsteps silent and his form a shadow amidst the labyrinthine corridors of the Chateau Frontenac. The darkness of the passageways embraced him, offering refuge to a man who had narrowly averted catastrophe, allowing him to vanish into the enigmatic obscurity of his mission once more.

In the wake of the tumultuous events inside the Chateau Frontenac, the security forces eventually rallied, wresting control from the clutch of chaos, and the immediate threat that had gripped the room receded like a retreating tide. The leaders and personnel, once caught in the throes of panic, gradually regained a semblance of composure.

However, in the aftermath of that fateful moment, Brian vanished into the ether, his mission of revenge cast aside like a heavy burden. He understood, with a solemn clarity, that he could never fully elude the far-reaching tendrils of the consequences that would inevitably shadow him. But in the crucible of decision, he had prioritized the lives of the innocent over the insatiable maw of vengeance that had once consumed him. It was a haunting act of redemption, a choice that would forever shape the trajectory of his existence, and a testament to the enduring power of humanity's capacity for selflessness and redemption.

As Brian slipped away into the inky embrace of the night, he bore with him the formidable burden of his past, a heavy yoke that rested uneasily upon his shoulders. The future, cloaked in shadows and riddled with uncertainty, unfurled before him like an enigmatic tapestry yet to be woven.

In the recesses of his heart, the memory of his love for Anastasia lingered like a bittersweet echo—a poignant reminder of the choices he had been compelled to make. Her image, a haunting presence in the corridors of his mind, tugged at the frayed edges of his resolve.

As he ventured further into the obscurity of the night, Brian couldn't help but grapple with an enduring question that resonated within him: Was redemption still attainable for a man ensnared by the specters of his demons, or had he embarked upon a path from which there could be no return? The uncertain journey ahead was fraught with enigmas, and he treaded the precipice of a fate that remained as elusive as the distant stars in the night sky.

Brian stumbled into a desolate alley, his labored breaths echoing through the stillness, a stark contrast to the tumultuous storm of emotions raging within him. His heart continued its furious cadence, the lingering residue of adrenaline coursing through his veins like a relentless current.

In the distance, the grand silhouette of the Chateau Frontenac stood sentinel, its imposing presence an indelible symbol of history and power. The iconic edifice loomed as a haunting reminder of the world he had so recently departed, a world now separated from him by a chasm of choices and consequences, leaving Brian to navigate the shadowy alleyways of an uncertain future.

Chapter Fourteen

B rian knew acutely that he could no longer linger within the confines of Quebec City. The audacious, failed attempt on the lives of Churchill and Roosevelt had left an indelible mark, an inescapable stain that would inevitably draw the relentless pursuit of authorities upon him.

Although he had abandoned his mission for vengeance, Brian understood he could not simply vanish into obscurity, free from the repercussions of his actions. The weight of his choices and the looming specter of consequences clung to him like a shroud, a shadow that would persistently track his every move, forcing him to navigate a treacherous path into an uncertain future.

In the shrouded confines of the dimly lit alley, Brian's senses were heightened to an acute pitch. He leaned heavily against the unforgiving embrace of the cold, stone wall, his form melding with the shadows that clung to the crevices. The night air, crisp and laden with tension, carried the dissonant echoes of sirens and frenetic shouts from the direction of the Chateau Frontenac, painting an eerie tableau.

Every second that slipped away was precious, and Brian was acutely aware of the need for swift, decisive action. The relentless pulse of urgency propelled him forward, interesting him to make calculated choices in the precarious dance of escape that lay ahead.

Brian's immediate priority was to obliterate any semblance of his former self. In a clandestine ritual, he fumbled in his pocket and retrieved a small, well-worn pocketknife. With hands that trembled with anticipation and the gravity of his predicament, he embarked on a precarious metamorphosis.

The scruff of his beard yielded to the blade's edge, falling away like a cascade of forgotten memories. Though his transformation was far from complete, the absence of the beard marked a symbolic beginning—a shedding of the old skin. In the dimly lit alley, he tugged a well-worn hat low over his forehead, casting a web of shadow that cloaked his features, veiling his identity beneath a shroud of anonymity. It was a fragile disguise, but it was a start on the path to eluding the relentless pursuit that awaited him.

Brian's heart pounded in his chest as he meticulously altered his appearance in a dimly lit hotel room. Beads of sweat formed on his brow, and his hands trembled with a combination of fear and determination. The room was suffused with tension, and he could hear the distant hum of the city outside, oblivious to the turmoil within.

With every change he made to his appearance — trimming his scruffy beard, dying his hair a different color, and donning nondescript clothing — Brian's mind raced, conjuring up a complex and meticulous plan to evade capture and slip away from Quebec City unnoticed. He knew the authorities would be relentless in their pursuit of anyone remotely associated with the recent, disastrous assassination attempt.

The weight of the situation bore down on him as he realized the gravity of the task ahead. His life depended on staying off the radar and avoiding recognition. He scanned the room, his eyes darting from one corner to another, searching for anything that might give away his identity.

The thought of capture filled him with dread, not just for himself, but also for those who had helped him on this ill-fated mission. He couldn't afford to leave any loose ends that could lead the authorities back to his allies.

Brian's mind whirled with strategies, considering every scenario and meticulously planning his escape route. He knew he had to leave no room for error. Each decision he made, from the choice of transportation to the cover story he'd use, was vital to his survival.

As he continued to transform his appearance, he couldn't help but wonder if he was outsmarting his pursuers or if they were closing in on him at that very moment. The city outside may have been oblivious to his plight, but Brian knew acutely that his every move had to be executed flawlessly if he wanted to elude capture and ensure his freedom.

Brian's heart pounded in his chest as he tiptoed out of the narrow, shadowy alley and onto the dimly lit streets that lay eerily deserted. The once-bustling city had been thrown into a state of frenzied chaos, its usual vitality silenced by the turmoil of recent events. Every footstep echoed in his ears, a stark reminder of the danger that lurked around every corner.

His every movement was marked by caution, his senses heightened to a razor's edge. The flickering streetlights cast eerie, shifting shadows that seemed to taunt him. Brian knew he needed to disappear into the chaotic backdrop of the city, to become a nameless face amid the clamor of uncertainty.

Then, like an oasis amid a desert, he spotted a small grocery store nestled between two abandoned storefronts. Its neon sign, though flickering, offered a beacon of hope. The decision was instantaneous; Brian realized it was time to replenish his dwindling supplies. In this unpredictable and perilous journey, he couldn't afford to ignore an opportunity to secure sustenance, not knowing when the next chance would present itself.

As he pushed open the creaking door, the faint jingle of a bell echoed through the empty store, announcing his presence. The shelves, once laden with an array of groceries, now bore the scars of looting, with many items missing or scattered on the floor. Brian moved silently, gathering what he could: canned goods, bottled water, and a few essential toiletries. Every choice was calculated, ensuring he could carry his haul without drawing attention.

Inside the grocery store, Brian's senses were on high alert. He moved with the precision of a seasoned spy, a well-practiced art of blending in. His first move was to grab a shopping basket, the dull clatter of the plastic handle against metal rails causing him to wince, fearing it might have drawn unnecessary attention.

In the dimly lit store, the shelves appeared as a battleground, plundered by desperate souls seeking sustenance amid the chaos that had engulfed the city. Brian knew his choices had to be swift and strategic, each selection a deliberate step in his quest for survival.

His gloved hands moved deftly, snatching items seemingly at random from the ravaged shelves. A loaf of bread, its plastic wrapper crinkling softly, was the first to find its way into his basket. It symbolized sustenance, a small yet vital lifeline for the uncertain journey ahead.

Next came the canned goods, their labels faded and stained, but their contents promised a source of nourishment in dire times. Brian's fingers grazed the metal, cold and unforgiving, as he added can after can to his growing cache.

A bottle of water, its cool surface beaded with condensation, beckoned to him. He knew the value of hydration on the treacherous path he was embarking on. It was more than a mere beverage; it was a lifeline in a parched landscape of uncertainty.

Every selection was a calculated choice, an essential piece of the puzzle to ensure his survival. He couldn't afford to appear conspicuous, so he refrained from overfilling his basket. Instead, he focused on the essentials, items that would sustain him on his harrowing journey through the unknown.

With each addition to his basket, Brian's heart quickened, aware that every second spent in the store increased the risk of discovery. He maintained a facade of normalcy, just another shopper navigating the wreckage of a city in turmoil. Little did the otherworldly chaos surrounding him know he was gathering the provisions not just for sustenance, but for a desperate escape into an uncertain and perilous future.

Approaching the checkout counter, Brian could feel the weight of his choices in the basket. The dim, flickering overhead light cast a pale glow over the scene, revealing the chipped and faded linoleum floor beneath his worn sneakers. He watched as the small pile of essentials lay there, a testament to his determination in the face of adversity.

Brian withdrew a handful of coins from his pocket, each one bearing the distinctive marks of wear and tear, a reflection of the turbulent times that had brought him to this point. He carefully counted them out, acutely aware of the cashier's scrutiny. The coins clinked as they hit the counter, their metallic echoes magnified in the store's silence.

The shopkeeper, an older gentleman with tired eyes, stood behind the counter. He wore an apron that had seen better days, and his once-pristine white shirt was now speckled with stains from countless transactions. The faint crackle of a radio broadcast filled the air, its disembodied voice narrating the unfolding chaos outside.

Brian kept his head down, a calculated move to avoid making eye contact. He knew that blending into the background was crucial, that drawing attention now would be disastrous. As he exchanged the coins for his meager grocery haul, the shopkeeper's gaze seemed to briefly flicker towards him before returning to the radio, engrossed in the news updates that continued to pour in.

With the transaction completed, Brian collected his purchases in a worn plastic bag, careful not to rustle it too loudly. The shopkeeper's attention remained riveted to the ongoing news bulletin, oblivious to the significance of this ordinary-looking customer and his basket of essentials.

As Brian slipped out of the store, the chilly night air enveloped him once more. The city's turmoil raged on, but he had secured what he needed, all while maintaining his inconspicuous presence. In the darkness, he became just another shadow, disappearing into the uncertain depths of the night, his steps determined, his destination unknown, but his resolve unwavering.

With the weight of his newly gained provisions on his back, Brian's thoughts turned to the next crucial step: transportation. He knew all too well that taking a bus, or a train was a perilous gamble. Authorities were closely monitoring such public transit, and he was a face they were likely eager to identify. In this city of chaos, blending in was paramount to survival.

After a moment of contemplation, Brian made a calculated decision: he would steal a bicycle. It was a choice that offered both mobility and discretion, a means to traverse the urban landscape while remaining unobtrusive.

As he ventured deeper into the city's labyrinthine streets, his eyes scoured the surroundings for an opportunity. Moonlight filtered through the looming buildings, casting long, eerie shadows that seemed to dance to an unsettling rhythm. The night was punctuated by distant sirens and sporadic flashes of emergency lights, painting a grim tableau of the city's turmoil.

It didn't take long for him to spot a potential target. A bicycle was chained to a lamppost, its frame glinting softly in the pale moonlight. It stood there, abandoned, a testament to the hurried escape of its previous owner. Brian's heart raced as he approached the two-wheeled prize, his gloved fingers deftly producing a set of lock-picking tools.

His nimble fingers worked in concert with the faint click of the lock tumblers, and after a tense moment, the chain fell away, freeing the bicycle. Brian mounted it swiftly, the worn leather of the saddle molding to his frame as if inviting him on a journey into the unknown.

With each pedal stroke, Brian's escape plan took shape. He had chosen a path less traveled, one where he could cover significant ground while remaining unnoticed. As he silently glided through the streets, his stolen bicycle whispered across the asphalt, carrying him further away from the city's chaos and deeper into the enigmatic night, where shadows concealed his presence, and the promise of escape beckoned on the horizon.

With a soft, almost ghostly creak, Brian pedaled away, his movements almost inaudible as he gained momentum. The world around him seemed to fade into the background, the noise of chaos in Quebec City replaced by the rhythmic hum of the bicycle's wheels against the pavement.

The outskirts of the city beckoned their quietude, a stark contrast to the turbulent heart of Quebec City. Brian knew that his survival hinged on putting as much distance as possible between himself and the metropolis. Each push of the pedal propelled him further into the unknown, away from the dangers that lurked in the shadows of the city he had known.

The night enveloped him like a shroud, concealing his movements as he followed the road toward an uncertain destination. With each passing moment, the city's chaos receded into the distance, and Brian felt a glimmer of hope. On this stolen bicycle, he was a solitary figure in the night, racing toward a future that remained shrouded in mystery and uncertainty. His only ally was the relentless rhythm of his escape.

Brian pedaled through the labyrinthine network of winding streets and narrow alleys, each turn carrying him deeper into the maze of shadows. The stolen bicycle glided almost soundlessly beneath him, the rubber tires whispering secrets to the moonlit night. With every passing second, his anxiety heightened, a gnawing sensation that he was not alone in this clandestine journey.

The sense of being watched weighed heavily on him, a shadowy presence that seemed to lurk at the periphery of his awareness. His eyes darted from passerby to passerby, scrutinizing their faces for any sign of recognition or suspicion. Each distant siren's wail pierced his psyche, sending shivers down his spine. The loudness of the city's chaos, once distant, now felt ominously close, as if it were a relentless specter haunting his every move.

Brian knew he couldn't afford to linger in the open for long. His heart raced, and beads of sweat formed on his brow despite the chill of the night. The stolen bicycle became his lifeline, propelling him further away from the danger he had left behind in the old Quebec City's turmoil. Yet, the unsettling sensation that he was being pursued refused to relent.

With a firm resolve, he navigated the complex streets, searching for a haven where he could momentarily evade the watchful eyes that seemed to track his every move. He knew that his next move had to be calculated, a decision that could determine his fate in this treacherous game of cat and mouse.

The stolen bicycle's tires hummed softly beneath him as he pressed on, determined to find that elusive refuge where he could catch his breath, lie low, and carefully assess his options. The city's shadows concealed his movements, but Brian knew acutely that time was not on his side, and the pursuit, real or imagined, was relentless.

The hours stretched into an endless night, marked only by the rhythmic cadence of Brian's tireless pedaling. The haunting specter of the failed mission for revenge hung heavy over him, an inescapable reminder that his world had unraveled irreversibly. There was no room for hesitation; the relentless pursuit of those who sought retribution compelled him to flee, vanishing into obscurity with each passing moment.

As the moon cast its silvery glow upon the forsaken road, Brian's resolve remained unwavering. He pedaled on, the bicycle beneath him becoming an extension of his will, each stroke of the pedals propelling him further into an uncertain future. With every hour that passed, he left behind the fragments of a life that had once been his, replaced by the chilling reality of a life on the run.

The city's chaos, the sirens, and the distant cries of desperation became echoes of a world that he was determined to leave behind. In the inky darkness of the night, he found a kind of solace, an anonymity that seemed to offer a glimmer of hope. The stars above bore witness to his flight, their silent guidance a distant comfort.

With every pedal stroke, Brian edged closer to the promise of an elusive freedom, even as the world he had known faded further into the rearview mirror of his stolen bicycle. The road ahead was uncertain, fraught with danger and uncertainty, but he was resolute in his determination to carve out a new existence, one that would forever be defined by his flight into the unknown.

Brian's desperate flight persisted into the unforgiving embrace of the early morning. With each passing minute, the shroud of isolation and uncertainty enveloped him further. He pedaled on, the stolen bicycle's wheels spinning tirelessly, the rhythm of his escape beating in time with his racing heart.

The urban landscape transformed as he traversed it, morphing from the turbulent heart of the city into the hushed calm of quiet residential neighborhoods. Here, the houses stood like silent sentinels, their windows shrouded in the pre-dawn gloom. It was a stark contrast to the chaos he had left behind, a world where his mission of vengeance had crumbled into failure.

Brian continued to ride, navigating the web of deserted streets, his breath visible in the frigid morning air. The eerie silence hung heavy around him, punctuated only by the rhythmic hum of his bicycle's tires on the pavement. Every pedal stroke brought him further away from the scene of the failed assassination attempt, a scene fraught with danger and betrayal.

He was driven by an unwavering purpose to put as much distance as possible between himself and the ghosts of his past. The city's dark secrets receded in his wake, gradually replaced by the promise of a new beginning, a chance to rewrite his destiny in the quiet anonymity of these empty streets.

As the first light of dawn cast long shadows, Brian's journey continued unabated. His flight was not just a physical one but a transformation, a rebirth into a life unburdened by the past. The stolen bicycle, his steadfast companion, carried him toward an uncertain future where he hoped to find sanctuary from the relentless pursuit that had forced him into this desperate flight.

As the first rays of dawn pierced the horizon, Brian found himself on the cusp of escaping Quebec City's grasp, the city's urban jungle slowly yielding to the serene embrace of the surrounding countryside. The night's turmoil was gradually replaced by the pastoral beauty of open fields and densely wooded forests, a stark contrast to the chaos he had left behind.

The stolen bicycle's wheels continued to hum softly beneath him as he pedaled onward, each stroke of the pedal propelling him deeper into the hinterlands. The city's tumultuous streets, once his battleground, now faded into a distant memory. In their place, vast open fields stretched out like a refuge, a sanctuary from the relentless pursuit that surely continued within the city's confines.

Brian's pulse quickened as he took in the rustic scenery, the verdant fields that whispered tales of serenity and escape. Dense forests, their canopies dappled with the morning light, beckoned like a sylvan sanctuary where he might find respite from the authorities who were undoubtedly scouring every nook and cranny of the city for any sign of the failed assassins.

The transition from the concrete jungle to the natural world was like a breath of fresh air for Brian. He knew that here, in the countryside's wilderness, he could disappear, his presence blending into the vast expanse of the landscape. Each passing mile brought him closer to the hope of eluding capture, the city's turmoil slowly becoming a fading specter in his rearview mirror.

As he ventured deeper into the countryside, the stolen bicycle became his trusted steed, carrying him further away from the chaos and danger that had defined his existence in Quebec City. With each turn of the pedal, Brian felt the weight of the world gradually lift, replaced by a burgeoning sense of freedom and the promise of a life defined by the tranquility of the natural world rather than the chaos of the city.

Brian's need for shelter, a respite from his relentless journey, and a sanctuary to regroup intensified with each passing moment. Amid the pristine natural beauty of the countryside, his eyes were drawn to a small, forlorn cabin nestled among the towering trees. It stood like a forgotten sentinel, a relic of a time long past, its weathered exterior and peeling paint bearing witness to years of abandonment.

Approaching the cabin, his every footstep was marked by caution, his senses attuned to any hint of recent activity. The surrounding forest seemed to hold its breath as he ventured closer, the underbrush rustling gently beneath his worn sneakers. Birds chirped in the distance, and a soft breeze whispered through the leaves, but there was no other sound to betray the presence of another soul.

Brian's hand brushed against the older wood of the cabin's door, and he scrutinized it for any sign of disturbance. The handle was cold and unyielding, and he could see no fresh marks or signs of intrusion. His pulse quickened as he decided, his gloved fingers gripping the handle tightly. With a determined effort, he forced the door open; the hinges protesting with a creak of long-neglected disuse.

Stepping into the dim, musty interior, Brian felt a sense of both relief and trepidation wash over him. The cabin bore the unmistakable marks of abandonment. Dust motes danced in the sparse beams of filtered sunlight that streamed through cracks in the wooden walls. Cobwebs clung to forgotten corners, and the air was thick with the scent of decay.

Brian knew he was alone, and that knowledge brought a semblance of peace. Here, in this forgotten refuge, he could finally catch his breath, rest his weary body, and plan his next moves. The cabin, a relic of a bygone era, was now his sanctuary, a place where he could regroup and plan his uncertain future in the wilderness's solitude.

Entering the cabin, Brian was met with the unmistakable air of neglect that clung to every surface. Dust motes danced in the dim light that filtered through the cracked windows, painting an eerie tableau of abandonment. He pulled the creaking door shut behind him, the heavy thud resonating through the cabin like a final seal against the outside world.

With each step, the floorboards groaned beneath his weight, as if the very structure of the cabin protested his intrusion. The room unfolded before him in its humble entirety, a one-room refuge from the chaos he had fled.

A rudimentary fireplace, its stone facade bearing the marks of countless fires long extinguished, occupied one corner of the cabin. It stood as a testament to the many winters this cabin had witnessed, providing warmth and sustenance to those who had sought shelter within its walls.

In the center of the room, a rickety table leaned precariously, its surface scarred and weathered from years of use and abuse. It was a relic of countless meals shared in this isolated sanctuary, a symbol of sustenance and survival.

A musty cot, its faded sheets bearing the imprint of countless restless nights, occupied a corner of the cabin. It beckoned as a place of rest, a refuge for a weary traveler seeking solace in the embrace of sleep.

Cobwebs hung from the rafters, their gossamer threads weaving a tapestry of time's passage. They swayed gently in the still air, a haunting reminder of the cabin's long solitude.

As Brian surveyed his surroundings, he knew that this cabin, despite its dilapidation, offered a sanctuary of sorts. It was a place where he could gather his thoughts, find a modicum of security, and plan his next moves in the quiet isolation of the wilderness.

Brian's body sagged with exhaustion, and the weight of his harrowing journey settled upon him like a heavy cloak. Emotionally drained and physically spent, he lowered himself onto the musty cot in a corner of the cabin. The cot groaned in protest, its faded sheets yielding to the weight of his weary frame as he sought refuge from the relentless trials of the past days.

The air inside the cabin was still and heavy, a silence that seemed to magnify the solitude of his surroundings. It was a refuge, a haven carved from the wilderness, where he could temporarily escape the pursuit that dogged his every step. Here, in the dim, dusty interior, he could allow himself a moment of lull, a chance to catch his breath and regain his strength for the challenges that lay ahead.

With deliberate movements, he reached into his bag, fingers fumbling in the dim light until they found what he sought—a map of the region, folded and worn from its journey with him. Carefully, he spread it out on the rickety table, the paper crackling softly as it unfolded. The map bore the marks of his previous attempts at planning, with hastily scribbled notes and annotations in the margins.

As he studied the map, Brian's mind raced with possibilities, each contour of the landscape a potential path to safety. He knew he couldn't linger here for long, that the cabin's dilapidated charm could only offer temporary solace. But at this moment, with the map laid out before him, he had the chance to chart his course, to plan his next move in the cabin's solitude's hushed embrace.

Brian's immediate aim loomed large in his mind: he had to put a vast expanse of distance between himself and the turmoil of Quebec City. His gaze fixated on the map spread out before him, the paper etched with intricate topography, its contours a web of potential routes to safety.

One option beckoned with a tantalizing allure: heading east toward the remote villages of Charlevoix. There, he reasoned, he might encounter sympathetic locals, individuals who were insulated from the chaos of the city and who could offer him refuge and help. The mere thought of a friendly face and a helping hand in those isolated hamlets provided a glimmer of hope.

Yet Brian's path forward was fraught with peril. He understood he couldn't afford to draw attention to himself. He had to remain inconspicuous, a ghost in the wilderness, a shadow slipping through the cracks of society's watchful gaze. Major roads, he knew, were patrolled, and monitored, their arteries feeding into the vigilant heart of law enforcement. He had to steer clear of these well-trodden paths.

The map became his canvas, and his finger traced tentative routes through the rugged terrain, avoiding the highways and byways that were ripe with potential hazards. His plan had to be as stealthy and elusive as his flight. Brian knew that success hinged on his ability to navigate the delicate balance between reaching out to sympathetic locals and staying hidden from the ever-watchful eyes of the authorities.

As he deliberated over his options, the cabin's solitude seemed to cocoon him in a world of possibilities and uncertainty. The map, now marred with his fingerprints and smudges from countless moments of contemplation, held the key to his survival. Brian's heart was heavy knowing that each decision he made would be a critical step toward his escape, his fingers trembling as he charted the intricate course that would lead him deeper into the unknown.

Brian harbored no delusions about the gravity of his predicament. The mission of revenge he had embarked upon had crumbled into ruins, its shattered remnants a stark reminder of the perils he faced. Yet, amid the chaos and uncertainty, one unyielding desire burned within him like a beacon: the desire for survival.

He knew that the comrades who had embarked with him on the ill-fated operation were now scattered to the winds, their fates uncertain. Some may have been captured, others might flee for their own lives, but Brian couldn't afford to rely on their help. The bonds of camaraderie forged in the crucible of their shared mission had been severed, leaving him to navigate the treacherous terrain of his escape alone.

At this moment, with the weight of the past bearing down on him, Brian realized that resourcefulness would be his greatest ally. He was adrift in a sea of uncertainty, with no clear path forward and no allies to lean on. Survival demanded that he tap into his deepest reservoirs of ingenuity, resilience, and determination, forging a path toward an uncertain future where each decision was a gamble, each step a test of his mettle.

The remnants of his mission, like ghosts of vengeance past, lingered in his thoughts. Brian had cast aside the pursuit of retribution, recognizing that survival itself was the ultimate prize. With each passing moment, he edged further into the unknown, a solitary figure in a world filled with uncertainty, where resourcefulness was his lifeline and the desire for survival, his unwavering beacon of hope.

Brian's eyes remained fixed on the map; its intricate details painted with the geography of his escape route. Yet, amid the contours and markings that dictated his path to safety, there was a pervasive ache in his heart, a presence that he couldn't ignore.

Anastasia, the woman he loved with a passion that had once burned fiercely, now haunted his thoughts. Her memory was a bittersweet melody that played in the recesses of his mind. He couldn't help but wonder about her fate, whether she was safe, or if the shadow of their failed plot had fallen over her as well.

The uncertainty gnawed at him, a relentless torment that tugged at his every decision. He wished he could reach out to her, to ensure her well-being, but the choice to disappear was not one he had made lightly. It was a choice born out of love, a desperate attempt to shield her from the storm of consequences that had arisen from his actions.

Brian knew his disappearance was not just a self-preservation tactic, but a sacrifice made for Anastasia's sake. He had severed the ties that bound them, to withdraw from her life, to protect her from the relentless pursuit that had become his reality. The weight of that decision bore down on him, each contour on the map a stark reminder of the distance he had put between himself and the woman he loved.

In the cabin's solitude, his heart heavy with the knowledge of what he had left behind, Brian pressed on with his plans. He knew that every step he took, every choice he made, was a testament to the love he felt for Anastasia, a love that had driven him to protect her even as it tore him away from her embrace.

With a deep and weary exhale that seemed to carry the weight of the world, Brian found himself on the brink of a daunting task: meticulously devising his escape route through the unforgiving wilderness. In this perilous endeavor, his very survival depended on the amalgamation of his honed survival instincts and an unyielding determination that had become the driving force behind his actions.

The path ahead was a harrowing one, fraught with obstacles and dangers at every turn. Brian knew that the journey he was embarking upon was riddled with treacherous pitfalls and unforeseeable challenges. It was a desperate gambit, one where each passing hour seemed to be a relentless echo of the one before it, but he had been cornered, with no alternatives but to venture into the unknown, fleeing relentlessly pursuing authorities.

As he meticulously charted his course through the rugged wilderness, Brian couldn't help but acknowledge the gnawing uncertainty that clung to his every step. Every rustling leaf and the distant cry of a wild creature was a reminder of the ever-present perils he faced. Yet, his resolve remained unshaken. He was prepared to confront these adversities head-on, drawing from the wellspring of his inner strength and the lessons of survival that had been etched into his very being.

With a heart that pounded like a drum and a spirit that refused to falter, Brian trudged forward into the vast, untamed expanse of the wilderness, where the next hour, much like the one before it, promised to unveil new tests of his endurance and determination. The wilderness would be his ally, his adversary, and his refuge as he continued his relentless flight, determined to elude the unyielding pursuit of the authorities that threatened to extinguish his freedom.

The hours seemed to drag on at a glacial pace as Brian found refuge within the confines of the forsaken cabin. Inside, time itself seemed to lose its sense of urgency, as he could hear the gentle sigh of the wind playing with the nearby trees and the distant serenades of birds whose songs echoed through the tranquil wilderness.

Brian knew acutely that he couldn't remain in this secluded sanctuary indefinitely. While the cabin offered a brief respite from the relentless pursuit that had brought him here, he knew that time was not on his side.

Every creak of the worn wooden boards beneath him served as a reminder of the fragile sanctuary he had found. His muscles ached from the ceaseless flight, and exhaustion weighed heavily on his eyelids. Yet, he resisted the seductive pull of sleep, for he understood that this stolen moment of respite was his chance to regather his strength and meticulously strategize his next course of action.

The cabin's worn, faded wallpaper whispered stories of a bygone era, its furniture covered in a shroud of dust. Brian took a moment to examine his surroundings, his eyes falling on an old, tattered journal left on a rickety table. Its pages, yellowed with age, held the secrets of previous inhabitants, offering a glimpse into the lives of those who had once sought refuge here.

Outside, the sun cast long shadows as it made its descent toward the horizon, casting a warm, golden glow upon the world beyond the cabin's weathered windows. The rustling leaves and bird calls painted a tranquil portrait of nature's timeless rhythms, a stark contrast to the turmoil that had brought Brian to this remote hideaway.

As he sat in solitude, the weight of his predicament pressed upon him. Brian knew that his respite was only temporary, and the outside world held both danger and opportunity in equal measure. With a sense of determination kindled by the solitude of the cabin, he charted his next moves, meticulously considering each step in his quest for freedom. The hours passed, but within the cabin's walls, Brian forged a plan that would set the course for his uncertain future.

Foremost on Brian's list of priorities was the imperative need to remain completely off the grid, a daunting task fraught with uncertainty. In the dimly lit cabin, he couldn't shake the nagging doubt that gnawed at him: did the authorities even realize he had survived the failed assassination attempt, and if so, were they actively hot on his trail?

The implications of his situation were dire, and his lack of information only added to the complexity of his predicament. A web of questions and anxieties swirled in his mind like a tempestuous storm. Had the relentless investigators connected him to the brazen attempt on a high-profile target's life? Or were they still piecing together the puzzle, unaware of the man they were chasing who had slipped through their fingers?

Brian knew that the answers to these questions held the keys to his survival. Every move he made, every step he took, had to be calculated with the utmost precision to evade detection. The cabin, while providing temporary shelter, was but a fragile fortress against an unknown enemy.

His fingers brushed against the journal's weathered pages, its secrets hidden in ink and parchment, a relic of forgotten stories. Brian realized that, for now, his life had become a page in a larger narrative, one he needed to control if he was to have any chance of rewriting his destiny. With the weight of uncertainty bearing down on him, he resolved to craft a strategy that would keep him off the radar and preserve his freedom in the face of formidable odds.

Brian's worn backpack held a precious cache of survival essentials, each item carefully chosen to prolong his existence in this unforgiving wilderness. Nestled inside, he had hoarded cans of preserved food, a compact yet indispensable water filter, a modest first-aid kit stocked with bandages and antiseptics, and a rugged hunting knife, its gleaming blade a stark symbol of both utility and potential danger.

The weight of these supplies pressed against his back as he contemplated their finite nature. Brian knew that his lifeline to sustenance was running perilously thin. The canned food, while sustaining him for now, couldn't stave off the inexorable march of hunger forever. His water filter had its limits, and his first-aid kit was only a buffer against injuries that might befall him in this perilous journey.

With resolve hardening in his heart, Brian realized the inexorable truth: he needed to restock his provisions, a venture fraught with its own set of dangers. It was a calculated risk he couldn't avoid. Gazing out of the cabin's window, he scrutinized the surroundings with a keen eye, hunting for any telltale signs of danger.

The world outside beckoned, a realm of untamed beauty and hidden perils. He felt the call of the wild, its mysteries and treacherous terrain lying in wait. Every rustling leaf and distant crackle of underbrush heightened his senses, serving as a reminder that danger could lurk behind every rock and tree.

Brian took a deep breath, centering himself, and with a shroud of caution, he stepped out into the unknown. His profile was low, a shadow melding with the natural world, as he ventured forth, a solitary figure poised between necessity and vulnerability. His journey to replenish his dwindling supplies was a dance with uncertainty, where every step brought him closer to sustenance, but also closer to the unseen threats that prowled in the wilderness.

The forest provided a tantalizing blend of sanctuary and adversity, offering Brian the opportunity to vanish amidst the lush, impenetrable foliage. However, this verdant realm also came laced with its own set of perils—nature's unpredictability manifested through the specter of wildlife, the treacherously uneven terrain underfoot, and the ceaseless, intricate need for navigation.

As Brian ventured further into the woodland, each step became a careful negotiation between the desire to evade pursuit and the acknowledgment of the formidable challenges that lay in his path. The underbrush teemed with life, an intricate ecosystem where the rustle of leaves could signify either passaging a cautious prey or the stealthy approach of a predator.

The terrain, too, was a relentless adversary. Hidden roots and rocky outcroppings conspired to trip him at every turn, and the ever-present risk of twisting an ankle, or worse, lurked with every stride. Every ascendant slope and precipitous descent demanded both physical stamina and mental fortitude.

Yet Brian navigated this untamed terrain with the seasoned confidence of one who had honed his survival skills through years of preparation. His senses, sharpened by experience, absorbed every nuance of his surroundings—the moss-covered boulders that acted as landmarks, the dappled sunlight filtering through the canopy that betrayed direction, and the distant calls of the forest's inhabitants, serving as an auditory compass.

With each cautious step, he wove together the threads of his knowledge—how to forage for sustenance, decipher the lay of the land, and expect the ebb and flow of wildlife. In the wilderness's heart, Brian was not merely a fugitive; he was a seasoned survivor, relying on his hard-earned expertise to navigate the dual worlds of concealment and peril that the forest presented.

As Brian trekked through the dense forest, his senses heightened to every rustle and whisper of the wilderness, he eventually stumbled upon a small, babbling stream. The serenity of this natural oasis beckoned to him, and with a cautious glance around to ensure he remained hidden from prying eyes, he dropped to his knees.

From his trusty backpack, he withdrew a well-worn canteen and a compact water filter, a lifeline to hydration in this unforgiving terrain. The stream's crystalline waters danced over smooth stones, a testament to nature's purity. Brian carefully dipped the canteen into the frigid embrace of the stream, its chilly touch sending shivers through his fingers.

With a deliberate sense of reverence, he watched as the water, once in its natural state, was transformed into a lifeline. The water filter, a marvel of modern ingenuity, began its work, stripping away impurities and ensuring that the liquid coursing into his canteen was safe to consume.

As the canteen filled, Brian couldn't resist the temptation to cup his hands and capture a handful of the cold, clear water. He brought it to his lips, taking deep, refreshing sips, allowing the rejuvenating sensation to wash over him. The purity of the stream's offering revitalized not only his body but also his spirit, fortifying him for the arduous journey that lay ahead.

With newfound vitality coursing through his veins, Brian used a few drops of water to wash his travel-worn face, cleansing away the grime and fatigue that clung to him. The water, cool and cleansing, was a balm to his senses, a moment of respite in the heart of the wild.

In this tranquil interlude by the stream, he was reminded of the delicate balance between survival and nature's abundant generosity. As he secured the now-filled canteen back into his backpack, he cast a silent vow to repay the wilderness for its sustenance by honoring his pursuit of freedom with every step he took.

Chapter Fifteen

As the sun's relentless march across the sky continued, Brian's unwavering determination centered still on one crucial aim: to put ever-increasing space between himself and the bustling metropolis of Quebec City. With each passing hour, he delved deeper into the heart of the untamed wilderness, leaving behind the familiar landmarks and urban clamor.

He meticulously charted his course, treading along the faintly etched game trails that wound through the dense underbrush. These enigmatic pathways, etched by generations of wildlife, offered him the dual benefits of cover and obscurity. Here, among the web of deer tracks and coyote trails, Brian minimized the chance of encountering other souls.

The choice to forsake established routes and delve deeper into the wilderness was not without its challenges. The terrain, already rugged, grew increasingly formidable as he progressed. Thorny thickets and jagged rocks tested his endurance, but Brian's resolve remained unshaken.

The forest, a sprawling expanse of ancient trees and whispered secrets, became his sanctuary. In the dappled sunlight filtering through the thick canopy, he found solitude and anonymity. The towering trees, guardians of this uncharted realm, embraced him in their silent watchfulness, their roots anchored in centuries of solitude.

Here, the constant hum of civilization was replaced by the gentle symphony of rustling leaves and the calls of unseen creatures. Brian reveled in the serenity of the wild, finding solace in knowing that he was a mere, inconspicuous presence amidst nature's grandeur.

With every step he took, Brian cast aside the shackles of his past life, embracing the uncertainty and exhilaration of his new existence. The forest's timeless embrace offered refuge from the relentless pursuit that had driven him into its depths, and he was determined to repay this sanctuary with the utmost respect and reverence as he continued his solitary journey into the heart of the wilderness.

As the day matured into late afternoon, Brian's relentless journey through the wilderness led him to an elusive refuge, concealed by the lush foliage and the enigmatic embrace of the forest. This secluded enclave, chosen with the precision of a seasoned survivalist, provided a much-needed respite from the ceaseless exertions of his flight.

In the shadowy embrace of the woods, Brian knew he couldn't sustain this clandestine existence indefinitely. The perils of nature and the specter of his pursuers loomed over him, reminding him that his sanctuary was fragile, temporary. His thoughts turned to the pressing need for a comprehensive plan that would chart his course through the treacherous waters of his predicament.

With meticulous care, he unfurled a mental roadmap, each destination a crucial milestone on his quest for freedom. New identification was a pressing priority, a key to escaping the relentless scrutiny of authorities. Accessing funds, a financial lifeline would be vital to sustain his flight, and Brian recognized he needed to find a way to secure these resources while staying under the radar.

The thought of eventually leaving the country weighed heavily on his mind. This endeavor was rife with complexities, from dodging border controls to gain passage to a foreign land. Brian understood the enormity of the task ahead, but he had no intention of letting it daunt him. Instead, he channeled his determination into crafting a plan that would not only guide his actions but also serve as a beacon of hope in the darkest of hours.

In the tranquil seclusion of his hidden haven, Brian wove together the strands of his escape strategy, mapping out the intricate steps that would transform his fugitive existence into a path toward a future unburdened by the shadows of his past.

The impending hour held a pivotal significance in Brian's tumultuous journey, as he found himself at a crossroads where the weight of his decisions bore heavily on his shoulders. This precious timeframe was dedicated to profound deliberation, a crucial interlude that could shape the trajectory of his newfound existence.

In a radical departure from the life he once knew, Brian had severed the last vestiges of his ties to the past. His relentless quest for revenge, once the driving force behind his actions, lay abandoned and forgotten. In its place, a singular, all-encompassing goal had crystallized survival and escape.

With laser-like focus, he had realigned his priorities, channeling his energy and resolve into charting an uncertain path forward. This path, fraught with uncharted territory and veiled by the shroud of uncertainty, beckoned to him like an enigmatic siren song. The stakes were staggering, and the challenges ahead appeared insurmountable, but Brian's determination remained unyielding.

He understood that the road he was embarking upon was bound to exact a toll, demanding sacrifices, and pushing him to the limits of his endurance. Yet, no matter the cost, he was resolute in his commitment to navigate this treacherous journey. Brian's unwavering resolve to embrace the unknown, to leave behind the specter of vengeance, and seize control of his destiny defined this critical hour as he steeled himself for the arduous odyssey that lay ahead.

As the sun's descent painted long, creeping shadows across the expanse of the dense forest, Brian found himself in a solemn moment of contemplation. Each elongating shadow seemed to mirror the gravity of the choices he faced, and as the day waned, the urgency of his situation became even more palpable.

The pivotal question that gripped his mind was that of identity. Brian recognized he couldn't remain a nameless, faceless fugitive forever. To escape the relentless pursuit of the authorities and vanish into the fabric of anonymity, he needed a fresh identity—a new life with a name, documents, and resources to sustain it.

As the forest's canopy filtered the fading sunlight, casting dappled patterns of illumination and shadow, Brian pondered the complex web of connections that might lead him to someone capable of providing the documents and resources. In the heart of this untamed wilderness, far removed from the trappings of civilization, his thoughts churned with the practicalities of securing the elusive keys to a new existence.

The forest, with its enveloping silence and the gentle rustle of leaves, bore witness to Brian's determination and the weight of his decisions. The journey ahead was fraught with challenges and peril, but it was a path he was resolved to tread. With each passing moment, the quest for a new identity became not just a necessity but a lifeline—a beacon of hope in the gathering shadows of his former life.

Brian's mind raced, a whirlwind of options and risks. His initial instinct was to reach out to his former comrades, the individuals with whom he had once shared a dangerous allegiance. Yet, upon deeper reflection, he realized that such recklessness could only spell disaster. The failed assassination attempt had exacted a heavy toll, claiming the lives of those he once called allies. He couldn't bear the thought of leading the relentless authorities to anyone else.

Resolute in his decision to protect those who might still live in the shadows, Brian shifted his focus to an alternative plan. He delved into the intricate web of the clandestine underground network he had once relied upon for information and supplies during his mission. This covert network was a subterranean world inhabited by enigmatic figures who thrived in anonymity and secrecy.

Within this shadowy realm, Brian knew he could find the help he needed to vanish into the abyss of anonymity. Individuals with the skills and resources to provide new identities and the means to evade the watchful eyes of law enforcement lurked in these murky corners of society.

The path he was embarking upon was not for the faint of heart, and Brian understood the risks inherent in placing his trust in the hands of these clandestine operatives. Yet, he also recognized that it was his best chance of eluding the relentless pursuit of the authorities and forging a new life in the unforgiving wilderness of anonymity.

Brian clutched a makeshift map, its hastily drawn contours etched in the margins of survival, and a weathered compass, both essential tools in his quest for a lifeline. The forest, which had become his labyrinthine refuge, sprawled around him, its secrets buried within the underbrush and the tangled canopy above.

His purpose was clear: he needed to navigate further into the depths of the wilderness, seeking a predetermined meeting point that held the promise of connection with a figure from his past. This rendezvous was more than a mere chance encounter; it was a lifeline, a carefully calculated thread woven into the fabric of his escape plan.

As the sun's descent cast a golden hue across the forest, Brian embarked on this critical expedition. Each step he took was a deliberate maneuver on the chessboard of survival, as he sought to pinpoint the elusive location that would serve as the bridge between his past and his uncertain future.

The meeting was scheduled for a precarious hour—just before the tapestry of twilight unfurled in the sky. In the dwindling light, he had to summon all his instincts and skills to ensure he reached the rendezvous on time and undetected, acutely aware that the gathering shadows held both the cover of concealment and the potential for peril.

With the makeshift map in one hand and the compass guiding his way, Brian's journey into the heart of the wilderness was a symphony of anticipation and trepidation, a dance with destiny that would shape the course of his newfound life.

As the daylight gradually waned, navigating through the labyrinthine wilderness became increasingly formidable for Brian. The encroaching darkness cast a shadowy veil over the forest, adding an extra layer of complexity to his journey. In these dire circumstances, his very survival hinged on his intuition and a profound understanding of the terrain he traversed.

With the sun's descent, the forest seemed to metamorphose, its character shifting from the familiar to the enigmatic. Each step he took was a testament to his resolute determination, as he relied on the finely tuned compass of his instincts to stay true to his course.

The forest, once a place of refuge and sanctuary, now appeared to close in around him, its towering trees becoming formidable sentinels of an ancient and silent realm. Their branches intertwined like an intricate tapestry, creating a dense canopy that absorbed the feeble remnants of light, leaving him shrouded in a world of shadows.

Despite the encroaching obscurity, Brian pressed on, his senses keenly attuned to the nuances of the terrain. His ears captured the symphony of nocturnal creatures awakening, their calls and rustling becoming familiar companions in the encroaching darkness. Each rustling leaf and whispered breeze served as a subtle signpost, guiding him along the path he had chosen.

In this perilous venture into the heart of the wild, Brian's reliance on his instincts and knowledge was not merely a choice but a lifeline—a testament to his indomitable will to forge ahead, even as the forest's depths threatened to engulf him in an abyss of uncertainty.

After a relentless journey through the darkening wilderness, Brian's tenacity brought him to the appointed location—a secluded clearing nestled beside an ancient sentinel, an oak tree that had borne witness to centuries of secrets. The small glade, bathed in the silver glow of the moonlight, was a sanctuary where past and present converged.

With the skill of a seasoned fugitive, Brian deftly concealed himself within the shadows, becoming one with the obscurity that shrouded the clearing. He understood the paramount importance of remaining invisible, a mere phantom lurking in the periphery, as he knew that even the faintest glimmer of light could serve as a beacon to those who hunted him.

The ancient oak tree, its gnarled branches reaching skyward like the hands of time itself, stood as a silent witness to the clandestine rendezvous. Its presence, both stoic and timeless, lent an air of solemnity to the meeting as if the weight of countless secrets bore down upon the gathering.

Patiently, Brian waited, his senses on high alert. He strained his ears, listening for any telltale signs of approach, every rustle of leaves and a distant hoot of an owl imbued with a sense of urgency. In the night's stillness, the clearing held its breath, as though nature itself awaited the unfolding of this clandestine chapter.

Brian's unyielding resolve, his ability to become one with the shadows, and his unspoken trust in the figure he expected the meeting coalesced in this moment of eerie stillness beneath the ancient oak. In this silent dance with destiny, he steeled himself for whatever lay ahead, knowing that the future hinged on the secrets that would soon be shared in the hushed conversations of the night.

The passage of minutes stretched into an interminable expanse, each second feeling like an eternity as Brian remained concealed within the shadowy confines of the clearing. His senses, honed to a razor's edge, stood on high alert, attuned to the subtlest shifts in the forest's symphony.

Every rustle of leaves, amplified by the stillness of the night, sent a jolt through his veins, making his heart race in response. The snap of a twig, like a gunshot in the silence, intensified the drumbeat of anticipation that thudded in his chest. He knew that the forest held its secrets close, and each sound could be a harbinger of danger or salvation.

Brian's unwavering vigilance was a testament to the stakes at hand. In this perilous moment, he couldn't afford to let his guard down, for his survival depended on the mastery of patience and vigilance. The clearing, bathed in moonlight, had become a stage where the future was cast in shadows, and he stood as its silent guardian, resolute in his determination to protect the secrets that bound him to the night.

Then, as if conjured from the depths of the night itself, a spectral figure materialized, emerging from the cloak of darkness that enveloped the clearing. The newcomer, a man clad in unremarkable attire that offered no hint of his identity, blended seamlessly with the obsidian tapestry of the night. His face remained veiled beneath the concealing shadows of a hat pulled low and a scarf drawn high.

Yet, despite the artful concealment, the stranger's eyes betrayed a keen intelligence, their piercing gaze assessing Brian with an intensity that sent a shiver down his spine. Those sharp, calculating orbs, like twin stars in the night, held the weight of knowledge and a subtle air of danger, as though they were a mirror reflecting the complexities of a life lived on the fringes of society.

As the two men regarded each other in the moonlit stillness of the clearing, the air was charged with unspoken understanding and mutual vulnerability. Brian recognized that this enigmatic figure held the keys to his escape, and the stranger seemed to acknowledge the depths of desperation that had brought Brian to this clandestine meeting beneath the ancient oak tree. In the hushed communion of their gazes, the fate of their futures hung in the balance, their destinies intertwined by the secrets they held and the shadows that enveloped them both.

Without uttering a single word, the mysterious figure extended a small package toward Brian, the offering cloaked in the weighty silence of their shared understanding. As Brian took the package into his trembling hands, he felt the rough texture of hope and apprehension intertwined within its confines.

Gently unwrapping the bundle, he revealed its precious contents: a meticulously crafted collection of forged identification papers, their authenticity a testament to the skill of those who operated in the shadows; a stack of unmarked cash, representing a lifeline to an existence off the grid; and a set of carefully written instructions, a roadmap to vanishing without a trace.

The papers bore his new identity, a mask to shield him from the prying eyes of the authorities, while the cash was both currency and security, a means to navigate the uncertain path ahead. The instructions, like a whispered promise, offered guidance on how to erase his former existence and become a phantom of the world, evading the relentless pursuit that threatened to consume him.

As Brian absorbed the significance of this clandestine exchange, he understood the package was more than just a set of tools—it was the cornerstone of his rebirth, the first step in a journey of perpetual escape. This enigmatic figure, a guardian of the underground world, had just handed him the keys to his new life on the run, a life defined by shadows and secrets, where survival was the currency and anonymity of the prize.

With a deft, almost ethereal retreat, the enigmatic stranger dissolved into the inky cloak of the night, leaving Brian in a state of profound ambiguity. The emotions that swirled within him were a complex blend of relief and apprehension, their discordant notes harmonizing in the symphony of his tumultuous existence.

In that fleeting moment beneath the moon's watchful gaze, Brian had taken his initial stride toward the elusive escape he so fervently sought. The package nestled within his grasp held the keys to a future unburdened by the shackles of his past. Yet, as the stranger vanished into the obscurity of the forest, Brian couldn't ignore the chilling reminder that the path he now trod was fraught with perils unknown.

The road ahead was a maze of danger and uncertainty, where every twist and turn held the potential for betrayal or discovery. To navigate this treacherous terrain, Brian understood he would need to summon every ounce of his wits and instincts, to become a master of evasion, a shadow slipping through the fingers of those who sought to capture him.

With the weight of his newfound identity and the enigmatic stranger's instructions firmly etched into his consciousness, Brian steeled himself for the harrowing journey that lay ahead. In the night's crucible, he had been handed a lifeline to freedom, but he knew acutely that it would be his wit, his determination, and his unwavering resolve that would ultimately carve the path to his escape, allowing him to remain perpetually one step ahead of the relentless pursuit that pursued him relentlessly.

With the shroud of darkness firmly draped over the landscape, Brian quietly extricated himself from the clandestine rendezvous point beneath the ancient oak tree. His steps, measured and purposeful, carried him away from the moonlit clearing, and he returned to his solitary pilgrimage through the enigmatic forest, venturing further into the uncharted depths of the unknown.

As he trudged onward through the wilderness, his senses acutely attuned to the symphony of nocturnal life that surrounded him, Brian knew that the next hour held the promise of profound transformation. The resources he had gained were more than mere possessions; they were the tools with which he would forge a new identity, a persona that would grant him sanctuary from a world that had become his enemy.

In the night's solitude, Brian's fingers traced the edges of the forged identification papers, a tangible manifestation of his rebirth. The unmarked cash nestled in his pocket was a lifeline, a key to unlock the doors of his escape. With each passing moment, he planned his metamorphosis, plotting the intricate steps that would lead him to a place of obscurity and safety.

The world he had once known had crumbled, reduced to a relentless pursuit that threatened to consume him whole. But as he pressed forward, guided by the secrets he now possessed, Brian was resolute in his determination to carve out a new existence, a life where shadows and secrets would be his allies, and freedom his most coveted prize.

In the next hour, Brian's efforts were a symphony of meticulous transformation. With unwavering resolve, he embarked on altering his appearance and crafting a fresh identity that would serve as his cloak of invisibility.

Each minute that ticked by carried the weight of urgency, a constant reminder that time was a currency he could ill afford to squander. The pursuit of anonymity was a relentless race against the clock, and every detail mattered.

Brian's hands deftly wielded the tools of his changing his looks—a razor to sculpt his hair, a change of clothing that stripped him of his former self, and cosmetics to subtly alter the contours of his face. His reflection, once a mirror of familiarity, was now a canvas awaiting the masterful brushstrokes of change.

He understood that this metamorphosis was his only chance at disappearing completely from the unforgiving radar of the authorities. His new identity had to be an impenetrable fortress, a mask that would deflect even the most astute scrutiny. The stakes were staggering, and failure was not an option.

In the dim, moonlit solitude of the wilderness, Brian's silent transformation was a testament to his unwavering determination. With each deliberate action, he etched the contours of his new self, forging a path to freedom where the shadows of his former existence would be left far behind.

Employing the meticulously crafted forged identification papers given to him by the shadowy contact, Brian embarked on the intricate journey of adopting a new identity, shedding his former self like a chameleon shedding its skin. From the cocoon of obscurity, he emerged as Robert Anderson, a name that would become his refuge, his shield, and his lifeline.

With painstaking precision, he embarked on the transformation, starting with his hirsute facade. His once unruly beard, which had once framed his face, was now meticulously trimmed to a precise, sculpted contour, leaving behind only a shadow of its former self. It was a careful calibration of change, a subtle evolution that marked the beginning of his rebirth.

In the moonlit stillness of the night, Brian's deft fingers wielded a bottle of hair dye, darkening his locks to a shade that felt both foreign and fitting. The reflection that stared back at him bore the echoes of his former self, yet there was a subtle but undeniable shift—a metamorphosis that transcended the mere physical.

The change, though subtle, was undeniably effective. In the mirror of his makeshift wilderness sanctuary, he beheld not the man who had once been entangled in the maelstrom of a failed assassination attempt, but the embodiment of his newfound identity. Robert Anderson was a mask, a persona crafted from necessity, a passport to a life untethered from the past.

With this transformation complete, Brian had taken his first definitive steps toward obscurity, his former self receding like a distant memory. In the wilderness, beneath the moon's watchful eye, he had become the embodiment of change, a testament to the human spirit's indomitable will to adapt and survive.

With the forged identification papers securely in hand, Brian turned his attention to the meticulously crafted documents that would breathe life into his new identity. He became an earnest scholar of these fabricated truths, absorbing every detail with a mixture of fascination and trepidation.

According to the papers, he was no longer Brian, but a Canadian citizen by the name of Robert Anderson, a birthright claimed in a small, obscure town nestled in the heart of British Columbia. The quaint, remote setting provided the perfect backdrop for his new persona, a place where the threads of his fictional life could seamlessly intertwine with the tapestry of reality.

His fabricated past was composed of a carefully constructed narrative—a background in construction work, a vocation that would furnish him with a plausible cover for his movements in the world he was about to enter. The documents spun a tale of sweat, labor, and toil, the kind that left its mark on a man but remained unremarkable in the grand scheme of things.

These papers, these crystalline fragments of fiction, painted a vivid portrait of Robert Anderson's existence, complete with a family history that served as the linchpin to his believability. His purported relatives and their addresses were etched into the documents with meticulous precision, lending an air of authenticity to the tale that was now his to embody.

As Brian delved deeper into this labyrinth of deception, he understood these documents were not merely sheets of paper; they were his ticket to freedom, his means of slipping through the grasp of his pursuers. Robert Anderson was not a figment of imagination, but a tangible existence, a mask behind which he could hide and, perhaps, begin anew.

In this clandestine sanctuary beneath the moonlight, Brian had become not just Robert Anderson but also the keeper of his fate, the sculptor of the life he would now assume. These papers were his arsenal, his weapon in the battle for obscurity, as he prepared to venture forth into a world where truth and fiction would blur, and survival would be the measure of his success.

With the meticulously constructed persona of Robert Anderson now firmly established, Brian's immediate priority became finding a haven for the night, a sanctuary where he could safely retreat from prying eyes. The prospect of remaining in any populated area was far too perilous, so he forged onward, deeper into the heart of the unforgiving wilderness.

Amid the wilderness, he possessed a whispered secret—a remote cabin that had once belonged to a trusted friend. This isolated refuge beckoned to him like a siren's call, offering a respite from the relentless pursuit that had hounded him. It was a place where he could blend into the obscurity of the natural world, far removed from the scrutinizing gaze of the authorities.

As he journeyed deeper into the forest, his steps resonated with the quiet assurance of someone who had traversed these woods countless times before. Each stride brought him closer to the coveted cabin, a hideaway that held the promise of reprieve from the relentless chase.

In the inky shadows of the night, Brian's resolve remained unwavering. With every step he took, he inched closer to the isolated sanctuary, a place where the walls would shield him from the world's relentless pursuit, where the solitude would grant him a moment's respite, and where, under the veil of darkness, he could redefine his existence as Robert Anderson—a name unburdened by the weight of the past, a name that would be his salvation in the unforgiving wilderness of anonymity.

Traversing the forest under the veil of darkness posed a formidable challenge, but Brian's survival skills were his guiding compass in this shadowy realm. With the moon's feeble light filtering through the canopy, he moved with an almost supernatural grace, a ghostly figure weaving through the labyrinthine underbrush, his senses acutely attuned to the intricacies of the terrain.

Every footfall was a whisper against the forest floor, each step a testament to the stealth he had honed over years of traversing this wilderness. He consciously steered clear of well-trodden paths, wary of any encounters that might shatter the cloak of anonymity he had carefully cultivated.

The night, with its cold, unforgiving grip, embraced him as he ventured deeper into the solitude of the forest. The eerie backdrop of the distant howling wolves only heightened the otherworldly atmosphere of his journey. Their mournful calls, echoing through the night, seemed like the voices of phantoms, shadowy companions that bore witness to his solitary trek.

Brian's awareness of the forest's dangers was keen, and he remained vigilant in his pursuit of safety. Each rustle of leaves, every rustling breeze, was both a potential threat and a whispered secret, guiding him through this nocturnal odyssey.

During this profound solitude, the wilderness offered no solace, no quarter. Yet, Brian's tenacity and resourcefulness had transformed him into a shadowy denizen of the night, a testament to the enduring spirit of survival that would propel him onward, deeper into the wilderness, as he embarked on this perilous journey toward an uncertain destiny.

After a relentless journey through the shroud of night, Brian's footsteps finally brought him to the hidden sanctuary of the secluded cabin. Nestled among the towering trees, it stood as a modest structure, a relic long forsaken by its previous inhabitants. For Brian, it had served as a trusted safe house on previous occasions, its covert location a well-guarded secret that had kept him concealed from the relentless gaze of those who pursued him.

With an exhale of relief, Brian crossed the threshold, stepping into the musty interior of the cabin. The air was heavy with the scent of solitude, a lingering testament to its abandonment. The dim moonlight filtering through the cracked windows offered only a muted glimpse of the space within.

As he settled in for the night, Brian's fingers brushed against the remnants of a life left behind—the canned food and bottled water left in a corner as provisions for emergencies. At this moment, they became his lifeline, sustenance for the weary traveler who had ventured into the heart of the wilderness.

The cabin, though modest, held the comforting embrace of familiarity. Its walls, once witness to countless tales of solitude and solitude, now cradled Brian in their protective embrace. As he huddled in the night's obscurity, he was grateful for this clandestine refuge, a place where he could momentarily set aside the burden of his flight and catch his breath.

With the canned food and bottled water as his companions, Brian prepared to spend the night in the company of solitude, knowing that the respite he found within these timeworn walls was a precious interlude in the ceaseless journey of his escape.

Seated within the hushed confines of the cabin, bathed in the muted glow of the moonlight trickling through the timeworn windows, Brian found himself ensnared in a labyrinth of introspection. In the night's quietude, his thoughts converged upon the tumultuous cascade of events that had inexorably led him to this shadowy sanctuary.

The haunting specter of revenge, once the driving force of his existence, now loomed like a sinister shadow on the periphery of his consciousness. He had embarked on a perilous journey, fueled by a thirst for vengeance, a journey that had unraveled into a twisted labyrinth of deceit and danger. Forced by circumstance, he had been compelled to abandon this dark path, a bitter relinquishment that left a bitter taste upon his tongue.

In the place of vengeance, Brian's singular focus now clung to the imperative of survival, the relentless pursuit of eluding capture by the authorities, who shadowed his every move. The chase had become his life, his constant companion, an unrelenting symphony of evasion that echoed in the chambers of his mind.

As he gazed into the enigmatic abyss of his uncertain future, Brian couldn't help but ponder the elusive concept of peace. Would it forever elude him, like a mirage in the desert of his existence, or was there a sliver of hope that one day, the specters of his past would be laid to rest?

In the cabin's solitude, with the night as his only confidant, Brian was left to grapple with these profound questions, to wonder if the pursuit of survival could ever lead him to a destination where the ghosts of his past would be silenced, and the echoes of his former life would finally find reprieve.

The night crept by at an agonizingly languid pace, and Brian's thoughts were an ever-churning tempest of uncertainty. Within the confines of the cabin, he lay on a makeshift cot, consumed by the heavy pall of ambiguity that shrouded his existence. The safety of this secluded retreat was an ephemeral refuge, a sanctuary amidst the tumultuous tempest of his newfound life.

Aware that he couldn't indefinitely tether himself to this cabin, the oppressive weight of his new reality bore down upon him. The wilderness, though an ally, was not without its dangers, its challenges, and hidden perils haunting his restless mind. Brian understood that, in this unforgiving world of shadows, complacency could be his most perilous adversary.

Yet, for now, he clung to the slender thread of security that the cabin afforded. Here, in the wilderness's heart, he was shielded from prying eyes and relentless pursuit. In the profound solitude of the night, he charted the complex course of his next move, a strategy to navigate the convoluted maze of his newfound life.

The forthcoming hour promised a brief respite, a stolen moment of rest amidst the ceaseless chaos that had become his reality. As the moon's delicate light filtered through the cabin's weathered walls, Brian closed his eyes, allowing the whispers of the night to lull him into a troubled slumber. In this interlude of stillness, he gathered strength, determined to face the approaching dawn with renewed vigor and purpose, ready to confront the ever-shifting challenges that awaited him beyond the cabin's fragile sanctuary.

With the first delicate tendrils of dawn weaving their way through the dense canopy of trees, Brian found himself at a crossroads, a juncture demanding a resolute decision. The cabin, though a welcome haven, could be naught but a transitory refuge—a mere waypoint on his tumultuous journey. The dawning realization weighed heavily upon him: if he were to escape the relentless pursuit and carve out a new existence under the guise of Robert Anderson, he needed a comprehensive, long-term strategy.

As the morning light gently bathed the world around him, Brian knew that his continued safety hinged upon his capacity to devise a meticulous plan, one that would lead him away from the cabin's limited sanctuary and toward the elusive horizon of his freedom. The wilderness, a fickle ally, held secrets of both salvation and peril, and he needed to master its complicated passages.

The hours that lay ahead were a canvas upon which he would paint his escape, a symphony of careful deliberation and calculated risk. Brian understood the stakes had never been higher; the identity of Robert Anderson was not merely a mask but a key to unlocking a future unburdened by the shadows of his past.

As the surrounding forest stirred to life by the rising sun, he contemplated the uncertain path that stretched before him. The decisions he would make in the coming hours would determine the course of his destiny, as he ventured forth, ready to embrace the challenges and victories that awaited on his journey to a life uncharted, to a world where the weight of his past would finally relinquish its hold, and Robert Anderson could emerge as a new and unencumbered soul.

Foremost among his concerns was the imperative to create a chasm of distance between himself and the perilous clutches of Quebec City, a once-familiar metropolis that had transmogrified into a sinister labyrinth. Its very streets, once trodden with familiarity, had become a perilous expanse, and Brian knew that the tempest of danger still swirled menacingly in its heart.

Yet Brian harbored no illusion that he could simply emerge from the wilderness, shedding the cloak of obscurity and seeking solace within the tapestry of society. The authorities, their watchful eyes honed to a razor's edge, were on high alert, their pursuit sharpened to an unforgiving point. The recent failed assassination attempt at Chateau Frontenac had cast a long and ominous shadow, a shroud of notoriety that clung to his very existence.

He understood that to evade their relentless pursuit required a strategy as calculated as it was audacious. The world beyond the wilderness was a perilous expanse, a terrain where he would need to become an unremarkable phantom, to cast aside his past like a chameleon donning a new skin.

The sun, now risen, cast a warm yet wary light upon the wilderness, illuminating the myriad challenges that lay ahead. Brian contemplated his options, knowing that the path to freedom was shrouded in the thickest of fog and the deepest of shadows. To traverse this treacherous course required not just his skill and cunning but also the audacity to defy the relentless pursuit of the authorities. It was a gamble, a high-stakes endeavor, and the dice were cast upon a table where the winner would be the one who mastered the art of disappearance and emerged, unscathed, into the enigmatic realm of anonymity.

The following hour unfolded as a meticulous symphony of preparation and planning within the confines of the cabin. Brian immersed himself in the intricacies of the new identity he was tasked with embodying, scrutinizing every facet of the fabricated life he had lived. Each detail, from the smallest anecdote to the broader strokes of his past, was etched into his memory with painstaking precision. He understood that this fictional persona had to become his second skin, a seamless veneer that would grant him passage through the world undetected.

As the minutes ticked by, Brian turned his attention to the supplies meticulously stashed within the cabin's aged walls. With methodical care, he inventoried the essentials—canned provisions, bottled water, a small first-aid kit, and other necessities. His assessment revealed that the cabin held enough resources to sustain him for several weeks, a critical buffer against the uncertainties of life in the wilderness.

In the somber solitude of the cabin, Brian's focus was singular, his determination unwavering. The identity of Robert Anderson was now more than just a mask; it was a lifeline, a passport to a future unburdened by the shadows of his past. As he committed the details to memory and secured his provisions, he knew that the next leg of his journey would test not only his survival skills but also the depth of his resolve.

After hours of meticulous preparation and a growing sense of confidence in the carefully constructed facade of Robert Anderson, Brian resolved it was time to depart from the cabin's sheltering embrace. The forest had served as his refuge, a sanctuary where he could lay the groundwork for his escape, but the next chapter of his journey beckoned with an urgency that couldn't be ignored.

With resolute determination, he ventured out into the heart of the wilderness once more, the dappled sunlight filtering through the swaying leaves serving as a bittersweet reminder of the world beyond. The forest, though a trusted ally, had its limitations, and Brian knew he needed to traverse the path that led to civilization.

His destination was a town—a realm where he could begin the intricate dance of establishing his new life under the name of Robert Anderson. The challenges ahead were formidable, and every step would be fraught with uncertainty, but Brian's tenacity remained unyielding.

The forest, with its echoing whispers and enigmatic shadows, receded into the background as Brian ventured forth, guided by a singular purpose. The world beyond the wilderness held the promise of anonymity, of a fresh start unburdened by the ghosts of his past. In that world, Robert Anderson would emerge from the shadows, a phoenix rising from the ashes, ready to forge a future untethered by the constraints of his former life.

Clad in a weathered backpack that held the tangible remnants of his newfound identity—forged documents, a modest stash of cash, and the bare essentials—Brian embarked on the next leg of his odyssey into the heart of the wilderness. Every step was imbued with purpose, each footfall a resolute declaration that he would no longer remain confined within the cabin's shadows.

The path he treads upon is fraught with doubt, winding through the intricate foliage of the forest. As he ventured deeper into the woods, the towering trees seemed to whisper secrets of the ages, their gnarled branches serving as ancient sentinels bearing witness to his passage.

The destination he sought was still a nebulous specter on the horizon—an elusive town nestled somewhere in the wilderness's embrace. It was there that he aspired to find the tethers to the outside world, to catch a train or board a bus that would propel him to a larger city, a realm of anonymity where he could breathe freely once more.

In this audacious gambit for escape, every twist and turn of the wilderness was a reminder of the unknown challenges ahead. The terrain was his compass, the wilderness his unforgiving mentor, and Robert Anderson, the moniker he wore like armor, his key to forging a path toward the world beyond. The journey was perilous, the risks innumerable, but with each determined step, Brian inched closer to the elusive promise of freedom that beckoned from the horizon.

With the relentless march of hours, Brian's odyssey unfurled amidst the sprawling expanse of the dense forest. This was no leisurely stroll but a cautious, calculated dance through nature's obscure realm. He dared not tread the well-trodden paths or approach any hint of civilization; instead, he adhered to the fringes, a phantom traversing the shadowy margins of the wilderness.

His survival skills became his guiding stars, his instincts honed through years of preparation and life on the precipice. Every movement was a choreography of caution, each step taken with the feather-light precision of a seasoned tracker. He moved in stealthy silence, a shadow among shadows, aware that the echoes of his past could not afford to reach prying ears.

The forest enveloped him in a symphony of nature's melodies—the rustling leaves, the murmurs of unseen creatures, the distant calls of birds—all weaving a harmonious tapestry that stood in stark contrast to the cacophony of chaos that had dominated his recent existence. Here, amidst the verdant tranquility, Brian felt a peculiar serenity—a reprieve from the relentless storm of his life.

As he continued his measured progress through the wilderness, passing time marked not just his physical journey, but a transformation of the spirit. In this place of solitude, the tempest within him waned, replaced by a quiet resolve, a determination to leave behind the remnants of his past and embrace the enigmatic future that beckoned from the depths of the forest.

As the sun ascended its lofty throne in the mid-morning sky, Brian's journey led him to a secluded road, a serpentine pathway that whispered secrets of the nearby town. This road, seldom traversed and shrouded in dappled sunlight, became his silent companion in the unfolding drama of escape.

Like a specter weaving through the fringes of existence, Brian clung to the shadows, his senses acutely attuned to the slightest hint of danger. Each step was deliberate, every glance a vigilant sweep of the surroundings, as he embarked on the precarious endeavor of navigating this tenuous threshold between wilderness and civilization.

The world beyond the forest's confines bore witness to a wary fugitive, one who watched for any telltale signs of authority—checkpoints, flashing sirens, or vigilant patrols. His existence had been cast into the crucible of secrecy, and he knew that the slightest misstep could precipitate his undoing.

Brian's progress was a symphony of caution—a ballet of avoidance, an intricate dance with the unknown. To draw attention to himself was curse, a gambit with consequences too dire to contemplate. In the road's silence, his very breaths were measured, each footfall a whisper against the ground.

In this uncharted realm between wilderness and civilization, Brian treads with an unwavering resolve. His fate hung in the balance, teetering on the precipice of discovery, yet he was determined to master this perilous terrain and continue his pursuit of freedom under the guise of Robert Anderson.

As Brian's measured strides carried him ever closer to the outskirts of the town, his heart quickened its rhythm, a discordant symphony of anticipation and apprehension. Each footfall felt like a resounding drumbeat, echoing the dichotomy of his emotions—a rising sense of hope for a new beginning intertwined with the dread of discovery lurking in the shadows.

The town, a mere breath away, symbolized the threshold to a realm where his rebirth as Robert Anderson could begin. It was a place where anonymity beckoned, where the shackles of his former life could be shed, and the tapestry of his future rewoven.

But with every step he took, the perils multiplied, the net of danger drawing ever tighter. The next hour, pregnant with potential, was also fraught with uncertainty. The promise of escape was juxtaposed with the weight of risk. Each decision, each choice, held the power to alter the course of his destiny.

Brian was now on an inexorable trajectory, a path of no return. The journey to reshape his life was treacherous, a tightrope walk suspended over the abyss of his past. He knew there was no turning back, no rewinding the threads of fate. With unwavering resolve, he ventured forth, bracing himself for the crucible of challenges and the crucible of transformation that lay ahead.

With the same measured caution that had guided him through the labyrinthine forest, Brian stepped into the small town that lay nestled on the outskirts of the wilderness. This unassuming hamlet, bathed in the dappled glow of sunlight, exuded an air of tranquility and anonymity—a stark contrast to the bustling, scrutinizing streets of Quebec City that he had so recently departed.

In this quiet, nondescript enclave, the rhythm of life moved at a leisurely pace. It was a place where everyone seemed to know their neighbors' business, where the gentle hum of daily existence was a soothing lullaby. Here, the mundane concerns of everyday life masked the secrets that lurked beneath the surface, offering a perfect cloak of obscurity for one seeking refuge.

For Brian, this serene atmosphere was a balm for his weary soul, a sanctuary where he could breathe freely once more. The town's familiarity and small-town intimacy were precisely what he needed—a space where his past could dissolve into the tapestry of collective memory, and where he could emerge as Robert Anderson, a face among many, a name lost in the chorus of life's quiet dramas.

As he ventured deeper into the heart of the town, Brian embraced the tranquil anonymity that enveloped him. Here, in this unassuming refuge, he dared to dream of a future unburdened by the relentless pursuit of his past—a future where the shadows of his former life would recede, and the dawn of a new beginning beckoned like a distant horizon, bathed in the soft, forgiving light of possibility.

Brian's initial imperative was to secure a haven where he could exist in obscurity, at least for a brief respite. Amidst the quiet streets of the town, an unassuming motel beckoned to him, its unpretentious facade an invitation to anonymity. Here, he checked in under the guise of his freshly minted identity as Robert Anderson.

Approaching the motel's reception with an air of calculated nonchalance, Brian was acutely aware of the significance of this pivotal moment. The exchange that followed held the potential to both shield him from scrutiny and to serve as a critical link in the chain of his new existence.

With a practiced ease, he slid a stack of cash across the counter, his eyes meeting the clerk's with an unwavering gaze. The transaction was conducted in silence, a tacit understanding that no paper trail would be left behind to betray his presence. The bills exchanged hands, an exchange of fleeting trust, a transaction that marked the birth of Robert Anderson's life within the town.

As he received the key to his nondescript room, Brian knew this motel would become his temporary refuge, a sanctuary in which he could navigate the intricacies of his newfound existence. With each step down the dimly lit corridor, he left behind the lingering specter of his past, embracing the possibility of an unburdened future. In this cocoon of anonymity, he would carefully plan his next moves, ensuring that every action bore the stamp of Robert Anderson, a name that would soon become synonymous with his escape and transformation.

Within the confines of his unassuming motel room, Brian finally allowed himself the luxury of a deep, exhaling sigh—a sound that echoed the long and arduous journey from the remote cabin to the welcoming embrace of the town. The exhaustion that had settled into his bones seemed to weigh him down, reminding him of the trials he had weathered.

With a sense of relief washing over him, Brian acknowledged the paramount importance of the moment. It was a brief respite, a window of opportunity nestled within the folds of time, during which he could unburden his thoughts, orchestrate the symphony of his next moves, and, just perhaps, reach out to Brendan or any surviving members of their clandestine group.

The room, unassuming like the motel itself, held the promise of solace. Its dimly lit ambiance provided a sheltering cocoon, offering him a sanctuary in which he could temporarily set aside the burdens of the outside world. Here, beneath the muted glow of lamplight, he would take stock of his newfound life as Robert Anderson and carefully craft the delicate tapestry of his future.

As he settled into the worn chair by the window, Brian gazed out into the quiet street below, the world outside seemingly oblivious to the enigmatic presence within the room. This was his interlude of contemplation, a moment to recharge his weary spirit and fortify his resolve, for he knew that the relentless pursuit of the authorities and the weight of his past were never far behind. In this haven of solitude, he would prepare for the chapters that lay ahead, where every action would be a testament to his resourcefulness, and where the shadows of his past would be held at bay, allowing Robert Anderson to rise anew.

In the cocoon of his motel room, Brian's thoughts immediately gravitated toward the turbulent aftermath of the failed assassination attempt at Chateau Frontenac—an event that had precipitated his desperate flight and the unraveling of the life he once knew. His immediate concern was to grasp the extent of the chaos left in its wake.

With a sense of urgency, he reached to turn the radio on which was perched on a weathered table, a portal to the outside world, a beacon of insight into the events that had set his life on its current trajectory.

Brian deftly tuned in to the local radio station explaining the news transitioning from static to a vivid depiction of the post-assassination landscape. The images that were described on the radio news broadcast greeted him were a stark reminder of the devastation that had unfolded—the shattered facade of the Chateau, the frenetic swarm of emergency responders, and the disarray that had gripped the once-picturesque scene.

The radio reporter, his voice tinged with a mixture of shock and speculation, dissected the event. They sought to unravel the enigma that was the motive behind the audacious attack and the identities of the assailants who had dared to breach the citadel's sanctity. The airwaves hummed with conjecture, as if trying to make sense of a puzzle whose pieces remained tantalizingly out of reach.

Brian listened with a solemn intensity, absorbing the fragments of information that filtered through the airwaves, aware that the events he had been entangled in had become a larger-than-life spectacle, a tempestuous narrative that he could no longer control. This was the world he had left behind, a world that was now intertwined with the shadowy figure of Robert Anderson, and he knew he must tread carefully in the days to come, lest the turbulent whirlwind of the past sweeps him up once more.

The room's atmosphere grew palpably tense as Brian fixated on the unfolding news coverage. The authorities, in the aftermath of the Chateau Frontenac debacle, had yet to divulge any concrete information about the elusive perpetrators. However, Brian harbored no illusions about the transient nature of this ambiguity.

He understood that, with each passing moment, the invisible net of investigation would inexorably tighten around the incident's enigmatic protagonists. The relentless pursuit of truth was a force that knew no respite, and he knew he couldn't afford to be ensnared within its voracious grasp.

As the minutes ticked away, the room's shadows deepened, mirroring the growing gravity of the situation. Brian's jaw clenched with a resolute determination, his mind coalescing around the unyielding need to remain a phantom, a figure cloaked in obscurity. He would meticulously chart his course through this precarious labyrinth, constantly aware of the tightening noose that threatened to encircle him.

The authorities might not yet have unveiled the identity of the assailants, but Brian understood that time was his most precious currency. He needed to stay ahead of the inexorable march of justice, to shape his destiny while remaining ever elusive, and to ensure that Robert Anderson remained an enigma in the shadowy tapestry of the unfolding narrative.

Brian's immediate focus shifted to the critical task of cementing his new identity as Robert Anderson. The path ahead was laden with formidable challenges, each demanding his unwavering attention. He knew that merely possessing forged documents wouldn't suffice; they had to withstand the scrutiny of the meticulous world beyond the motel room.

The blueprint for his changing of his features was clear: he needed official identification, a source of income, and a secure abode—all seamlessly aligned under the guise of Robert Anderson. The forged documents, though a foundation, were merely the first brushstrokes on the canvas of his new life.

With meticulous precision, he dissected the documents, scrutinizing every detail, every nuance. Each imperfection, each seam in the carefully woven tapestry of his fictitious past, had to be ironed out. The photographs, the birth certificate, the employment history—they all needed to exude an air of authenticity as if Robert Anderson had existed in the world for years.

Brian knew acutely that he was navigating treacherous waters, and the forgery had to be impeccable. Any hint of suspicion could lead to his undoing. His very survival depended on his ability to blend into society as Robert Anderson, an entity unburdened by the sins of the past.

With every passing hour, Brian's commitment to this transformation grew more steadfast. The confluence of his wits, his determination, and his unyielding resolve was a crucible in which the future would be forged. In the dimly lit room, he meticulously molded the contours of his new life, ensuring that the chiseled identity of Robert Anderson would emerge as a masterpiece of deception, impervious to the probing eyes of those who sought to unmask his secrets.

In a rare moment of contemplation, Brian allowed himself to peer into the rearview mirror of his past. The life he was leaving behind resembled a complex tapestry—a mosaic woven from threads of secrets, allegiances, and simmering vendettas. It was a life fraught with intrigue, where loyalties were forged in the crucible of necessity, and trust was a commodity traded cautiously.

Now, as Robert Anderson, he stood at the face of his new identity, a blank canvas stretching endlessly before him, eager to be adorned with the hues of recent history. The weight of his decisions, the sacrifices made, and the uncertainty of the future converged upon him, like a heavy cloak that clung to his shoulders.

The mantle of Robert Anderson, the nom de guerre under which he had chosen to re-emerge, was both liberating and daunting. It offered him a chance to shed the skin of his former life, break free from the constricting bonds of his past, and craft a destiny that was unburdened by the shadows that had once loomed large.

Yet, as he stood on the cusp of this transformation, Brian couldn't ignore the palpable gravity of his choices. The future was an enigmatic terrain, and the path he had chosen was fraught with uncertainty. The name Robert Anderson was not just an alias; it was an identity he would wear like armor, a persona that would define his every action, a shield against the relentless pursuit of his past.

In the motel's stillness room, Brian grappled with the profound weight of his decisions, aware that he was embarking on an odyssey into the unknown. This was a journey where the canvas of his existence would be splashed with vibrant strokes of deception and survival, a tapestry in which the threads of the past would be woven into a new narrative—an epic tale of a man reborn, unshackled from the sins of yesterday, and resolute in his pursuit of a future shrouded in the mists of possibility.

With the next hour passed, Brian's thoughts coalesced into a meticulous mental checklist, each task a pivotal stepping stone on the path to solidifying his new existence as Robert Anderson. The challenges that lay ahead were manifold, demanding his strategic finesse and unwavering resolve.

Foremost, he recognized the pressing need to secure stable employment—a means of sustenance that would underpin his newfound identity. A job, like a bridge, would link him to the rhythms of this unfamiliar town and provide a crucial cover for his activities. It was a task not to be taken lightly, for it would serve as both his livelihood and his alibi.

Simultaneously, Brian understood that his temporal refuge within the motel had its limitations. He needed to find a permanent place to live, a shelter that would serve as the foundation for his reinvented life. This residence had to be unassuming, discreet, and above all, unsusceptible to prying eyes that might unveil the ruse.

As he plotted his course forward, Brian also recognized the imperative of establishing connections in this foreign terrain. Friendships, however fleeting, would provide him with insights, information, and a sense of belonging that could serve as a bulwark against isolation and suspicion.

The hours that lay ahead were undeniably critical, akin to the strokes of a master painter on a canvas yet to be filled. Each decision he made, each connection he forged, would shape the course of his new life, an intricate mosaic of choices that held the power to transform a fugitive into a citizen, a blank slate into a man with purpose.

In the dimly lit room, Brian steeled himself for the obscure journey that awaited, knowing that every task, every decision, carried the weight of his future—a future in which Robert Anderson would emerge as a phoenix from the ashes of his past, navigating the tightrope of deception, and forging a destiny shrouded in the veils of obscurity.

Amidst the whirlwind of tasks and decisions that lay ahead, Brian couldn't escape the heavy weight of his past—a past that included Anastasia, a love that had once been an inseparable part of him. Her memory lingered in the recesses of his heart, a reminder of the sacrifices he had made in his desperate pursuit of justice.

With a somber introspection that seemed to echo through the quiet room, Brian thought about Anastasia. Her name, once whispered with affection, now carried the undertone of regret. He knew his actions had wounded her deeply, leaving behind a trail of emotional scars that mirrored the ones he bore.

As he contemplated the tumultuous wake of his mission, Brian couldn't help but wonder if Anastasia had been ensnared in the chaos he had wrought. He feared that the vortex of danger and intrigue had touched her life, dragging her into the maelstrom of consequences that had followed his ill-fated quest for vengeance.

The thought gnawed at him, like an unresolved chord in a haunting melody. Anastasia was a chapter of his past that he could never fully close, a love story that had been torn asunder by the currents of his obsession. The pain of leaving her behind, the hurt he had inflicted, and the uncertainty of her fate weighed heavily on his conscience.

In the motel's solitude room, Brian carried the bittersweet burden of love lost, knowing that the path he had chosen had exacted a heavy toll on both his soul and the heart of the woman he had cherished. As he embarked on the arduous journey of his new life as Robert Anderson, he couldn't escape the specter of Anastasia—a reminder that, even with a different look and Identification, the echoes of the past would always linger, shaping the contours of his future.

Chapter Sixteen

B rian harbored an unshakable determination to vanish without a trace, to embark on a fresh start in a realm where the echoes of his name and the specter of his past held no sway. Deep within the clandestine networks of the underground world, he possessed valuable contacts—individuals adept in the art of disappearance, those who could orchestrate his vanishing act with deft precision.

Yet, the cost of this radical transformation was exorbitant. It demanded the severing of all ties, not just to the life he had once known, but also to the cherished possibility of reconciliation with Anastasia. Their shared history, the tendrils of their love story, were inextricably bound to the man he had once been, and to erase that man was to extinguish the flame of hope for a future with her.

The gravity of this decision weighed heavily upon Brian's soul. It was a choice that defied the comfort of nostalgia, a decision to traverse the treacherous path of solitude, where the past would be consigned to the annals of memory, and the future held the promise of anonymity and liberation.

As he contemplated the enormity of this sacrifice, Brian knew acutely that he was about to embark on a journey into the abyss, where the price of redemption was the forfeiture of the very connections that had once defined him. In the end, the promise of a new beginning beckoned to him, tantalizingly distant, like a faint glimmer on the horizon—an elusive hope that he would chase, even at the cost of leaving behind the fragments of a love story that had once burned brightly in his heart.

Navigating the hushed streets of Quebec City, Brian found himself ensnared in the cocoon of an overwhelming emptiness. He had made the excruciating decision to relinquish his mission of vengeance, an endeavor that had once consumed him entirely. But in doing so, he had paid a grievous toll, one that weighed heavily upon his heart.

The void within him was cavernous, an aching chasm that had swallowed not only his vengeful purpose but also the facets of his life that he held dear. He had surrendered his love—the love he had shared with Anastasia, a love that had once been the guiding star of his existence. In that departure, he had severed a tether that bound him to warmth and tenderness, leaving behind an abyss of desolation.

More than that, Brian had forfeited his sense of self. The man who had embarked on the perilous journey of revenge was no more, replaced by a shadow of his former identity—Robert Anderson, a name that would be his shield and his shroud. This transformation, though necessary, was akin to shedding a skin, a metamorphosis that left him feeling raw and vulnerable.

As he walked the streets of the city, Brian was haunted by the echoes of the past. The alleys, the buildings, the very air seemed to bear witness to the weight of his choices. The cityscape was a tapestry woven with memories, each thread an indelible mark of what he had been, what he had lost, and the indomitable emptiness that now enveloped him.

Amid this quietude, Brian grappled with the enigma of his existence, standing at the crossroads of life irrevocably altered. The pursuit of revenge had given way to an arduous odyssey of self-discovery, and the path ahead was cloaked in uncertainty. It was a journey that demanded not only his resolve but also his capacity to redefine himself in the vendetta's absence that had once defined him.

The future loomed before Brian, an enigmatic expanse fraught with uncertainty, much like the labyrinthine streets of Quebec City he had traversed. He carried with him the weight of the choices he had made, each one etching its indelible mark upon his conscience. These decisions, borne of desperation and remorse, had cast long shadows over his life, and he knew their specters would haunt him endlessly.

In the night's solitude, however, Brian clung to a fragile ember of hope—a belief that redemption, though elusive, was never beyond reach. He understood it was possible to forge a path back to the light, even after being ensnared by the consuming darkness of revenge.

As he faded into the obscurity of the night, his footsteps echoing softly on the cobblestone streets, Brian held on to the fervent desire that someday, somehow, he might find a means to make amends for the transgressions that had led him astray. It was a beacon of optimism that pierced the shroud of his uncertainty, a faint but unwavering glimmer in the vast expanse of the unknown.

With each step into the velvety blackness, he embarked on a journey of self-discovery, a quest for absolution that he knew would be fraught with trials and tribulations. Yet, he was resolute in his determination to find a way back to the path of righteousness, to emerge from the abyss that had once held him captive.

The night, with its mysteries and uncertainties, cocooned Brian as he ventured into its depths. It was a journey where the past was a specter; the present was a crossroads, and the future was a realm of infinite possibilities. And though redemption remained elusive, it was a destination he would relentlessly pursue, driven by the fervent belief that even in the darkest of hours, the flicker of hope could illuminate the way home.

Brian's escape from the relentless pursuit of the authorities had been a calculated miracle, a feat made possible by his deep-rooted connections within the clandestine underbelly. Under the shroud of darkness, he had meticulously assumed a new identity, one that allowed him to fade into obscurity, away from the piercing gaze of those who sought to bring him to justice.

With the skillful aid of his underground allies, Brian had painstakingly stitched together the fabric of his new existence. He became an unassuming figure, a solitary man who had found refuge in a serene coastal enclave on the tranquil east coast of Canada. This small, forgotten town, nestled by the gentle embrace of the sea, had become his sanctuary, a place where the tumultuous tides of his past could recede into insignificance.

The years flowed past him like the waters that kissed the town's shore, and Brian made a deliberate choice to distance himself from the harrowing memories of his troubled past. In this quiet coastal haven, he sought solace in the simple joys of life—the rhythmic cadence of the ocean's waves, the whisper of wind through ancient trees, and the warmth of the sun's caress on his weathered skin.

Time became a companion, gradually erasing the sharp edges of his past, transforming them into faded echoes. Brian's focus shifted from the relentless pursuit of vengeance to the pursuit of an unburdened existence, one free from the shackles of his former life. It was a life wherein the mundane moments held profound beauty—the laughter of children, the aroma of freshly baked bread, and the starlit canvases that adorned the night sky.

And so, he drifted through the years, his footsteps tracing the sands of a life shaped by resolute choices. In the cocoon of his coastal refuge, he marveled at the transformative power of time, grateful for the sanctuary he had discovered, and cherishing the tranquility of a world that had once seemed so far beyond his reach.

Brian forged a new life on the edges of the world, securing employment as a humble fisherman. Each day, he ventured out into the boundless expanse of the open sea, where the briny tang of the salt-laden air and the endless, cerulean horizon gave upon him a profound sense of peace—tranquility he had yearned for amidst the chaos of his former existence.

The rigors of a fisherman's life immersed him in an immersive blend of labor and nature. The mornings unfurled with the sun's gentle kiss on the water's surface, beckoning him to the waiting vessel. His hands, once accustomed to the unforgiving grip of weapons, now grasped the sturdy lines and rusted nets that bound him to the rhythm of the ocean's tides.

The physicality of his new vocation demanded his full attention, serving as a therapeutic balm for a mind haunted by memories of treacherous pursuits. Hauling in heavy nets teeming with silvery bounty became an anchor that tethered him to the present while navigating the capricious waters provided a reminder of life's unpredictable currents.

The relentless dance between man and nature was a symphony that echoed through his days, harmonizing his body and spirit. With each dawn, he discovered solace in the steady cadence of his labor, the stark beauty of the open sea, and the symphony of gulls that soared overhead.

As the sun dipped below the horizon, casting fiery hues across the undulating waves, Brian found himself at peace with the world—grateful for the simplicity of his life as a fisherman, content in the profound serenity of the open sea, and resolute in his determination to leave behind the turbulent past that had once ensnared him.

Despite the valiant effort to forge a new life, Brian couldn't entirely outrun the relentless ghosts of his past. In the tranquil solitude of his coastal existence, memories of a different life still lingered, casting their long shadows across his consciousness.

Anastasia, a name etched in his heart, continued to occupy his thoughts. He wondered, often in the night's stillness, if she had moved forward, beyond the turbulent chapters they had once shared. The uncertainty gnawed at him, a question without a simple answer, like an unfinished symphony echoing in the chambers of his heart.

It was a melancholic refrain that played in his mind—an ode to a love that had been, a melody punctuated by the silence of their separation. Brian questioned whether she, too, bore the indelible scars of their shared history, whether the wounds of their love had left their marks upon her soul.

In the quiet moments, when the sea whispered its secrets and the stars kept their watchful vigil, Brian couldn't help but wonder about the woman he had left behind. It was a bittersweet yearning, an ache for the closure that had eluded them both, a poignant reminder that even in the sanctuary of his newfound life, the specter of Anastasia and the shadows of their past remained as indomitable as the tides that kissed the shore.

As he gazed out at the vast expanse of the sea, its depths mirroring the mysteries of his heart, Brian knew that the memories and questions would forever be a part of him, a testament to the love and loss that had shaped the contours of his life.

On a tranquil evening, Brian found himself ensconced within the confines of his modest, weathered cottage, a shell of solitude where he had sought refuge from the world's tumultuous embrace. The ambient flicker of candlelight cast a dance of shadows across the timeworn wooden walls, painting the room in an intimate image.

As he sat ensconced in the warmth of his sanctuary, the harmony of solitude was abruptly shattered by an unexpected knock on the door. It echoed through the room, an intrusion into his quiet reverie, and set his heart to a frantic rhythm. His hand, in that unguarded moment, trembled slightly as it sought the cool, reassuring grasp of the doorknob.

With a measured breath, Brian approached the portal, his mind awash with a maelstrom of apprehension and curiosity. The door, when he finally opened it, revealed a tableau he had scarcely dared to imagine—a pair of eyes that bore a striking familiarity, like twin constellations in the vast cosmos.

It was a moment that defied explanation, a convergence of past and present that left him momentarily bereft of words. The eyes that met his gaze held a history, a connection, that transcended the confines of time and distance. In the hallowed threshold of his cottage, the boundaries between what had been and what was now blurred, and Brian found himself standing on the precipice of a revelation—a reunion that would unravel the threads of his carefully constructed solitude.

The encounter, like a tempestuous wave crashing upon the shore, heralded a new chapter in his life—a chapter that bore the promise of answers, closure, and the rekindling of a connection long thought lost. As the eyes bore into his, the past and present coalesced, and Brian braced himself for the secrets and emotions that lay dormant, waiting to be unearthed in the wake of that unexpected knock.

"Brian," the name escaped Anastasia's lips in a whisper, a fragile melody that hung in the air like a secret long held. Her voice bore the cadence of astonishment, a symphony of emotions woven into its tapestry—surprise, relief, and an unspoken longing. In the soft illumination of his cottage, she appeared before him, a vision of time's passage etched upon her features.

Her visage had been marked by the years, her once-youthful countenance now bearing the weathered imprints of life's journey. Lines had etched their narratives upon her skin, and her eyes, while reflecting the same incendiary determination, that held within them the tempered wisdom of experiences lived.

Yet, despite the visible passage of time, the essence of Anastasia remained unaltered—a flame that had weathered the storms of existence but still burned with the same fervor. The spark in her eyes, an unquenchable fire, held the same luminosity as if it had defied the relentless march of years to preserve the essence of her spirit.

In that fleeting moment, a bridge between past and present was forged—a connection that transcended the boundaries of mere time. As they stood there, reunited after a chasm of separation, their shared history was an unspoken undercurrent, an echo of emotions that pulsed through the room. Brian found himself drawn into the depths of her gaze, recognizing in her eyes the profound tapestry of their past, a tapestry that held within it the promise of reconciliation and the possibility of rediscovery.

The reunion, like an exquisite refrain in a long-forgotten melody, was a testament to the enduring power of connections forged in the crucible of time. It was a moment that defied the years and promised to rewrite the chapters of their shared history, as they navigated the uncharted territory of their rekindled connection.

"Anastasia," Brian's response was scarcely more than a breath, a reverberation that reverently brushed the air. He took a hesitant step back, allowing the threshold of his abode to embrace her presence, and she crossed the invisible boundary into his world, her delicate fingers closing the door with a soft click.

There they stood, in the heart of that hallowed space—a room illuminated by the soft flicker of candlelight, a realm where time seemed to stand still. Their gazes converged, an intermingling of emotions as if they were two celestial bodies that had once orbited each other in an intricate and fateful dance.

It was a poignant tableau, one laden with the gravity of their shared history. Two souls, once deeply intertwined in a complex tapestry of secrets and betrayals, now confronted one another in the intimate confines of Brian's sanctuary. The years had wrought their transformations upon them, had left their imprints in the lines etched upon their faces, and the experiences that had sculpted their hearts.

Yet, the space between them brimmed with unspoken narratives—the whispered words and silences that had characterized their tumultuous past. At that moment, Brian and Anastasia found themselves at the precipice of a juncture—an opportunity to unravel the secrets that had bound them, to forge a path towards understanding and, perhaps, a measure of redemption.

The silence that enveloped them was pregnant with history, the weight of their shared past settling upon their shoulders like a shroud. It was a pause, a breath suspended in time, as they navigated the uncharted waters of this unexpected reunion—a collision of destinies, fraught with the promise of revelation and the healing potential.

At last, it was Anastasia who dared to shatter the fragile bubble of silence that enveloped them. Her voice, though laden with a haunting vulnerability, bore the cadence of determination as she spoke, the words resonating with a profound longing and a tinge of trepidation.

"I've been searching for you for years," her voice hung in the air like a fragile plea, a testament to the unrelenting quest that had driven her. "I needed to know if you were okay if you had found peace."

The words, like a fragile bridge over a chasm of uncertainties, revealed the depth of her concern, the genuine worry that had been the compass guiding her relentless pursuit. Her eyes, the same eyes that had once held his heart captive, bore a raw vulnerability, a longing to decipher the enigma of his absence and to discover whether the passing of time had been kind to him.

Their reunion, thus, was not only a convergence of souls but also a reckoning with the unanswered questions that had lingered between them, like specters of the past. It was a moment where the echoes of their shared history hung in the balance, poised to unravel the mysteries and to, perhaps, illuminate the path toward understanding and reconciliation.

A solemn nod rippled through Brian's frame, a measured affirmation that carried with it the weight of years lived in solitude and reflection. His eyes, now glistening with tears that seemed to hold the echoes of countless regrets, bore the scars of a past he could never fully escape.

"I'm alive, Anastasia," his voice trembled with a vulnerability that mirrored the rawness of his emotions, "but I can never forget the past or the choices I made." Each word carried the heavy burden of the secrets he had borne, the weight of decisions that had forged his path through the wilderness of guilt and remorse.

In the depths of that moment, the room seemed to hold its breath, as if suspended in a sacred pause between their intertwined destinies. Brian's confession was a testament to the indomitable imprints of their shared history, a recognition that the past could neither be erased nor denied.

The tears that welled in his eyes were the silent testimonies of a soul that had wrestled with its demons, a spirit marked by the irrevocable choices that had defined his journey. It was a moment of revelation, a recognition that their reunion was not a restoration of the past, but a reckoning with the enduring echoes of the decisions that had forever altered the course of their lives.

Anastasia's touch, as gentle as a whisper of warmth, graced Brian's cheek, her fingers a tender caress against his weathered skin. In that intimate moment, her touch bore the silent promise of understanding and compassion, a silent affirmation that their shared history, no matter how fraught, had forged a bond that could not be shattered.

"Neither can I," her voice, soft as the breeze that rustled through autumn leaves, carried the same weight of memories and remorse. Her words hung in the air, a poignant acknowledgment of their shared burden. "But we can't change what happened. All we can do is try to make amends, find a way to move forward."

The simplicity of her words masked the profound complexities of their situation, the intricate tapestry of emotions that lay beneath. Anastasia's gaze, unwavering and sincere, held within it the hope that amidst the fragments of their past, they might unearth the possibility of redemption.

Their reunion, in that fragile moment of connection, became a crossroads—a juncture where the specters of their shared history and the promise of an uncertain future converged. The path ahead was shrouded in uncertainty, yet their determination to reconcile, seek forgiveness, and forge a way forward was a testament to the enduring power of human resilience and the indomitable spirit of those who dared to confront the shadows of their past.

In the hushed space between them, the room seemed to pulse with the weight of unspoken truths. Brian and Anastasia, locked in a gaze that bridged the chasm of their shared history, recognized the daunting journey that lay ahead—a path cloaked in shadows and steeped in uncertainties. The room bore witness to the echoes of their past, as if the walls themselves held the secrets of their tumultuous journey.

In that charged moment, their unspoken acknowledgment of the formidable challenges they would face hung in the air like a manifesto of their resolve. They understood the immutable nature of the past—it was a canvas already painted; a narrative irrevocably etched. What they could control, however, was the future—a blank slate upon which they could inscribe a different story, one shaped by the lessons of their shared history.

The room, bathed in the soft luminescence of their shared revelation, became a sanctuary where past and present converged, where the ghosts of their history were welcomed rather than shunned. Brian and Anastasia had profoundly realized—that they couldn't rewrite the past, but they could harness its teachings to build a different future together.

Their shared determination was a pledge, a covenant with the uncertain road that lay ahead. It was a testament to the resilience of the human spirit and the capacity for redemption. As they faced the nebulous horizon, they did so knowing that no matter how formidable the challenges were; they were bound by the unbreakable thread of their shared history—a history that, though marked by shadows, held the promise of transformation and the potential for a brighter future.

As the heaviness of their shared history lifted like a shroud, Brian and Anastasia, their hearts yearning for release from the burdens of the past, drew each other into an embrace that transcended words. In the tender refuge of each other's arms, they discovered a sanctuary where the tempestuous echoes of their journey were momentarily stilled.

Their embrace was a testament to the human capacity for healing and redemption, a communion of two souls who had long carried the weight of their regrets and sorrows. In the warmth of their connection, they found solace—a respite from the tempestuous storms that had raged within them for so long.

With their foreheads gently pressed together, their breaths harmonizing in the moment's quietude, they dared to dream of a different future—a future where the wounds that had haunted them might, against all odds, heal. It was a fragile hope, but it was hope—a beacon that pierced through the shadows of their past.

As they clung to each other, the world beyond their intimate cocoon of embrace ceased to exist. In that suspended moment, the scars of their shared history seemed to fade, and they dared to believe that, just maybe, they could mend what had been broken, reconcile what had been torn asunder, and rekindle a flicker of light in the darkness that had for so long defined their lives.

In the days that unfurled into weeks, Brian and Anastasia embarked on a journey of reconnection, a delicate dance that led them through the labyrinthine corridors of their intertwined pasts. Their newfound connection was a lifeline, one they clung to with unwavering determination, as they traversed the landscape of memories, both bitter and sweet.

Hours upon hours were spent in fervent conversation, their voices weaving a tapestry of stories and recollections. They delved into their pasts, unearthing the painful memories that had once been locked away, and dusting off the moments of happiness that had glimmered like fleeting stars before the tempestuous descent into chaos.

The process was emotional—a release of pent-up emotions and unspoken truths that had been shackled for far too long. With each shared memory, each whispered confession, they unburdened themselves of the heavy loads they had carried in solitude. It was a reckoning with their past, an acknowledgment of the wounds that had festered, and a chance to offer solace and understanding to one another.

The room they inhabited, now imbued with the echoes of their shared narratives, bore witness to the emotional tides that ebbed and flowed. It was a sacred space, a sanctuary where the fragments of their history were sifted through and pieced together anew.

Through these conversations, Brian and Anastasia discovered that their past, though marred by tumultuous events, also held within it the seeds of resilience and hope. They were forging a bridge from their shared history toward a future where the scars of the past could serve as a foundation for healing and transformation.

In the quiet intimacy of their conversations, Anastasia unburdened herself with the intricate narrative of her life following their separation. Her words flowed like a river, tracing the contours of her journey—a journey marked by resilience and unwavering determination.

She spoke of her unwavering commitment to her role within the Royal Canadian Mounted Police (RCMP), a vocation that had become both a calling and a mission. Her voice, a melodic cadence that carried the weight of her convictions, recounted the path she had chosen.

Through the years of their separation, Anastasia had remained within the ranks of the RCMP, her dedication unshaken by the tumultuous events that had torn them apart. It was a choice driven by a deep-seated desire to make a lasting, positive impact—a determination to prevent the tragedies that had marred their shared history.

With each passing year, she had ascended the ladder of her profession, her ascent not merely a career pursuit but a means to an end. Her position had become a platform—a podium from which she could advocate for justice, fairness, and the unswerving adherence to principles she held dear.

The story she shared was a testament to her unyielding spirit, a narrative etched with the contours of resilience and courage. Through her unwavering commitment to the RCMP, she had harnessed the pain of their shared history, channeling it into a force for change.

Anastasia's journey, as she recounted it, was not merely the story of her evolution; it was a revelation of the strength that could be found in the face of adversity and the transformative power of unwavering dedication to a cause greater than oneself.

In the gentle ebb and flow of their conversations, Brian wove the tapestry of his journey, a life carved from the elemental simplicity of a fisherman's existence. His words, like the rhythm of ocean waves, revealed the profound solace he had discovered amidst the quiet routines of his daily labor.

He spoke of the intimate connection he had forged with the sea, its vastness stretching beyond the horizon, a boundless expanse that had become his silent confidante. Each day spent navigating the unpredictable waters had offered him a refuge—a respite from the cacophony of the world beyond.

The coastal landscape, with its rugged beauty and endless vistas, had etched itself into the very core of his being. The sight of sunrises painting the sky in hues of gold, and the soothing lullaby of waves breaking against the shore at twilight, had become the balm for his soul.

Yet, amid the serenity of his newfound life, the specters of his past actions loomed large, like shadows that refused to be dispelled. The memories of choices made and consequences faced were a constant companion, an enduring reminder of the tumultuous path he had walked.

Above all, the memory of his brother—the loss of a kindred spirit and the agony of separation—hovered in the recesses of his heart like a silent lament. It was a wound that had never fully healed, a presence that was felt in every quiet moment of introspection.

In the juxtaposition of his tranquil existence and the ghosts of his past, Brian's story became a poignant exploration of the human capacity for solace and reconciliation. It was a narrative that underscored the paradox of finding refuge in simplicity while grappling with the echoes of a complex and tumultuous past—a testament to the intricate interplay between healing and remembrance.

Amidst the intricate dance of their emotions, Brian and Anastasia found themselves at the crossroads of yet another formidable decision—one that would shape not only their shared path, but also the course of justice itself. The information they held, like a dormant time bomb, possessed the power to rewrite the narrative of their lives.

Over the years, the fire of Brian's vengeful desire had mellowed, its flames flickering into a tempered resolve. The passage of time had quenched the thirst for retribution, revealing in its place a yearning for accountability—a desire to see those responsible for the tumultuous events at Chateau Frontenac brought to answer for their actions.

In the shadowy recesses of their shared history, Brian and Anastasia grappled with the question of what to do with the information they possessed. The need for truth and justice remained a palpable force, a call they could not ignore. The past, it seemed, had woven its intricate threads into their lives once more, demanding their reckoning.

Their shared decision reflected the complex emotions that swirled within them—a recognition that the pursuit of justice could no longer be borne solely by the fires of revenge, but must be guided by the steady compass of accountability.

As they ventured into this new chapter of their intertwined lives, the choices they made would hold the power to illuminate the shadows of the past and, just perhaps, pave the way for a future where healing and justice could coexist.

With the weight of their shared history and a deep-seated commitment to justice guiding her, Anastasia unveiled a carefully crafted plan. Drawing upon her formidable expertise in intelligence operations, she outlined a path that held the potential to right the wrongs of their past without the shadows of violence looming overhead.

Her proposal, like a well-orchestrated symphony, unfolded in intricate detail. They would embark on a discreet journey of sharing the damning information they possessed with select individuals within the government—figures who stood as unwavering sentinels dedicated to the noble cause of rooting out corruption and ensuring unflinching accountability.

The strategy was a dance of shadows, a diplomatic maneuver that would harness the levers of power and bureaucracy to bring indirectly those responsible for the tumultuous events at Chateau Frontenac to the doorstep of justice. It was a testament to the belief that the rule of law, wielded with precision and tenacity, could be a formidable force capable of dispelling the darkness of their past.

Faced with this proposal, Brian and Anastasia found themselves at a juncture where their commitment to justice was unshakable, yet their resolve to avoid further bloodshed remained unwavering. It was a choice that would test the boundaries of their partnership—a choice that, if successful, could be the culmination of their arduous journey toward redemption and accountability.

Brian, after a period of soul-searching and reflection, profoundly realized—revenge, like a hollow promise, could never truly heal the wounds of their shared past. It was an epiphany that bore the weight of years of introspection and the wisdom that only time could give.

With his commitment to a path of healing and accountability firmly established, Brian aligned his resolve with Anastasia's plan. Together, they embarked on the intricate journey of orchestrating the release of the damning information, a symphony of secrecy and discretion that would unveil the truth and right the wrongs of the past.

Their combined efforts, drawing upon the intricate web of connections they had nurtured over the years, ensured that the information would reach the right hands—the individuals within the government who were unwavering sentinels of justice, dedicated to the cause of rooting out corruption and upholding accountability.

The process they embarked upon was neither hasty nor impulsive; it was a deliberate and unhurried dance through the corridors of power. Their patience became their ally, a virtue that allowed them to navigate the intricate web of bureaucracy and secrecy with the grace of seasoned diplomats.

With each carefully orchestrated step, Brian and Anastasia moved closer to the culmination of their mission—an endeavor that would ultimately unveil the truth, hold those responsible to account, and offer a semblance of closure to the wounds that had long festered.

As time flowed steadily onward, months melted into years, and the fruits of Brian and Anastasia's patient labor unfurled like a tapestry of reckoning. Their carefully orchestrated plan had set in motion a cascade of events that would reshape the narrative of their shared history.

Investigations, like beams of light penetrating the darkest corners, were launched with meticulous precision. The truth, long veiled by the shroud of secrecy, gradually emerged, casting long shadows upon those who had once gathered within the walls of Chateau Frontenac.

Accountability measures, akin to a fortress of justice, were painstakingly erected. The leaders, once shrouded in the cloak of power and impunity, stood upon the precipice of a reckoning. Questions, sharp as daggers, pierced the veil of silence that had protected them for so long.

The inquiries delved into their actions during the war, peeling back the layers of deception and evasion that had shielded the truth. It was a process marked by the relentless pursuit of answers, the unearthing of buried secrets, and the inexorable march of justice.

In the corridors of power, the once-mighty leaders faced the echoes of their past—a past that had been hidden away, but whose specter now demanded confrontation. The emergence of the truth was a testament to the power of determination, patience, and the enduring commitment of two individuals to the cause of justice.

As the years passed, the wheels of accountability ground forward, ushering in a reckoning that would forever alter the course of their history—a reckoning that would finally expose the deeds and misdeeds of those who had once wielded unchecked power.

The unfolding of justice, like the turning of ancient gears, was far from flawless. It was a process marked by its imperfections, where not every individual was held to account for their actions. Brian and Anastasia, like silent sentinels, observed from the sidelines as the intricate web of accountability took shape.

It was a journey where the light of truth occasionally cast long shadows, and the pursuit of justice encountered obstacles and veiled corners. The scars of the past, like indelible marks, lingered despite the unfolding reckoning.

Yet, even in the face of these imperfections, Brian and Anastasia remained resolute. Their commitment to the cause of justice transcended the confines of time and circumstance. They understood that their actions, while unable to change the past, served as a beacon—a testament to the enduring quest to prevent the recurrence of such tragedies.

From their vantage point on the sidelines, they bore witness to the transformative power of accountability, a force capable of shaking the foundations of impunity and, in its wake, erecting the pillars of responsibility.

Their hope, steadfast as the North Star, was that the lessons learned, and the truths uncovered in this imperfect process would serve as a bulwark—a safeguard against the repetition of history's gravest mistakes. It was a legacy they aimed to leave behind, etched in the annals of time, a testament to the enduring human capacity for change and the relentless pursuit of a more just world.

As the sands of time continued their relentless march forward, Brian and Anastasia found that their shared mission for justice had an unexpected consequence—it drew them inexorably closer, forging a connection that transcended the boundaries of romantic love. What had once been the fire of passion had strengthened into a profound and abiding bond, one rooted in the soil of shared experiences and a joint commitment to the pursuit of redemption.

Their journey, marked by the twists and turns of fate, had woven the threads of their lives together inextricably. The complexities of their past, once a chasm that had threatened to tear them apart, had become the foundation upon which their partnership was built.

They had weathered the storms of adversity, standing side by side as they navigated the treacherous waters of justice and accountability. The trials and tribulations they had faced had not weakened their connection but had, instead, fortified it, as steel tempered in the fires of adversity.

Their love, though transformed, remained a constant presence—a beacon of warmth and solace amid the turbulent sea of their endeavors. It was a love that had matured, deepening with each passing day, as they continued to walk the path of redemption together.

In the quiet moments of introspection, as they contemplated the echoes of their past and the uncertainties of their future, they found solace in each other's presence. It was a bond that transcended the boundaries of romance, a partnership forged in the crucible of shared purpose and the unwavering commitment to making amends for the tumultuous history they had once shared.

Brian, with the backdrop of the endless ocean as his daily canvas, continued his life as a fisherman. However, his existence had undergone a profound transformation—one marked by closure, a sensation that had long eluded him like a distant star. The vast sea, once a refuge from his turbulent past, now mirrored the tranquility he had found within himself.

Anastasia, unyielding, remained dedicated to her role within the RCMP. Her commitment was not solely confined to seeking justice from the shadows, but extended to a mission of reform from within the organization itself. Her position served as a fulcrum for change, a vessel through which she worked tirelessly to ensure that the mistakes of the past were not condemned to repetition.

Their separate paths, while distinct, were bound by a shared purpose—a shared commitment to a future where the lessons learned from their shared history would shape a world less burdened by the weight of its own misdeeds.

Brian's life, once steeped in turmoil and haunted by memories, had now settled into a rhythm of quiet contentment, as the tranquil ebb and flow of the tides mirrored the newfound peace within his heart.

Anastasia's relentless efforts from within the corridors of power represented a beacon of hope—a testament to the enduring belief that positive change could be cultivated from even the most entrenched systems.

Together, they stood as living testaments to the transformative power of resilience, love, and the unwavering pursuit of justice—a legacy that would ripple through the currents of time, affecting change in ways they could have never imagined.

Their journeys had taken them on divergent paths, like two streams meandering through a vast landscape, only to converge once more at a place of profound acceptance and healing. It had been a transformative odyssey, one that had carried them from the abyss of betrayal and the tumultuous waters of revenge to a newfound beginning—a beginning bathed in the gentle, hopeful light of a future untethered from the shackles of their past.

The scars of their shared history, once open and raw, had now healed into the tapestry of their lives—a tapestry woven with threads of resilience, redemption, and forgiveness. They had confronted the shadows of their past and, in doing so, had emerged stronger, their bond unbreakable.

Their journey was a testament to the indomitable human spirit, a testament to the power of love and the capacity for healing. From the depths of despair, they had risen, not as individuals scarred by their history, but as a united force—a force of acceptance and hope.

In this new beginning, they found not just a sense of closure, but a profound peace with their past. It was a peace that flowed through their lives like a gentle river, carrying with it the promise of a brighter future—a future unburdened by the ghosts of yesterday, and illuminated by the potential for a world in which forgiveness, healing, and hope reigned supreme.

The passing of the Destounis, Anastasia's parents, marked the somber conclusion of an era that had been marred by a profound sense of disappointment. The weight of their unfulfilled hopes and dreams, stemming from the events at Chateau Frontenac, had been palpable, casting a long shadow over their familial bonds.

Yet, beneath the veneer of disillusionment, the Destounis had always remained loving parents—guardians who had cherished the vision of a future filled with the laughter of grandchildren and the happiness of their beloved daughter. Their hearts had been indelibly imprinted with the contours of their shared dreams, dreams that had been, regrettably, left unfulfilled.

The passing of the Destounis was not just the end of an era, but also a poignant reminder of the complex tapestry of love, disappointment, and unspoken understanding that had defined their family. In the wake of their departure, Anastasia carried with her the bittersweet memories of their aspirations and a deep longing for the future that had never come to pass.

The passing of Anastasia's parents plunged her into a profound and unyielding grief. They had not merely been figures in her life; they had been the very bedrock upon which her existence had been built. Their loss was a chasm that seemed to swallow the world around her.

In the depths of her mourning, she reflected on the profound role they had played. They had been her anchor, the unwavering presence that had steadied her through the storms of life. Their love, unconditional and boundless, had been the fortress in which she had sought refuge during her darkest hours.

Their dreams for her, dreams that had once sparkled with hope, had been eclipsed by the relentless march of history. They had yearned to witness her marriage, to embrace the joy of seeing her start a family of her own. Yet these dreams had been dashed by the turbulent events of the past, leaving behind a bittersweet ache in their wake.

As she navigated the complex terrain of grief, Anastasia found solace in the cherished memories of her parents. Their love remained an eternal flame, illuminating the path ahead, a testament to the enduring bonds of family and the profound impact of their unwavering support and love.

Amidst the profound waves of grief that enveloped her, Anastasia sought solace in the cherished memories of her parents—their laughter, their wisdom, and the values they had diligently instilled in her from her earliest days. In their absence, those memories became her sanctuary, a place where their love lived undiminished.

Their legacy, one built upon a bedrock of service and unwavering commitment to justice, served as a guiding light during her darkest hours. It was a legacy that ran deep within her, flowing through her veins like a steady current, and it became the foundation upon which she rebuilt her life.

With a resolute heart, she continued her work within the RCMP, steadfastly upholding the principles of justice, integrity, and accountability. In every action, she saw herself as an extension of her parents' legacy, a torchbearer carrying their values forward into the world.

She knew, beyond any doubt, that this was what they would have wanted—a continuation of their commitment to service, a testament to the enduring impact of their love, and a way to honor the values that had shaped her into the person she had become.

The Destounis family's disappointment had cast a long and shadowy pall over Brian's heart. Once welcomed into their fold, he had inadvertently become a harbinger of disillusionment through his actions. Their loss weighed heavily upon him, like an anchor tethered to his soul, a constant reminder of the profound consequences of the choices he had made in his past.

Their passing, a solemn and poignant event, acted as an unyielding mirror, reflecting the repercussions of his actions with unflinching clarity. He had not only betrayed the trust of his beloved Anastasia but also of her family, who had extended their embrace to him. Their dreams, like fragile glass, had been shattered by the storm of history he had helped create.

As he mourned their loss, Brian could not escape the haunting memories of their disappointment—the somber looks in their eyes, the unspoken questions that lingered in the air, and the weight of unfulfilled expectations. Their absence served as a stark reminder, etching into his soul the indelible lesson that choices made in haste and anger could leave scars that stretched far beyond one's existence.

Yet, amidst the shadows of remorse, there remained a glimmer of hope—a resolve to honor their memory by forging a path toward redemption. It was a burden he willingly accepted, a quest to amend his past transgressions and to bring healing, not just to his wounded spirit but also to those he had unwittingly wounded along the way.

As time passed, Brian and Anastasia leaned on each other for support. Their bond had grown stronger through the trials they had faced together. They knew they couldn't change the past, but they were determined to honor the memory of the Destounis and make the most of the future.

Hand in hand, they embarked on a journey toward a profound sense of closure and a rekindled sense of purpose. Their shared path, marked by the jagged edges of pain and the haunting echoes of betrayal, had paradoxically led them to a place where understanding and redemption blossomed like resilient flowers amid the ruins.

The trials they had faced together had honed their resolve, forging an unbreakable bond that had emerged from the crucible of their experiences. With unwavering determination, they set their sights on making the most of the second chance in life that had been given to them—an opportunity to chart an alternative course through the labyrinth of existence.

While the past remained an indelible chapter in their lives, they carried its lessons as lanterns to illuminate the path forward. The darkness that had once shrouded their souls had given way to a hopeful dawn. Together, they sought not just to heal their wounds, but to create a legacy of love, resilience, and forgiveness that would transcend the boundaries of time.

In their quest for understanding and redemption, they discovered that the most profound transformations often arose from the crucible of adversity. They stood on the precipice of a brighter tomorrow, their hearts ablaze with the promise of an unwritten future—a future where their shared journey would be marked not only by the shadows of the past but also by the enduring light of hope, purpose, and the boundless capacity for renewal.

Brian and Anastasia approached the dawn of a new chapter in their lives with resolute determination and a profound sense of purpose. Having navigated the tempestuous waters of betrayal, loss, and the painful toll of personal sacrifices, they stood on the face of a fresh beginning—a beginning defined by their unwavering commitment to rebuild what had been shattered and to shape a future that held the promise of redemption.

The storms of adversity they had weathered together had not broken their spirits; instead, they had steeled their resolve. With a laser-like focus, they directed their energies toward the arduous but necessary task of reconstructing their lives, brick by brick, thread by thread. Each scar borne from their experiences became a testament to their resilience, a symbol of their unyielding determination to move forward.

Their collective vision was not one of mere survival but of forging a path toward a future that held the potential for transformation and renewal. The scars of betrayal had become the battle scars of warriors who had emerged from the battlefield with newfound wisdom and strength.

As they embarked on this journey of reconstruction and renewal, they were bound by a shared commitment to work tirelessly, not only for their healing but also to contribute to a world marked by compassion, justice, and the enduring belief in the power of redemption.

Anastasia remained steadfast in her role within the RCMP's Left Wing division, a commitment that had only grown stronger. Her dedication to ensuring that justice prevailed had taken on extra dimensions, fueled by the enduring memory of her parents and their legacy of service to their country.

As she delved into each case, her resolve was unwavering. The memory of her parents, who had exemplified values of integrity and dedication, acted as both a guiding compass and a driving force. With each investigation she pursued, she felt an even deeper connection to their memory, as if they were beside her, whispering words of wisdom and encouragement.

The responsibility she bore to honor their legacy weighed on her, but it was a weight she carried with pride and determination. She was driven by a profound desire not only to make her parents proud but also to ensure that their values and commitment to justice continued to shine as beacons in a world that sometimes lost its way.

In her pursuit of justice, Anastasia became a living tribute to her parents' memory, an embodiment of the unwavering belief that the pursuit of truth and accountability could make the world a better place. With every case she closed, every wrong she set right, she knew she was upholding a legacy that transcended time—a legacy rooted in love, dedication, and an unshakeable commitment to making the world a more just and compassionate place.

Brian had undergone a profound transformation, letting go of the consuming quest for revenge that had once defined his existence. He had starkly realized that this relentless pursuit had ultimately led to naught but anguish and destruction. With newfound wisdom, he redirected his energies toward a different, more life-affirming path—a path he now walked hand in hand with Anastasia.

His transition into a new life was marked by a shift in priorities, as he sought solace in a quieter and more serene existence. Embracing the tranquil ambiance of Quebec City, he carved out a niche for himself, finding work that allowed him to relish the simple joys of life. Gone were the days of relentless vengeance; instead, he reveled in the steady rhythm of his daily routine, where peace and contentment took center stage.

The union between Brian and Anastasia had become a bedrock for their shared aspirations. With the specter of their tumultuous past fading into memory, they could now dare to dream of a future intertwined, a future filled with promise and hope. Together, they laid the foundation for their new chapter, nurturing the seeds of love, understanding, and the enduring commitment to a life marked not by revenge but by finding happiness and fulfillment.

Their love had not only survived the crucible of their turbulent past but had thrived, emerging stronger and more resilient than ever. United in their shared resolve, they were now steadfast in their commitment to construct a life imbued with the profound joys of happiness and fulfillment.

Their days were often punctuated by serene visits to the park that skirted the gentle banks of the St. Lawrence River. Here, amid the rustling leaves and the soothing melodies of nature, they found solace and renewal. As they strolled hand in hand, they reveled in the simple yet profound pleasure of reminiscing about their shared memories—the trials, the triumphs, and the moments that had sculpted the landscape of their intertwined lives.

These moments were not just a chance to reflect on the past, but also an opportunity to create new, cherished memories together. In the tranquil embrace of the park, they nurtured their love, a love that had withstood the test of time, and they reveled in the beauty of the present, holding tight to the promise of a future filled with endless moments of shared happiness and enduring fulfillment.

The leaders of the Allies had come and gone, leaving Chateau Frontenac behind. The war was over, but Brian and Anastasia had found their peace. They understood that life was precious, and that love had the power to heal wounds and mend broken hearts.

As they looked out at the river that had witnessed so much of their journey, they knew that their love was stronger than any adversity. With hope in their hearts and a shared commitment to a brighter future, they walked hand in hand, ready to face whatever challenges lay ahead.

Brian and Anastasia discovered themselves ensconced in their private realm of jubilation and profound relief. The heavy burden of their tumultuous past, marked by betrayals and agonizing sacrifices, now lay eclipsed beneath the radiant promise of a future bathed in brilliance.

The world had witnessed their odyssey, a journey fraught with trials and tribulations that had tested their resilience and resolve. But, as the jubilant chorus of triumph reached their ears, the past was consigned to the annals of history. In its place emerged a new horizon, aglow with the possibility of hope, reconciliation, and boundless potential.

Amidst the clamor of global celebration of the anniversary of the end of World War 2, they stood as living testaments to the indomitable human spirit. They had weathered storms and emerged from the crucible of adversity, their love and partnership now etched with an enduring strength, ready to face the promise of a brighter and more hopeful future.

Brian, his arms wrapped securely around Anastasia, found himself overwhelmed by a surge of euphoria that threatened to spill over. The weight of his past transgressions, a burdensome load that he had borne for what felt like an eternity, had finally been lifted. With the long, grueling war finished years ago now relegated to history, the promise of a future imbued with tranquility and love beckoned like a beacon.

As he gazed deeply into the pools of Anastasia's eyes, he sought not only her companionship but also the absolution he yearned for. It was a silent plea for understanding and forgiveness, an unspoken acknowledgment of the regrets and mistakes that had marred their shared journey. The intimate connection they shared transcended words, a testament to the enduring power of their love, which had weathered the darkest of storms and now stood as a beacon of hope in the radiant dawn of their new life together.

Brian's voice quivered with vulnerability as he spoke, laying bare the depths of his remorse and longing. The weight of his past actions, which had not only betrayed his country but also the woman he loved with every fiber of his being, hung heavily in the air between them.

With sincerity etched across his face, he addressed Anastasia with a heartfelt plea, revisiting a question he had asked before but which held renewed significance in this moment of redemption. "Anastasia," he began, his voice carrying the weight of his past and the hope for a future together, "I know I've asked you before, and I not only betrayed my country but the woman I love. Would you consider marrying me?" His eyes, filled with a mixture of contrition and a burning desire for a fresh start, locked onto hers, awaiting her response with bated breath.

Anastasia's countenance transformed into a radiant, heartwarming smile that seemed to light up the entire room. Her eyes, glistening with love and unwavering sincerity, remained locked onto Brian's, conveying a depth of emotion that words alone could scarcely capture.

With a voice that carried a hint of laughter and an abundance of affection, she responded to his heartfelt plea. "Brian," she began, her words imbued with the certainty of her heart, "I said yes the first time you asked, so why should I change my answer now? Yes, of course, I'll marry you. I'll love you until I die." Her words uttered with unshakable devotion, sealed their fate with a promise of enduring love and a future that brimmed with the possibility of happiness and redemption.

Emotion surged through Brian, his arms around Anastasia tightening as though he sought to forge an unbreakable bond in that moment. It was an embrace filled with an intensity that spoke of his reluctance to release her ever from his hold.

Their lips met in a passionate kiss, a testament not only to their undying love but also to the solemn commitment they made to a future illuminated by the brilliant light of hope. It was a kiss that bore witness to their mutual forgiveness, a profound understanding of the mistakes of the past, and a profound appreciation for the peace they had yearned for so ardently. In that shared kiss, they found solace, redemption, and the promise of a love that would endure through the ages.

The enduring imprints of their experiences would forever shape the narrative of their shared history, each scar telling a unique story of trials and tribulations. However, as they stood side by side, they were armed with resilience and determination, prepared to embark on a new chapter of their lives. In this uncharted territory, they clutched each other's hands, finding solace in the warmth of their touch.

Their collective journey forward was illuminated by the twin beacons of love and happiness, serving as their guiding stars. These two forces, as boundless and effervescent as the universe itself, promised to illuminate the darkest corners of their lives and lead them toward a future filled with joy, laughter, and unwavering companionship. Each step they took was a testament to their unwavering commitment to one another and their shared vision of a future built on the foundations of their past experiences, and the strength they had found in each other's embrace.

Brian and Anastasia found themselves immersed in heartfelt reconciliation. They had weathered the storm of war and time, both fighting the external battles of life and their inner turmoils that emerged from the crucible made them stronger and more resolute.

In the aftermath of such a transformative era, where the world bore the indelible scars of conflict and upheaval, Brian and Anastasia stood on the precipice of a new beginning. Their hearts, once weighed down by the anguish of war, were now filled with the promise of a brighter future. Their shared dreams and aspirations took shape as they meticulously laid the foundation for their life together.

They envisioned a future characterized by unwavering love, where every moment was infused with hope and the belief in the human capacity for resilience and renewal. It was a world where they would not only create a haven of love for themselves, but also contribute to the healing and rebuilding of a world that had been forever altered by the ravages of war.

With each plan they made, they carried with them the lessons learned from their wartime experiences, drawing strength from their shared history. Their commitment to one another was not just a testament to their love but also a declaration of their determination to carve out a future that stood in stark contrast to the dark days they had endured. It was a future built on the principles of peace, compassion, and a steadfast belief that, despite the scars of the past, love would always prevail.

As they charted the course of their shared future, one of their initial and heartfelt decisions was to retrace their steps back to Montreal, the city that had long held a special place in their hearts. The prospect of returning to Brian's beloved hometown stirred a wellspring of emotions within them, for Montreal was not just a geographical location but a repository of memories, both poignant and cherished.

Brian, in particular, carried with him a deep longing to reconnect with the city he had left behind. The St. Lawrence River, which meandered through the heart of Montreal, held a poignant allure for him. It was on the tranquil banks of this majestic river that he and his brother had forged bonds of camaraderie through countless fishing trips. Each ripple on the water's surface seemed to echo with the laughter and shared stories of those days. Brian's heart swelled with anticipation as he envisioned revisiting those hallowed fishing spots, where the memories of his brother lived in the whispering winds and gentle currents.

Anastasia looked forward to the prospect of reuniting with old school friends and acquaintances who had been a part of her life before the tumult of war had separated them. The city streets and neighborhoods held the promise of familiar faces and warm embraces, rekindling the social bonds that had temporarily faded into the backdrop of wartime chaos. She envisioned heartwarming reunions, animated conversations, and the rekindling of connections that had once brought joy and solace during more innocent times.

Their decision to return to Montreal was not merely a geographical choice but a profound emotional journey, an opportunity to navigate the intricate tapestry of their past and present, weaving together the threads of nostalgia and anticipation as they embarked on the next chapter of their lives.

As Brian and Anastasia embarked on their poignant journey back to Montreal, they were greeted by the city with open arms, an embrace that resonated with both the scars of war and the spirit of resilience that had endured. The city, like an old friend, had weathered the turbulent storm of conflict, and though it bore the visible marks of the war's impact, there was an unmistakable aura of renewal and rebirth that hung in the air.

As they strolled through the streets of Montreal, they encountered a cityscape transformed by the indomitable spirit of its inhabitants. Though the scars of war were etched into the architecture and the collective memory of the city, there was an undeniable sense of resilience that pervaded every corner. It was as if Montreal had risen from the ashes, strengthened by the adversity it had faced, and was now poised to embrace a brighter future.

The warm welcome they received from the people of Montreal was a testament to this spirit of renewal. The city's inhabitants, like old friends reuniting after a long separation, extended their hospitality with open hearts. Brian and Anastasia felt a deep connection to their hometown, not just as a place of nostalgia, but as a living testament to the unbreakable human spirit that could overcome even the darkest of times.

Their return to Montreal marked not only a physical journey but also a profound emotional one. It was a journey of rediscovery, of reconciling with the past while forging ahead into a future filled with the promise of healing and new beginnings. As they navigated the streets and landmarks of their beloved city, they were reminded that history and hope could coexist and that even in the wake of war, the human spirit could find its way back to the light.

With unwavering determination, Brian and Anastasia made a profound choice to embark on a fresh and resolute journey of renewal. Brian's shadowy history, marked by his involvement with IRA sympathizers, was now firmly relegated to the past, and he harbored no desire to resurrect it. The weight of his past choices and affiliations had become a burdensome anchor that he was determined to cast off.

Brian understood that the path to true justice was not in revisiting the tumultuous world of political conflict and clandestine allegiances. Instead, he believed that genuine justice could be found in the steadfast commitment to rebuilding their lives and the ardent dedication to honoring the memory of those who had been tragically lost during the war.

Their quest for renewal was not merely a symbolic gesture, but a tangible pledge to carve out a future that stood as a testament to the enduring human spirit. It was a future where the echoes of gunfire and the divisive ideologies of the past were replaced with a harmonious cadence of life, love, and unity. Brian's resolve to put his past behind him was reflected in his belief that the greatest tribute to the fallen was to forge ahead, making the most of the precious gift of life they had been denied.

In this new beginning, Brian and Anastasia were determined to build a life characterized by compassion, reconciliation, and a relentless pursuit of healing. Their decision was not an act of forgetting, but a conscious choice to channel the lessons of the past into a brighter and more hopeful future. As they moved forward hand in hand, they carried with them the weight of history and the promise of a tomorrow where the scars of war would give way to the blossoms of peace and renewal.

Their quest for a fresh startled Brian and Anastasia to discover a charming house nestled in the tranquil suburbs of Montreal. This cozy abode, surrounded by lush greenery and a sense of serenity, seemed like the perfect canvas on which they could begin painting the portrait of their shared life. It was a place where every nook and cranny held the promise of a new beginning, and they embarked on the journey of making it their own.

Brian's newfound path saw him taking on the role of a carpenter, channeling his craftsmanship and skills into creating not just a house but a home where their future family would grow and flourish. Each swing of the hammer, every carefully measured cut of wood, and the meticulous attention to detail he poured into his work were a testament to his commitment to building not just physical structures but also the foundations of a loving and nurturing family life. His hands, once accustomed to the tools of conflict, now crafted the pillars of stability for their family's future.

Anastasia continued her career within the Royal Canadian Mounted Police (RCMP), but her focus had shifted. Instead of dealing with the complexities of larger geopolitical issues, she was now dedicated to maintaining security and order within their community. Her unwavering commitment to justice found a new purpose as she worked tirelessly to ensure the safety and well-being of their neighbors and fellow citizens. Her role as a guardian of their local community resonated deeply with her, reflecting her belief that genuine change began at home.

Their life in the suburbs of Montreal was not just a physical relocation; it was a manifestation of their collective desire to create a haven of love, stability, and security. Together, they embraced their respective roles with a sense of purpose, knowing that every nail-driven and every security measure implemented was a step towards the harmonious life they had envisioned. As they settled into their new home and community, they were writing a new chapter in their lives, one that celebrated the power of resilience, love, and the commitment to making a positive impact on the world around them.

As the relentless march of time carried Brian and Anastasia forward, the bonds of their love deepened with each passing year. Their journey together had been a profound one, fraught with challenges and obstacles that tested the very foundations of their relationship. Yet faced with adversity, they stood as an indomitable and united front, their love emerging stronger than ever.

Life had not spared them from its trials, but Brian and Anastasia confronted these challenges with a shared resolve, a testament to the enduring power of their love. Their experiences had imparted to them a profound understanding of the importance of forgiveness and second chances. They had learned that the ability to forgive, to let go of the weight of past transgressions, was the key to unlocking a future filled with promise.

Their love story, once marred by the shadows of betrayal and concealed secrets, had undergone a remarkable transformation. It had developed into a narrative of resilience, where trust had been rebuilt brick by brick, and their commitment had weathered every storm. Theirs was a love that had not only survived the trials of time but had thrived in the crucible of adversity.

In the quiet moments of reflection, they recognized the profound significance of their journey. Their love was no longer defined by the mistakes of the past, but by the strength they had discovered in each other's arms. It was a love that had been tested and tempered, a flame that had burned brighter in the darkness of their shared history.

Together, they bore the scars of their past, but those scars were not marks of shame or regret; they were symbols of their resilience and the enduring power of their love. As they looked to the future, hand in hand, they knew that their love story was not just a tale of redemption but a living testament to the capacity of the human heart to heal, to forgive, and to love unconditionally.

Their wedding day dawned as a radiant celebration, a momentous occasion that drew together family and friends who had been witness to their enduring bond through every triumph and tribulation. The scars of their tumultuous past had gradually, but not entirely, faded, for they served as a poignant reminder of the hurdles they had overcome. Yet, these scars were no longer symbols of pain but marks of resilience, each telling a story of a shared journey toward healing and hope.

The wedding ceremony was a tapestry of emotions, where laughter mingled with tears of joy. Their families, who had watched them navigate the turbulent waters of life, rejoiced in the love that had blossomed amidst adversity. Friends, old and new, gathered to celebrate the union of two souls who had forged an unbreakable connection.

As Brian and Anastasia stood at the altar, the weight of their past seemed to dissolve in the radiant light of the present. They looked into each other's eyes, their gazes filled with a profound understanding of the trials they had endured and the strength that had emerged from those trials. They clasped each other's hands with a sense of purpose and resolve, ready to embrace the future they had always dreamed of.

Their wedding was not just a union of hearts, but a testament to the transformative power of love and forgiveness. It was a celebration of their unwavering commitment to each other, a commitment that had carried them through the darkest days and into the embrace of a brighter tomorrow. As they exchanged vows and sealed their promises with a kiss, they embarked on a new chapter of their lives, their love story now marked by the enduring themes of resilience, hope, and the boundless capacity of the human heart to heal and love anew.

Against the backdrop of the very city that had borne witness to the trials and triumphs of their love story, Brian and Anastasia embarked on the next chapter of their lives, a chapter brimming with the resplendent promise of love, the profound grace of forgiveness, and the enduring, redemptive power of second chances.

The cityscape that framed their new beginning was a mosaic of memories, each street and building holding a fragment of their shared history. It was a place where their love had been tested and tempered, a city that had seen them at their lowest ebb and witnessed the remarkable ascent of their love from the ashes of the past. The very cobblestones and skyline seemed to whisper tales of their journey, a journey marked by resilience, mutual understanding, and the unyielding pursuit of a brighter future.

As they embarked on this fresh chapter, Brian and Anastasia carried with them the weight of their experiences, the scars of their past no longer a burden but a source of strength. Their love had weathered the storm, emerging from the tempest stronger and more enduring. It was a love that had been tested and found unwavering, a testament to their commitment to each other.

Faced with uncertainty, they embraced the future with open hearts, their love story now etched with the promise of renewal. Their journey was a poignant reminder that even in the wake of mistakes and regrets, the human heart could forgive, heal, and love again. And so, hand in hand, they walked into the horizon, ready to explore the uncharted territory of their future, secure knowing that their love was a force that could withstand any trial and emerge triumphant, just as it had against the backdrop of their beloved city.

Sources

"—-." *www.SecondWorldWarHistory.com*, www.secondworldwarhistory.com/operation-jubilee-invasion-of-dieppe.php.

Wikipedia contributors. "Dieppe Raid."*Wikipedia*, Aug. 2023, en.wikipedia.org/wiki/Dieppe_Raid.

"Dieppe Raid." *The Canadian Encyclopedia*, www.thecanadianencyclopedia.ca/en/article/dieppe-raid.

—-."St. Lawrence River." *Wikipedia*, Sept. 2023, en.wikipedia.org/wiki/St._Lawrence_River.

—-. "Victory in Europe Day." *Wikipedia*, Sept. 2023, en.wikipedia.org/wiki/Victory_in_Europe_Day.

Don't miss out!

Visit the website below and you can sign up to receive emails whenever Newman Skyles publishes a new book. There's no charge and no obligation.

https://books2read.com/r/B-A-BWBZ-HYOQC

Connecting independent readers to independent writers.

Did you love *Dieppe's Revenge*? Then you should read *White-Noise Conspiracy*[1] by Panayotis!

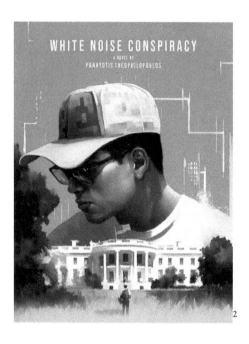
[2]

Juan was determined to destroy the infrastructure of the United States through computer hacking. When he found himself involved with a family of terrorists. Juan ended up on the run from the FBI, wanted for murder.

---

1. https://books2read.com/u/3ydDLB

2. https://books2read.com/u/3ydDLB

Also by Newman Skyles

Peter Carter & The Seekers
Peter Carter & The Seekers - The Lost City of Atlantis
Peter Carter y los buscadores - La ciudad perdida de la Atlántida
Peter Carter & The Seekers Alexander The Great's Treasures

Standalone
Time Eclipse

Peter Carter y los buscadores Los tesoros de Alejandro Magno
Eclipse de tiempo
Dieppe's Revenge

Watch for more at https://www.spartankingenterprises.com.

About the Author

Retired and Living In Florida.

   Read more at https://www.spartankingenterprises.com.

Milton Keynes UK
Ingram Content Group UK Ltd.
UKHW020247221123
432980UK00016B/924